# INTO PIECES

NICOLE BANKS

Copyright © 2015 by Nicole Banks. All rights reserved. No part of this book may be used or reproduced in any manner whatsoever without written permission from the author, except in the case of brief quotations embodied in critical articles and reviews.

Editing done by Rosemi Mederos

Book cover design by Professional Publication

## Author's note:

While this book is completely fictional, it does contain adult themes. This novel is intended for mature readers only.

Novel contains a rape scene. While the content isn't overly graphic to some, reader discretion is advised.

# DEDICATION/ACKNOWLEDGEMENT:

First and foremost I must thank everyone I drove crazy picking out the cover for this book. I love you guys I really do.

My mom, who now needs a new pair of eyes. Lol. Hopefully this gets easier as we go. My monsta, who actually didn't pick this cover, it's okay I still love you anyway. Jen, thank you for our three o'clock chats (Maybe Jason will find out who he really is by the time this book releases lol) and letting me flood your phone with hot girls and not so hot guys. Though, given the fact you've tried to kill me on more than one occasion I'd say I'm allowed to drive you crazy.

The Batman- You are who you are and I couldn't ask for a better person to share in this craziness with.

Short stuff and Mama Gina aka my assistances and the wives lol. Thank you a million times for your support it means the world to me.

Tina and Heather- my two new fave people I've had the pleasure of getting to know on my journey as an author. You two ladies have no idea how much I appreciate you. You've both have become an extension of my team and I value both of your opinions. You two deserve all the goodness in the world.

Lastly, my readers: Thank you for being patient with me. I know it hasn't been easy but I promise you it's worth it. Now sit back and get comfy and enjoy the continuation of Angel and Jas' story.

"We are all searching for someone whose demons play well with ours."

-Unknown

# CHAPTER 1

*Jasmine*

There was something so intoxicating about having a man at your mercy, specifically your man.

I had Angel's wrists tied tightly to his bedpost. He was sprawled out naked, just the way I liked him. It gave me enough time to sit back and admire his magnificent body.

My eyes could never get enough of him. Angel was gorgeous. The nipple piercing and dragon tattoo, which ended just above his penis, only added to his raw sex appeal. He looked good enough to devour and I planned to do just that.

His body tensed every time I ran my palms across his exposed skin. Angel's long thick penis twitched every time I ran my tongue across my lips. Like it was begging for my attention. A wicked smile spread across my face. Soon, I'd taste him again. I would make him wild and lose that tight leash he had on his control.

I loved the way his green eyes watched my every move. They turned a mossy green color when he was aroused. They darkened the more turned on he became.

The heat that shone in his eyes was enough to turn me into a puddle at his feet. Judging by his cocky grin, he knew exactly what he was doing to me and he enjoyed it.

"You know, Love. I love the way those beautiful brown eyes of yours go darker with your need to have me." He smirked. "You keep looking at me like that and I'm going to cum."

I blushed. "We can't have that, now can we?"

He licked his lips. "How about you come here so I can taste just how sweet you are?"

His eyes traveled from my face, slowly going over every inch of my body. He couldn't physically touch me, but I felt his caress touching every single inch of me.

When his eyes finally made their way back to my face he whispered, "I can't seem to get enough of you."

"Angel–"

"Now, Jasmine."

The authoritative tone in his voice almost made me jump at his request. How could he be tied up and still have control? I mentally shook my head, I knew better. Angel at his core was a predator. He'd always be one even when he was at a disadvantage.

"This was supposed to be about me pleasing you, Angel. I was supposed to be the one in control."

He flashed that heart-stopping grin of his. "You are always in control, Jasmine. Don't you ever forget that. I'm the one always begging to touch and taste you. Nothing would make me happier than to be buried in between those luscious legs of yours. I want to lick and taste every inch of you. Let me taste how wet you are for me, my love."

# Chapter 1

I contemplated his request. I loved the way his lips and tongue felt against me. It was a pleasure like I've never experienced. But I knew the second I let him use his mouth on me I would be gone, mindless to the pleasure, lost to whatever he wanted.

"Angel, this is supposed to be about you. You can't tell me you'd rather eat me out then have me suck you off."

"You can do that later, promise." He winked. "I'm always hungry for you, Love. I can spend a lifetime in between those long legs of yours, whether it's my dick or my tongue. And right now, I want to bury my tongue deep inside you, so I can consume every single drop of cum I make you spill."

As if on cue, my body responded to his words. I felt a surge of liquid rush straight to my core. My clit throbbed painfully, demanding to be touched, tasted and pleasured.

"Come here, Jasmine."

His voice was husky with desire, and my body instinctively moved toward him. I couldn't fight the pull anymore than he could.

I straddled his face. He quickly turned and bit the inside of my thigh. "Hey, stop that."

Angel chuckled. "Then hurry up and take a seat. I've been dying to make you scream with my mouth."

I lowered myself slowly, letting the anticipation build. "Jasmine." Angel growled in a warning tone. I knew he wanted me to plop down and ride his tongue till I came. But I wanted to hold on to whatever control I thought I had for just a bit longer.

I was barely an inch away from his mouth. I heard Angel take a deep inhale and felt him nuzzle my core. He let out a muffled sigh as he inhaled again. Now that he was dragging this out, I wanted him to taste me already. I didn't have the patience to wait.

I called his name but it turned into a moan as his tongue made a small swipe in between my folds. We both groaned.

Angel started licking and burying his tongue deep inside me. He found his rhythm. It was that masterful rhythm that drove me insane with pleasure. I could hear his deep murmur of approval. I began to rock my hips into him, meeting him half way. The pressure started to build again. It shocked me how, no matter how many times I came, Angel had the ability to build me up again and again.

If we both kept this pace, I'd explode from the inside out and cum quickly. I tried to pull back a little; I selfishly didn't want this to end. I wanted to drag this winding tension out a little while longer. The reward for it, I knew, would be exquisite.

Angel growled. He bit firmly into my thigh again. A small moan escaped my lips, surprising me. I didn't expect the pain his bite caused to bring another wave of pleasure flowing through me.

I was hot all over. I felt like my senses were expanding. The sound of the headboard hitting the wall as I rocked my hips into Angel was deafening. Each swipe of Angel's tongue

# Chapter 1

felt like a thousand volts of energy shocking me to my core and bringing me closer to my orgasm.

Angel continued his torment with his face buried between my legs. Why did I tie him up again? I wanted his hands on me. I needed to feel him touching me while I came.

I rocked into his torturous tongue harder. Just one more stroke. "Angel please–" I desperately pleaded.

He growled and I faintly heard wood snap. In one swift movement I was on my back and Angel was buried deep inside me causing an explosion of pure ecstasy. I cried out as I clung tightly to him, riding out wave after wave.

As soon as my orgasm started to dwindle, Angel began to thrust into me, causing new ripples of pleasure to explode throughout my body. He was dragging this out. It felt too good. I was suddenly overcome with an emotion I didn't have time to dwell on as I fought to keep any tears from spilling. Being in his arms felt right. Like I was always meant to be here. I couldn't let anything ruin this.

### *Angel*

Jasmine had quickly become my own personal heaven and hell. Or maybe she always had been. I just never looked close enough before. All I knew was this felt right. It was addicting in the best possible way. I had no problem being strung out on her brand of drug.

The greedy walls of Jasmine's warm slick heat continued to milk my cock, trying to coax my own orgasm out. I was right on the edge and was holding on by a thread. Jas fit like a glove, like she was made specifically for my dick.

The second I slide inside her, my orgasm snuck up on me and threatened to knock me out. I tried to hold back. I wasn't quite done with her yet. I had this deep-seated need to make her cum countless of times before I even got my nut. It was awe inspiring to watch Jasmine come unhinged.

When I finally had some type of control, I began thrusting into her. Jas' eyes rolled to the back of her head and she started murmuring incoherent words. A smug smile spread across my face. I did this to her. I made her feel free enough to lose control. I gave Jas her greatest pleasure.

Jasmine blindly grabbed my face and pulled me towards her lips. I would never deny her anything. Whatever she wanted I would give to her.

I groaned the instant our lips connected. I felt it again. Like an electric shot to my system. I was drowning in her. Every time I touched and tasted her. I was sinking even more and I had no intentions of being saved.

"Angel, I'm close. Cum with me please. I need to feel you this time," she murmured.

She didn't have to tell me twice. I picked up my pace getting lost in the little sounds she made in the back of her throat. She was getting close.

I grabbed a fist full of her hair. "Look at me, Jasmine."

## Chapter 1

I heard the growl in my own voice. I was inhuman, an animal, when I took her like this. The caveman wanted nothing more than to mark her and claim her.

"I want you to see what it is you do to me."

Her brown eyes heavy from arousal were locked on mine. "Cum for me, Jasmine. Cum for me so I can cum for you."

I swallowed her moan in a brutal kiss as I felt her shatter in my arms. My orgasm came right behind hers. It damn near knocked the wind out of me. The sex was always better than the last. I could only pray we wouldn't destroy whatever this was between us.

I collapsed, falling to my side so I wouldn't crush her with my weight. Though, judging by the way Jas was just laying there, limp and fully sated. I didn't think she would have minded my weight too much.

I smiled before pulling Jasmine close to me. She murmured something and snuggled right into the crook of my arm. I sighed. For the first time in a long time, I was content. There truly was something peaceful about having her here like this.

I was glad to see she hadn't fully pulled away from me yet. I feared whatever progress we made over the last couple of weeks had completely slipped away the day we made love for the first time.

*I found her, huddled in the corner of her kitchen pale and shaken. Some situations required you to act first, question* later. Going by the state I found Jasmine in, the questions that were pounding in my brain were forced to take a back seat.

I carried her back to bed. Her body curled right into mine as a sob wracked her entire frame. I cursed under my breath as I laid her in her own bed. I hesitated. At first, I wasn't sure what to do. Jas cried again, and my body went to her on its own accord. But the second I got close to her, she torpedoed out screaming like someone was hurting her.

Whatever high I was riding from my orgasm was gone. I felt like complete shit. I thought I was the reason for her melt down. I was sure I hurt her.

I didn't touch her. I didn't want to spook her anymore than I already did. I just continued to call out her name hoping something would register. When it finally did, Jas quickly apologized and threw me out. I wanted to stay and push but I knew that would only make things worse. So I tucked tail and left. If she needed some time to sort shit out, fine. Who was I to push? I let her be for a couple of days and when she was ready she'd let me in and tell me how to fix it so I wouldn't hurt her again.

But when she finally came back around it was as if nothing happened. She begged me to let it go and promised I didn't do anything wrong.

"I can hear your mind going a mile a minute. It's disrupting my sleep," Jasmine mused.

I made lazy circles across her back, and I felt her shiver as she pulled herself closer to me. I smiled; we had come a long way in such a short time. "I'm sorry for disrupting your beauty rest, Love."

She giggled. "What are you thinking about anyway, Angel?"

"If you're ever going to tell me what happened in your kitchen that night after we made love."

## *Jasmine*

For all of Angel's faults, being persistent was his worst one. He could never let anything go. I knew he worried and was probably racking his brain about what caused my freak out. I knew he thought he hurt me in some way when we made love. I told him a million times it wasn't him or anything he did. He was perfect, just like I knew he'd be.

The damn package Marcus sent had paralyzed me. Any happiness I felt in Angel's arms was destroyed the second I opened that box. My one moment of happiness was ripped away. I finally felt safe enough to let go and somehow Marcus found his way back into my life ruining everything.

Once the initial fear and panic subsided, it was replaced with blinding anger and hatred. I was pissed. The one thing I was promised, the one guarantee I had, managed to show up in my house waving a bright red flag in my face.

I called Tony the second Angel left. He swore Marcus wasn't coming back, that he couldn't. Those were the terms all parties had agreed to. The package was sent because someone cleaned out his old house, and Marcus knew they were sending any items that didn't belong to him back to their original owners. Well, that was really sweet of them.

Apparently Marcus enjoyed keeping little souvenirs from the girls he raped. I shuddered thinking about how many other girls got the same surprise I did.

Tony assured me that Marcus was just trying to scare me. Ya think? I ended up freaking out and went crazy on Angel. I ruined what possibly was one of the best moments of my life, and all for what? Tony promised me there was no way Marcus could come back.

He handled everything dealing with the rape and my brother's death too. I trusted him. He always kept me informed, at least he tried to. So when he told me I had nothing to worry about I trashed everything and went about my business. I saw no reason to dwell on it. I promised myself I wouldn't be a victim and I wasn't going to be. Marcus wasn't here; he wasn't going to be here. So why give him any more power over me?

"Are you gonna tell me, or just stay in that pretty little head of yours?"

I pushed up on my arm to look into his gorgeous face. It baffled me that I was here with him like this. We were kids, we grew up together. I always thought I'd be Jay's baby sister to everyone forever. I should have known, though, that Angel would be the one to see past it. I really hoped we wouldn't destroy each other.

## Chapter 1

"It's nothing, Angel. Promise. I thought it was something but it turned out to be nothing. You worry too much you know that?"

He placed a kiss on my nose and brought his hand up to caress my cheek. "Someone has to. There's a lot that can and will cripple us as individuals and as a couple. I don't want that, Jasmine. I don't want us shutting each other out when we can help each other." He traced his thumb over my bottom lip and I shivered. "I need you to trust me."

His eyes were pleading. This was important to him. I was important to him and he was important to me too. For us to have a shot at this, we'd both have to trust each other in all ways.

"I know, Angel. I'll try harder." And I would try harder. I wanted this. "Can I ask you a question?"

"Anything, my love."

Deciding to lighten the mood, I asked, "How the hell did you break the bedposts?"

He started laughing. "Trying to change the subject?" I nodded. "They were already broken, Jas."

He lifted the piece of wood in question and forcefully put it back in place. Then, with a little shove, the wood popped out.

"One time in high school, I was with this chick and she handcuffed me to my bed. We ended up losing the key." He chuckled at my jaw-dropped expression. "Let me tell you, it's kind of embarrassing having your parents not only come home early but have to help break you out of a pair of handcuffs. Needless to say, I made a few faulty spots on my bed just in case I got stuck, again."

I couldn't hold my laughter in. That definitely tops a most embarrassing situation list. I would have died of mortification. "You know, Angel. I think you've had entirely too much sex."

With a wicked grin, Angel rolled me over, pushing me on my back. He started kissing my neck. "I don't see you complaining, Love." He was already half hard as he pushed himself against my core.

Angel groaned. He lifted his head looking at me with something close to awe in his eyes. "Always so wet for me."

His eyes started to turn into that mossy color I was growing accustomed to. I felt him swell fully against me.

"You are a machine."

He chuckled. "It's you. It's how you feel beneath me, over me. How you feel when I'm inside you. Your taste, those little sounds you make when you're close to coming. It's the way you let yourself completely go, getting lost and crazed by every touch, every sensation. It's how you trust me to know exactly what you need and when you need it."

My breath quickened as he kept rocking into me. This was complete torture. Angel was teasing me; he rubbed his penis against my core but he wouldn't slip it inside where I desperately craved him. Why did he insist on driving me crazy?

CHAPTER 1

He rocked his hips forward, and I brought my hips up to meet his. I was trying to push him towards giving me what I needed.

He paused, a smug smile tugged at his lips. "You are always so impatient, you know that? What is it that you need, Love?"

He knew already what I needed; I didn't have to say it. I tried again to bring my hips up at the same time he rocked into me but he gripped my hips forcefully, holding me in place. I growled and it only caused Angel to chuckle in response.

"You don't say it, Jasmine, you won't get it. What is it that you need?"

I caved uncaring how desperate I would sound. I wanted relief and I needed him inside me sooner rather than later.

"You, Angel. I need you."

His smirk died and the intensity in his eyes sparked a new fire inside of me.

"And you will always have me."

Angel thrust inside of me and I winced at the sudden intrusion. I was sore and swollen from the previous rounds. Maybe I should have taken it a little easy. Angel placed small kisses on my lips, my check and my neck.

"See why it can be bad to be impatient? I will always be here; you don't have to rush. Are you okay?"

## Into Pieces

Every time we had sex, he was always endearing. He refused to hurt me. At every wince he would stop and ask if I was okay. It was sweet sometimes; at that moment, though, that's not what I wanted. "I will be once you start moving, Angel."

He grabbed a fist full of hair and kissed me hungrily as he pulled all the way out and pushed all the way back in. I moaned deep in my throat. I was sensitive all over. I felt him everywhere at once. Down from my toes to the tips of my nipples.

He pulled back out again and I broke the kiss on a whimper.

"You're close aren't you, Jasmine? I can feel your greedy walls hugging my cock. You see what you do to me? You feel how hard I get for you?"

He thrust back into me. We both moaned and groaned loud and deep as our orgasms blindsided us. I was struggling to keep my eyes open, and I couldn't get my lungs to work properly. I was tingling all over; the sensation was overwhelming stealing whatever breath I had left. But it felt amazing. I felt like I was flying. I was on an orgasm high I didn't want to come down from.

Angel collapsed on top of me, and I was too tired to do anything but welcome his weight. He placed small kisses on my cheek and whispered, "Better and better." If only we could stay like this forever.

## Chapter 1

My sex-filled haze was interrupted by a hard knock on the door. I groaned. Great, the real world had come knocking, literally.

"Listen you two, there are people in the house now. It's disgusting if we have to hear you bumping and grinding. Try and keep it down, please. I don't want to hear what you're doing to my best friend; that's just nasty."

Angel leaned in a little with a smirk on his face. He went to speak, but he was cut off by another knock on his door. He groaned and picked up whatever he could find and threw it at the door. "Go away, Kris."

"Fine. I will not tell you there's pizza here for you when you two decide to join civilization. Also you have mail, Angel. It's a letter or some shit. Rude ass people."

We heard Kris' footsteps retreating as she grumbled loudly about inconsiderate people. We both started laughing. I guess it was time to get back to the real world.

INTO PIECES

# Chapter 2

### *Jasmine*

I was in the kitchen with Kris while Angel took a shower. He tried to get me to join him, and I was all for a little rub down but my stomach had other plans. It growled loud enough for us both to hear, which made him force me into the kitchen to eat. I didn't realize how hungry I was till I was about half way through one pie by myself.

"Bottomless pit today huh, Jas? My brother does remember to feed you, right?"

I blushed. "Of course he does, you little gremlin. I did eat, just apparently not enough."

Kris started laughing as her father walked in. "Oh nice to finally see you, Jasmine. I thought Angel was going to have you locked up in his room forever."

My face turned beet red. This was exactly why I wanted to stay at my house. No one was home. It was the closest thing we had to privacy, but Angel insisted we stay here. If I was being honest I felt a little safer over here then I did at my house.

Thanks to Marcus and the package he sent, I was constantly looking over my shoulder in my own home. I knew I could tell myself I wasn't a victim all I wanted but it didn't stop the fear from coming every once in a while. I knew I had nothing to worry about, but somehow Marcus still managed to scare me.

Angel's deep rumble interrupted my thoughts. "Well, pops, that had been the plan. I have to make up for lost time, you know? But people do have to eat."

I turned around to see Angel standing in the doorway wearing only basketball shorts and nothing else. They hung low enough on his hips that I could see the little love bite I left him.

A trickle of water slowly ran down his broad chest and his smooth ripped stomach. I licked my lips, imagining licking every single drop of water off him.

When my eyes traveled back up his body and finally reached his face, Angel was wearing a wolfish grin. I watched as his eyes darkened to a mossy green color. He looked good enough to eat.

My body instantly hummed in anticipation. I couldn't wait to feel Angel's body against mine again giving it untold pleasure. The chemistry between us kept growing. Even now, after going how many rounds was it? Four, maybe. The current in here completely shifted. I was vibrating with anticipation and the need to have him touch me.

How could he possibly get my body to spark for him like this time after time? He hadn't even touched me yet, and I could feel how soaked I was already.

Angel made his way towards me. His strong legs eating up the distance between us in a matter of a few breaths. My heart beat a little faster and louder. I was sure Angel could hear it too. What would he do this time? How would he make it better than last time?

He wedged himself between my legs. I reached out to touch him, unable to keep my hands to myself. He stepped back shaking his head. I couldn't help my pout. He wasn't playing fair.

Angel chuckled as he leaned his lips towards my ear placing a small kiss right at my pulse. My body leaned in closer seeking more of his touch.

"You know, my love. I can still smell myself all over you. It makes me hard knowing I've marked you inside and out. It makes me want to strip you out of my shirt, spread your incredible legs wide and fuck you senseless right here on this kitchen table."

"Dude! I can't hear you, thank God. But I'm trying to eat. Can we not do that at the table? The kitchen is for eating not seducing while there's company."

I swear my face was going to be permanently red the way I seemed to blush all the time. I completely forgot we weren't alone. It amazed me after everything I've been through; Angel had the ability to make me forget. My good senses were thrown out the window when he was around.

Angel started chuckling. "You're a brat, Kris. You know you've caught me in worse situations."

"Ah, yes, but see, you weren't with my best friend then, and I'm still going to therapy over that handcuff situation. Thanks again, bro."

He rolled his eyes. "You complain a lot. You weren't even home for that incident. Where'd you put my mail?"

He sat down, taking the pizza off my plate. "Hey, I wasn't done, fatty."

Angel grinned. "Yeah, well, I worked up an appetite too."

Kris threw two envelopes in his direction. "*Maldita sea!* Come on already! You two were just humping like rabbits, can you at least pretend to be worn out and take all that shit you're oozing down a notch? Geez, I'm trying to finish my food here."

Angel laughed loudly. "I'm impressed you can even hear or see anything. Your head barely passes the table."

I almost choked on my water. I was unable to control the laughter. Looks like Angel had some jokes left in him after all.

Kris shot me a menacing look before addressing her brother. "Keep with the short jokes, bro, gonna bite your ankles and I'm gonna get your little girlfriend too."

Angel and I both laughed, as he opened the first letter. "I thought you said there was only one letter, Kris. I see two here, you forget how to count?"

She stuck out her tongue. "Don't make me cut you. I can count shit head. It probably got stuck together."

He read over the contents of the first letter and a small smile appeared on his face. "I guess we have a wedding to go to."

"Who's this 'we' you speak of? And who do you know that's getting married?" I asked.

## Chapter 2

"One of the guys from my unit, also the last person I'd expect to ever walk down the aisle. And the 'we' is us"

He looked a little unsure of himself before he focused his attention on Kris. "You can come too, brat. If you want." He tacked on the ending.

Kris beamed. "Duh!" She loved weddings; well, she loved any reason to party. "Can Chase come too?"

Angel smiled looking a little relieved. "Of course, who else is going to keep me sane dealing with the two of you?"

I couldn't help but smile at Angel. This was the Angel I remembered. The lighthearted nature was coming back, slowly. He smiled more, and those emerald green eyes of his, though they still looked haunted, no longer looked as guarded as they did when he first came back.

He reached over, grabbing my hand in his. "You good, Love?"

I nodded as he took my hand to his lips and placed a small kiss at the center of my palm. Goose bumps spread across my entire body. Angel smirked and bit down gently. I couldn't suppress the shiver that ran down my back. "Angel?" I said in a husky whimper.

Angel's grin was all knowing. My body was his own personal instrument, and he knew exactly which strings to pull to get me to respond in the way he wanted.

He dropped my hand to read the second letter. I shook my head, trying to clear the lust haze I seemed to always be in when he was around. The man was incorrigible.

Angel scanned the contents of the second letter, and his whole demeanor changed. Gone was his smile and the mischievous gleam in his eyes. His whole body went rigid. I could practically hear him grinding his teeth in clear frustration.

I placed my hand on his arm. "Hey, you okay?"

He jerked out of my touch as if I burned him. I tried not to let the hurt show, but it wouldn't have mattered anyway. Angel was up and across the kitchen ripping the letter to shreds before throwing it out. What the hell?

I got up and went towards him. I wanted to help him. I wanted to ease whatever frustrations he had. But before I got close to him, his hand went up to stop me in my tracks. "Jasmine, don't." His voice held no emotion, which concerned me. His whole body radiated aggression, but he spoke with utter calmness.

I was a little unsure of what to do. I wanted to press, but I remembered we weren't alone. Kris and their father were both still in the room. I wasn't trying to embarrass him or myself.

He let out a frustrated breath and pulled out his phone. Oh, so we weren't going to talk about this, but he had time to answer his phone? I stepped closer and that's when I saw it. The phone he held was actually mine.

"Hey, wait. Why do you have my phone?"

## Chapter 2

He completely ignored me, and his face scrunched up as he continued to look through my phone. Nosey much? What the hell was he reading? I went to snatch the phone away, but he moved it out of my reach.

"Um, you want to give me my phone back? Why do you even have it?"

He grunted. "Is it a problem, Jasmine? You wouldn't be hiding anything from me would you?" Angel sounded like a total dickhead.

"Is there a reason you're acting like a jackass? Why do you even have my phone, Angel?" I repeated a second time, hoping to get through to his thick skull.

"All phones look the same and this shit keeps vibrating. I thought it was mine." His lips turned up into a nasty sneer. "But since it's not mine you want to tell me what the fuck this shit is?"

He shoved the phone in my face. I squinted trying to scan the contents. My eyes opened wide before I could school my expression. Oh shit! I tried to be indifferent as I read the text message. But I couldn't suppress the dread that crept up my spine.

*"My sweet girl. I know I've been gone awhile, but is that any reason to misbehave? Has he fucked you yet like I have? I bet he can't make you scream the way I can. Don't worry, baby, all in due time. But know this, the more you play, the worse things will be for you."*

Fuck, fuck, fuck. This couldn't be happening. Tony just promised me he wasn't out. How the fuck was he texting me?

*Breathe Jas.* I had to get out of here, ASAP. I needed to talk to Tony face-to-face. Clearly one of us missed something. Tony had a lot of shit he needed to sort out for me because, if this text was from Marcus, shit was about to hit the fan.

First things first, though, I had to calm Angel down and get my phone back. I wasn't ready to tell him about Marcus. Especially after he all but shut me out about the letter.

"Um, that could just be, um a wrong number? I'm sure it happens all the time."

Shit, my voice cracked and Angel's eyes narrowed as he crowded my space. "If this happens all the time, I think you need to change your number."

Okay, poor choice of words, Jas. Though somewhere in the back of my mind, something was telling me this was, in fact, just the beginning.

"It doesn't happen often. I'm sure if we just ignore it, the person will take the hint that it's the wrong number and leave me alone." I hoped.

"Jasmine, I highly doubt that. The shit came in blocked. Clearly whoever is doing this knows what they're doing and wouldn't be texting the wrong person."

Shit, if Marcus kept this up, Angel would know about him before I was ready to tell him. Angel's eyes narrowed even further, and I swear he was ready to call me on my bullshit but he crossed his arms instead. He looked like he was waiting for me to give him some type of answer. I hope he wasn't holding his breath for it.

I snatched my phone back. The plan was to go home, change and physically face Tony. He promised Marcus was gone over the phone and I believed him. Now I needed to see the truth face-to-face when he told me.

Anyone could lie over the phone, it was a lot harder to look someone in the eyes and do it. Unless, of course, you were a grade A asshole, and Tony was the furthest thing from that.

"I need to go."

I moved past Angel, but he grabbed my arm. "I thought we were done running, Jasmine. Always in a rush to run or push people away when things go south. But, you know what? Go ahead, keep running, keep with your secrets; they ain't gonna do shit but tear us apart."

I stood there completely baffled. Keep secrets? A humorless chuckle bubbled up out of my mouth. So now he was going to preach to me after the shutdown I just received prior to all this? Oh, okay, double standards. No problem. I see how it is.

I looked him straight in his eyes, and they held a lot of animosity and anger. I would be lying if I said that didn't hurt. But I brushed it off, holding on to my own anger.

"Wise words, Angel. I hope you remember all that shit you just spewed the next time I ask you to let me in. Maybe you should practice what you preach."

INTO PIECES

# CHAPTER 3

*Marcus*

I was whistling some annoying show tune that I couldn't get out of my head. I walked up Jasmine's walkway, straight to that brown door that haunted my dreams at night. But nothing plagued me more than the girl who lived beyond it.

I placed my hand gently on the door inhaling, hoping to catch Jasmine's scent. All I got was the smell of the grass in her front lawn. I sighed. I wasn't really expecting much. I was just here to drop off another gift.

It was her necklace, the one she left at my place the night we made love. It ripped off her during our little foreplay; it even had a tint of her blood still on it. I couldn't bring myself to clean it. I closed my eyes getting lost in the memories of that night. It always played in my mind so vividly. I knew the second she came knocking on my door what she was there for.

*Jasmine had on these little short shorts and this shirt that bared her soft stomach. I couldn't wait to run my hands across her soft skin.*

*She was shy at first, but that was a given. She had no experience but I knew, I could feel it; she was hungry for me. My dick instantly hardened at the sight of her just standing there waiting for me to take her.*

*I really wanted to take things slow with her. I had this night all planned out since the moment I laid eyes on her. But the second she mentioned Angel's name, something inside of* me snapped. *How dare she bring him into this house, into our time?*

I charged at her, catching her by surprise. I snatched her by her hair. "You belong to me." I whispered before I flung her on my bed. There was fear in her eyes, and it only heightened my arousal. I loved it when they showed fear. That power exchange, that understanding that I had complete control over them was intoxicating.

I stripped all my clothes away as Jasmine watched avidly. She may have been a little fearful but she wanted me. She wanted me against her and inside her with no barriers.

I would make sure she would never forget this, or me. I would mark her in everyway I knew how. Everyone would know who she belonged to.

"Now, Jasmine. Since you're mine, I will not have you talking about Angel or any other guy for that matter. This is our time."

I loomed over her, finally ready to take what was mine when she swung connecting with my jaw. She scrambled off the bed. "Don't fucking touch me, Marcus. I didn't come here for that."

I spit blood and smiled. This was another reason why I wanted her. She liked my brand of foreplay; a little pain for a little pleasure. My jaw throbbed in pain but I fucking loved it.

"Ah, but you did, my sweet Jasmine. Why else would you come here? I know Angel told you to stay away. But you still

## Chapter 3

came. You wanted this. You want us, me. Why else would you be here?"

"The hell I do. You need to stop this, Marcus."

There was a challenge in her eyes. So Jasmine was going to fight me? My dick swelled even more at the thought. This was going to be too good. I'd force her to submit. I would show her I was the only one who could give her what she wanted. I was the one who could control her body.

I licked my lips. The other girls fought me too. But none would be like, Jasmine. I would enjoy breaking her in, and she would break. They always did.

\*\*

It took longer than I expected, but I finally had her subdued. She didn't go for the obvious hits. She was looking for weak spots, as I made sure to guard my dick at all cost. It would suck to have to postpone this on the account of my dick going soft.

Her shirt ripped in the process. Or maybe I tore at it, a little impatient to see her without her clothes on.

Her breathing was so erratic it caused her chest to rise and fall in rapid succession. The movement had me glued to her, watching her small perky breasts rise to meet me. I could see through her bra that her nipples were puckered, begging for my attention. Ah, my sweet girl, could she be more perfect?

I reached out and pinched her nipples hard, tweaking them a little. Jas cried out her pleasure. The sound was music to my ears. She was so responsive to me.

My hand slowly dipped into her shorts; these had to come off. I grabbed the hem of her shorts and she swung at me again. I backhanded her. Her lip was already bloody and the hit made it worse. How did she still have any fight left in her?

"I really do hate to mark you like that, Jasmine, but it's time you behaved. Don't make me restrain you."

She spit blood at me. "Then let me go. Please don't do this, Marcus. Just stop."

"You are mine, Jasmine. In all ways you are mine, and I will take what I want from you."

"Marcus, please don't do this," she begged.

She was beginning to piss me off. She wanted this. I knew she did. She came to me. Me! She wasn't supposed to beg me to stop. She should be begging me to continue.

I ripped her shorts off. "Marcus, please. Just stop."

"Shut the fuck up, Jasmine. If this were Angel's dick, you'd be begging to have it in your tight little cunt just like every other girl out there." I grabbed her jaw hard forcing her to look at me. "He doesn't love you, Jasmine. No one will, not once I'm done with you."

I dipped my fingers into her pussy and groaned when I found her soaked with need. "Look at how wet you are for me, my sweet girl. You may want to fight me, but your cunt is just begging me to fuck it."

I slipped my fingers out. I couldn't wait any longer; I needed to be inside her. I ripped off her panties and shoved my dick deep inside her.

Holy shit! The sensation was enough to make me cum right on the spot. I didn't move right away. I couldn't; if I did, this would be over too quickly and I wanted this to last.

I got my breathing under control. Jasmine was so tight; she squeezed my dick like a glove. It was like she was made for me; perfectly crafted to be mine.

I moved slowly, stretching her out getting lost in her. This was too good, too right. Every girl I've fucked I've always used a condom. I was glad tonight I decided against it. I was able to experience Jasmine skin to skin, there was nothing separating us. There never would be. I would be her first and her only.

I heard Jasmine cry out. My name was the one on her lips– no one else's. I finally won.

"Marcus, please just–"

"Shhh." I brushed the hair from her face. I needed to see how I made her feel. I wanted to watch her face as I took my pleasure.

"Shh, my sweet girl. I'm going to fuck you until I break you. And once you're broken you will finally understand who *it is you belong to. No one will want you once I'm done with you, Jasmine. I can promise you that."*

I slowly opened my eyes, trying to control my breathing. Every time I went back to that day, my body hardened to the point of the most pleasurable pain. But now wasn't the time for that. The last thing I needed was for some nosey neighbor to report a suspicious male standing in front of a door with a hard on. That would just ruin everything.

I took my hands off her front door with a little too much pressure and it popped open. *Well, look at what we have here.* I contemplated peeking in. This really wasn't part of the plan and I knew better than to deviate, but this was the closest I was going to get to her right now. That little flashback made me miss her even more.

I walked in. I knew Jasmine wasn't home. Angel's bitch ass had her. God forbid the prick leave her alone. That arrogant shit was trying to own what was already mine.

A small smile tugged at my lips. I wondered if he knew someone already had the pleasure of experiencing Jasmine, before he did? Did he understand that every inch of Jasmine's sweet, soft skin was engraved with my touch? Did he know that every time he tasted any part of her, my lips and tongue were already there making her beg and scream? I shook my head; I doubted it. Angel never liked fucking with anything that wasn't untouched.

I paused in the center of her foyer. Son of a bitch! Of course Angel thought to go after her. The little cunt didn't tell him I was her first. How dare she deny me? I meant something to her, damn it! I had to have meant something; I know I did. I was the first person to stretch out that tight pussy of hers. She begged for it, practically screamed for it. Jasmine belonged to me. She loved me.

Angel didn't love her. He was going to use her up till she no longer served her purpose to him. I would love her for as long as I lived. Why couldn't she see that?

Angel was a pathetic loser who did nothing but destroy everything around him. He discarded things once he grew tired of them. His friendship with Jay? As soon as he had no use for him, he made sure to destroy their "brotherly bond."

No one was safe from getting used and discarded by Angel. Even his last girlfriend, Janet got dismissed just as quickly as he had agreed to be with her. She was the one girl I honestly thought would make Angel settle down. But, true to form, once Angel got what he wanted, he tossed it to the aside.

Janet was heartbroken; she was so in love with him. She couldn't fathom how he could just up and leave her all by her lonesome. I mused; Janet had been easy pickings after that. She practically threw herself at me.

I licked my lips remembering how delicious she was. I had to give Angel some credit. He always knew how to pick his girls. They had a tough exterior but always tasted so sweet.

I walked further into Jasmine's home. From what I could remember, the place hadn't changed much. It wasn't like I spent endless amount of time here. Jasmine's bitch of a mother didn't allow me in her house, and she was very blunt about it. Only Angel was allowed to come and go as he pleased. Someone always managed to come before me. Her mother didn't understand how good I was for her daughter, no one did. Apparently, I was the bad guy.

I heard the creak of a door being opened. Shit! No one was supposed to be here, let alone come back yet. I was sure Angel would have kept Jasmine a hell of a lot longer than this. I sneered. Maybe Angel was tired of her already.

I wanted to stand here and watch her walk in. I wanted her to see I was indeed here for her now and always. She would never get rid of me. What I wouldn't give to watch her face light up with surprise when she saw me.

I missed so much. I missed seeing what her face looked like when she received my package. I missed her expression as she read the text message I sent. Surely she'd be overjoyed to know she was still on my mind.

I wanted nothing more than to stay right here and personally hand her necklace back. But that would ruin everything. It wasn't time yet. I had to give her a chance to come back to me.

I moved throughout the house trying to find a hiding spot. I passed her brother's room. The door was left open, and I couldn't help but take a quick peek inside. It was an empty shell of what it once was. A little pang of remorse shifted through me. I never had a problem with Jay. Actually, I never really cared for him; he tried to play nice with me every once in a while. He was polite like that. But in the end, he had to go; he only ended up getting in the way.

Disposing of Jay had been a necessary accident. An accident I wish didn't happen. Jay's death hurt Jasmine. It

## CHAPTER 3

hurt her to the point that she was practically thrown into Angel's arms. Fucking Jay; man never should have gotten in my way.

I heard the door slam shut, and I shot into the next room available. I stopped dead when I noticed it was Jasmine's room. I didn't have time to look around and appreciate what it was I was looking at. A voice I assumed belonged to the person who entered this house sounded closer. I wasn't in the mood to get caught yet.

I headed for her closet, and the second I stepped in, I was engulfed by her raspberry scent. I was instantly thrown back to when I fucked her. How delicious she tasted, how she moved her lean body against mine. I grabbed one of her shirts and inhaled deeply; God, I missed her. I spent entirely too much time away from her. I should have come home sooner. Angel wouldn't have been in the picture, yet.

I inhaled again, stifling a groan. How, after all this time, did she still smell the same? Did that mean she would taste the same? Would she feel the same against me? My dick throbbed painfully at the thought.

A moment of sheer insanity passed through me. Why the waiting game? Jasmine was mine. She belonged to me. I would not be denied what was mine.

I stepped out of the closet when her voice carried into the bedroom. I quickly stepped back, closing the door slightly.

"I don't care, Tony. No, no you told me I had nothing to worry about….I'm not stupid….Yeah, well, if it wasn't him, then who? No, genius, the number was blocked...Angel saw it! No, I didn't tell him....Look, I'm coming over, give me a few."

She stepped into her room throwing her keys and phone on the bed. Her shirt came over her head next. She had nothing underneath and my breath caught in my throat. "Still so perfect."

Jasmine had always been slim. But now, her slim body had extra weight to it. It wasn't fat; oh, no, she was toned. She actually looked like the fighter I knew she was.

My dick throbbed painfully; the fight in her had to be stronger than ever now. I licked my lips and hummed low in my throat careful not to make a sound. God, her submission would be so much sweeter this time around. I couldn't wait to take her again.

Her nipples were out begging for my attention. I loved that her body still responded to me after all this time. It knew I was here watching her. She was tempting me, like she always did. I wanted to step out of the closet and take her.

I palmed my dick stroking as I watched her body move. I could cum right here just from watching her. Day in and day out, I jerked off to the memory of Jasmine's tight cunt around my dick. Nothing could compare to the real thing.

My feet were moving me further out of the closet, closer to her. My body was answering her siren's call.

She moved to her dresser and threw on a sports bra and tank top. She grabbed her phone and keys off the bed, pausing before heading out.

## Chapter 3

She inhaled deeply. "Why the hell am I smelling roses?"

She looked around. Her eyes came to a stop at the closet door. She was looking directly at me. *Come on, Jasmine. Come take a peek.*

She took a step forward then shook her head. She mumbled something under her breath I couldn't hear and headed out.

It wasn't until I heard the front door slam that I stepped out of the closet. I had to take a couple of deep breaths, trying desperately to control my need to chase her down and fuck her. I needed to be smart about this whole thing. I wanted her to come to me like before; she had to.

I picked up the shirt she'd been wearing. This time I didn't bother suppressing my growl of frustration. Of course she would be wearing Angel's shirt. I spotted another shirt on the edge of her bed. The shit was Angel's too. My anger was getting the better of me. I wanted to destroy everything in sight. This motherfucker was always everywhere touching and tainting shit that didn't belong to him.

The insistent ringing of my phone temporarily brought me out of my rage. I didn't even bother to check the Caller ID. There was only one person who called this number. "Hello, brother."

I picked up Angel's other shirt taking it with me as I left. A back-up plan was beginning to formulate. There were other less drastic ways to get rid of Angel. I couldn't pull the same shit I did with Jay; Angel was a Marine now. I didn't think my

INTO PIECES

father had enough money left to cover up anything if Angel had a spot next to Jay in the cemetery.

# CHAPTER 4

*Tony*

I slammed my phone down hard on the kitchen counter, hearing it crack under the pressure of my hand. Great! I was going to need another phone–again!

I was a six-foot-plus, two-hundred-pound grown man, and Marcus always reduced me to feeling as helpless as a newborn. Why couldn't he just leave well enough alone already? What was it about Jasmine that had him so fixated?

I was agitated. I needed to do something, so I paced the length of my kitchen. My strides were quick and sharp as my legs ate the short distance. I was at a loss with Marcus. I didn't know what I could possibly do to diffuse this situation before it got even more out of hand. I really couldn't let him roam around like this. But, thanks to my father, I wasn't supposed to do anything. "We protect what's ours. That's it. He won't bother anyone, so don't tell anyone shit."

Yeah, okay, pops! He wasn't going to bother anyone except for Jasmine. I knew it and my father knew it, and yet he didn't seem too concerned about it.

This situation was so fucked up. He wanted me to continue to cover for him like I did when we were younger. I didn't have a problem with it then because he was my brother. A half-brother, but he was still my brother, which made him family.

## INTO PIECES

At a very young age I was instilled with the whole 'blood is always thicker than water' thing. I also had this fairytale image that it was going to be me and Marcus against the world. Even though I always knew something was off about him.

I would constantly catch Marcus doing things a young boy shouldn't do. On numerous occasions I would walk in on him having my dog lick his dick till he came. I told my pops, because that shit couldn't have been normal. My father told me to mind my own business, and that's what I did. If my father wasn't worried about it, why should I be? Who knew that shit was just the beginning of how much worse Marcus would get?

I remember the first time I actually witnessed him hurting someone. It was at one of our many parties; my father always threw parties back then as a way to introduce himself to all the new female occupants of the neighborhood. Apparently, for him, he could never be satisfied with just one lady in his life.

I walked into the room I shared with Marcus, and he was there with the neighbors' eight-year-old daughter. I didn't react at first; I stood there frozen. She was naked and so was he. She was crying and shaking with her hands covering her mouth. Marcus stood behind her, his fingers disappearing inside her.

He didn't even stop his movements or looked the least bit concerned when I walked in. Marcus looked at me and smiled. *"Do you want a taste?" He pulled his fingers from her and brought them to his mouth. He had his other hand gripped tight around the back of her neck, keeping her in place. He closed his eyes humming, his appreciation.*

## CHAPTER 4

"So good. I think you should have a piece of her, Tony. She's amazing. All sweet and untouched."

That was when I lunged for him and punched him in his face. The little girl screamed and tried to run out of the room, but my father caught her before she could get any further. His gaze swept the room in a swift motion. He didn't say anything at first; he just grabbed a shirt to cover her up and whispered something in her ear before pushing her outside of the room.

He came in and looked us both in the eye. "*Not a damn word is to be spoken about what just happened here. So help me, I so much as hear a peep about this shit, I will beat the both of so bad you won't be able to sit for a week. You both wanted a brother; well you've got one.*"

I tried to protest. "*No, Tony! Not a damn word, he's family we protect family always. Neither one of you will say anything about this, understood?*"

We both nodded and my father walked out my room slamming the door behind him.

The neighbor's daughter was the first in a long list of girls Marcus hurt, and my father willingly threw his money around to cover it up time after time. My father always told me he was getting help. That Marcus was really trying to curb his appetite. That had been a crock of shit.

My father let him run loose. Maybe he felt bad for him; like he was hoping Marcus would find himself in a ditch somewhere. All I knew was that Marcus wasn't getting any better. He seemed to be getting worse. Instead of fixing the situation, we just put a Band-Aid on it and covered it up with money. What was my pops going to do when the money ran out?

Looking back, especially after I found out he hurt Jas, I wish I had told someone about Marcus. I guess a part of me always thought he'd out grow this. He'd get tired of the games, tired of the bullshit, tired of hurting these innocent girls. I think a small part of me still believes he'll out grow it. God knew I prayed hard enough for it to happen.

Every girl Marcus raped took a little out of me. Jasmine had been the worst. I never knew the other girls the way I knew her. Jasmine was like my baby sister, and I had to watch her go from an innocent and carefree child to a badly damaged and beaten-down woman. She changed so much after Marcus; it was like night and day. It made me sick to my stomach knowing I played a hand in her suffering.

I went to sit down but there was a knock at the door. I already knew who it was, so I remained standing. "It's open." Jasmine barged in. She slammed the door so hard I thought it came off its hinges.

She stomped her way to where I stood, getting right in my face. Jasmine was tall for a girl, but she barely passed my shoulders. My sheer body mass alone engulfed hers, making her look tiny and vulnerable in comparison.

I smirked. Here she was standing toe-to-toe with me ready to clock me if she didn't like what I had to say. It looked like the fight in her was simmering on the edge. Seeing her like this made me believe deep in my heart she'd find a way to be okay.

## Chapter 4

Jas titled her chin; her pretty brown eyes a mix of hurt and fear. "Tony, I'm going to ask you one last time and so help me I find out you're lying to me. Is Marcus out?"

Her voice started out strong, only to break into a plea at the end. My heart broke for her. She tried, boy did she try to put on a brave front but she was scared.

I cupped her face; something inside me breaking even more as I watched the array of emotions play in her eyes. She was hopeful yet dreading the worse.

"I promise you, Jasmine. Marcus will not come after you again."

"You know damn well that's not what I asked you, Tony. Let me repeat myself since you're a little hard of hearing, is your brother out?"

Her voice grew stronger and steadier with every word she said. Her resolve to find out the truth calmed her. Too bad the truth was something I couldn't give her.

I shook my head. "No, Jasmine. Marcus is not out." I had to swallow the bile that rose up. I hated lying to her.

"Tony."

She stepped back shaking her head. The warning was clear in her voice. She crossed her arms over her chest. "I need you to be one hundred percent sure. I can't afford for you to be wrong."

More lies. "I am one hundred percent sure, Jasmine. Marcus is not out."

She dropped her hands. "If he's not out, then I need you to explain to me how the hell he's contacting me. I remember the terms of the agreement, do you? Does your father? If not, I can jot them down for you."

I went to her and she only stepped back further. She was slowly losing her trust in me. She had good reason to but it still hurt.

"Calm down, Jas. I told you what that package was about."

She scoffed. "You told me, don't mean I believe you seeing as how I got this message from a blocked number."

She threw her phone at me. I scrolled through the message shaking my head. Of course Marcus would do this shit. He never went back to any female; he used them and moved on. Jasmine was the only one he plotted to have and plotted to keep. It looked like he was plotting yet again to have her. I had to try and derail him this time; I couldn't let him hurt her anymore.

I handed Jasmine back her phone. "You have proof it was him, Jas?"

She cocked her eyebrow. "Oh, so you want proof? Okay. Yes. Let's take a drive up to where he supposedly is and ask him face-to-face if he's the one who sent me the text message. Should we take your car or your father's?"

I shook my head. The look in her eyes told me she was crazy enough to face him again. Just to see if he was actually where I said he was. I had to do my best to persuade her she had nothing to worry about.

## Chapter 4

"Come on, Jas. You know I can't do anything on an assumption. I know he's not out. You have nothing to worry about."

She started pacing and mumbling under her breath. I snatched her up by the arm turning her to face me before she could wear a hole in my floor.

"Breath, Jas. Look, I know and understand what you've been through. I know what he put you through and what we asked you to do afterwards. You're like a little sister to me, why would I want to see you hurt anymore then you have been?"

She pushed me and I dropped my hold on her. Whatever fear she might have felt was gone and was quickly replaced with animosity.

"I'm like a little sister to you? So much so that you allowed this shit head into my life knowing what he does to females. Do you honestly think I'd be standing here–better yet, don't you think Jay would still fucking be here if you or your father put Marcus on a leash or caged him?"

The words hit me harder than any blow could. I took a step back, staring at her, watching the hurt she dealt with day in and day out from the loss of her brother wash over her again. She hated me and she hated herself for the events that unfolded leading to Jay's death. I could tolerate her hating me because, by protecting Marcus, I ended up killing her and her brother both physically and emotionally. I helped hurt her and my father wouldn't allow me fix it.

I continued to stare at her. I couldn't speak; there really wasn't much to say. I fucked up by bringing him around. I knew better, Marcus had a thing for younger girls and bringing him around her was just asking for a shit storm to happen.

Jasmine let out a long breath before taking a seat at the kitchen table. I followed suit. "It's not your fault, Tony. He's your brother; I get it. You only saw what you wanted to see. I blame myself actually." She put her hand up stopping my protests. "Let me finish. I should have known to stay away from him when I saw that Angel didn't like him."

My eyebrow shot up in surprise. Jas tended to do as she pleased. Her and Kris had been a handful back then. "Um, hate to break it to you, Jas but even if Angel told you to stay away from him, you wouldn't have listened. Why does it matter now?"

She chuckled a little. "Angel actually told me to be careful with him. He knew if he or anyone for that matter flat out told me not to hang out with him, I would have been attached to Marcus' hip."

I cringed. That was all Marcus needed. He would have gotten to Jasmine a hell of a lot sooner and who knows how much more he would have destroyed her.

"I really should have listened to Angel's warning. He's always had an uncanny knack for knowing when someone was bad news."

That was the damn truth. The second I introduced Marcus to everyone; Angel took one look at him and told me not to bring him around his sister or Jasmine. I couldn't understand why Angel saw what no one else could, but I should have heeded his warning.

## Chapter 4

I thought bringing Marcus around us and other people would help him be normal. But all it ended up doing was put Jasmine in Marcus' crosshairs. The second he laid eyes on her, he was hooked. He never explained to me what it was, or I just wasn't listening. But Jasmine had become his fixation from the very first moment he saw her.

Jasmine's phone vibrated across the kitchen table. She looked at me before flipping it over. "Oh look, Tony, another anonymous text message. I wonder who it could be from this time." She handed me the phone without reading the text. "Would you like to read it out loud? I'm dying to know what it says."

Before I could even read the message Jasmine hopped out of her chair and snatched the phone back out of my hand. "Actually, Tony, fuck it. Don't even bother reading it. How about we go for a drive and ask Marcus himself what it is he can possibly still want to take from me?"

I didn't have time to respond, my back door swung open. Jasmine didn't bother to turn around; she was too busy spitting fire at me to notice the shift in the atmosphere.

"Well, hello, Jasmine. It's so nice to see you again."

Jasmine froze. The color drained completely from her face. "No, no, no, you just promised, Tony. You promised–please don't be here. God, not now please not now."

INTO PIECES

# Chapter 5

### *Kristal*

Well that was awkward. My father and I were both staring in the directions Angel and Jas had stormed off in. My father whistled and shook his head. Yea pops, my thoughts exactly.

Angel was such a private person. Any female relationship problems and arguments he had, he always kept behind closed doors. No matter the circumstances. It was a little odd for me to see my brother come unhinged like that in front of us.

My father started off in the direction Angel went. I jumped up, stopping him before he could go any further. Angel didn't seem like he would be in the mood to have another chat with Dad, especially since the first one ended the way it did.

Pops gave me his stern look. You know, the one that's supposed to entice fear and get me to do as I was told. I giggled. Those "looks" hadn't worked in a long time. They damn sure weren't going to work now.

He laughed taking a step back. "You know, Kris, when you were a kid, all I had to do was give you that look and you knew to behave." He chuckled to himself. "So, you're really not going to move?"

I shook my head. "Nope."

"Kristal!"

He said my name in that tone that meant business. The little kid in me almost made me relent. There was no sense in getting in trouble trying to save my brother's ass from talking with Dad.

I took a breath, trying a more mature approach. "Look, Dad. I don't think you should go after him. Given his mood, I don't think he's going to respond well to you and there's no need to have another screaming match today."

He stepped back, running a hand down his face and exhaled loudly. "They're going to destroy each other, Kris."

His statement stunned me. My father had been Team Angel and Jasmine since as long as I could remember. Now he was over here thinking they were going to destroy each other? I glanced back in the direction Angel had left. What changed? What did he see that I couldn't?

I looked back at my pops. "You don't really believe that, do you?"

He looked at me long and hard before responding. "Now, yes I do. There's just too much, Kris. They've both been through too much. I can't believe they have an ounce of who they use to be still with them. I know, I know, your mother and I were all for these two to end up together. But come on, Kris. Have you ever seen Angel have an outburst like that? He has always been a private person. This shit we witnessed, that's not him. That was not my son."

He stormed over to the kitchen table and took a seat with his head held in his hands. I watched as he took long deep breaths. This man was one of the most relaxed men I knew. He rarely ever stressed or got pissed off about anything. My father always looked youthful. But since burying Jay and watching Angel get shipped off to the Marines, life made him appear older than he was.

He looked up towards the ceiling. "I just got him back. I can't lose my son again."

I rubbed a hand across my chest trying to ease the pain those simple words caused. I hurt for my father. He was worried when Angel came home–we all were. We weren't sure who or what we were getting when he came back. Angel might have been here physically, but that didn't mean he would ever be here mentally or emotionally.

The worry that was etched on my father's face matched what I felt inside. He wouldn't survive burying Angel in any capacity. I wouldn't survive it either.

I turned, intent on going to find Angel when my father called out to me. I stopped turning back to face him.

"You're going to talk to him?"

That was the plan; whether or not either one of us would do any talking remained to be seen.

"Yeah, dad. That's where I was headed now."

He let out a hefty laugh. "Right and you were worried about him not being responsive to me? How do two of the most stubborn people I know even begin to have a conversation?"

I smiled. "Duh. I'm his baby sister. Angel has no choice but to play nice."

My father chuckled. "You don't believe that anymore than I do. But, if you think it will work, knock yourself out. Just don't throw anything okay?"

"Hey! I don't always throw things!" My father gave me a leveled look. "Okay, I do, but that's because people take advantage of the height."

I was bullied a lot because I was a midget in this land of giants I lived in. Sometimes, my only weapon was whatever I could throw. I couldn't be held responsible. I didn't choose the short life; the short life chose me.

Dad smiled as he walked over to me. "Just like your mother, always throwing things. Just go easy on him, okay? He's been through a lot in such a short time." He paused putting his hand on my shoulder. "You all have."

And wasn't that the truth. How could life be cruel enough to deal the cards they dealt to Angel at such a young age and expect him to survive unscathed? Maybe that was the point to all this. You weren't supposed to survive what life threw at you intact. You were supposed to be battered and bruised, creating a thick skin. This way when life really knocked you on your ass, you'd be able to get up and politely state, you hit like a bitch. And deep down you'd know you'd be okay.

My father placed a kiss on my forehead before turning to leave. I stood there awhile finally understanding what my father had gone through with Angel's departure and Jay's death. I guess kids never really understand the stress they put on their parents.

Looking to diffuse another stressful situation, I pivoted, heading straight for my brother's room.

I expected the door to be closed. Angel had a knack for shutting people out. But when I got there, the door was wide open. Angel was standing in front of his bed, and I could hear him breathing heavily.

I leaned up against the doorframe, waiting him out. I loved him, but I didn't want to deal with him outright. I wanted him to calm down a little bit. The whole point to this was to try and get through his thick skull. I couldn't do that if he was still foaming at the mouth.

Angel bent down and picked up what looked like Jas' shirt. He brought it up to his face and inhaled deeply before whispering, "My sweetest sin. What am I going to do with you?"

I scrunched my face up. Ew! Okay, maybe now wasn't the best time to talk to him. I turned around to leave when Angel spoke. "Took you long enough to come check up on me."

"Who says I'm here to check up on you?"

We both turned to face each other. Angel had a smirk on his face. "And here I was expecting Dad. How'd you beat him here?" The smirk quickly faded and was replaced by a scowl. "He's not going to check up on Jasmine is he?"

He made a move towards the door, and I threw up my hands to block him off. "No. He's not, Angel."

At least I hoped he wasn't. It wasn't like our father to meddle, but after that admission earlier, who knew?

"I just told him not to come talk to you. I figured you didn't want him here lecturing or giving you some life lesson. You're welcome, by the way."

He crossed his arms over his chest and his scowl deepened as he stared me down. "Who says I want you here doing the same, Kris?"

I rolled my eyes. "*Ay*, please, you give yourself way too much credit. Who says I have time for any of that?"

"No other reason to be here, Kris. But I'll make it easy for you; Jas and I had a little disagreement– nothing to worry your pretty little head about. You can leave now."

He leaned into me with his whole body, doing his best to surround me. Ah, good ol' Angel trying to bully me out of his room just like when we were kids. I had to laugh a little; it was nice to see some things wouldn't change.

I faked a yawn and looked at my nails; definitely time for a manicure. I looked back up at my brother and smiled. "I know you've been gone a long time, bro, but in case you forgot, I don't scare easily. You want me to leave, you're just going to have to ask nicely."

A deep rumble emanated from his chest and I grinned harder. I know it's stupid to poke the bear, especially since his temper has only gotten worse. But I was throwing caution to the wind. I made the mistake of treating Jasmine like glass, assuming she was healing on her own time when she wasn't. I would not do the same with Angel. I wasn't going to tip toe around him because he was having his own pity party. If we had to go toe-to-toe, then so be it. I be damned if he became just a shell of himself. I would not lose him, not if I could help it.

### *Angel*

If I stood here long enough growling and shooting daggers at her, maybe she'd get the hint and walk the fuck away. I had no time for my sister and her antics. Her being here almost made me wish our dad had come to check in on me instead. I loved my little sister, but holy shit, did she know how to get under someone's skin.

I pressed into her more, crowding her space. *Come on, Kris. Take the hint and leave already.* She continued to look at me with this shit-eating grin, and it made me want to choke her little ass out.

I blew out an annoyed breath. When it came to my sister, I learned quickly how to pick and choose my battles; I wasn't winning this one. Kris was as stubborn as I was and honestly, I was too tired to challenge her on it. I gave up and headed towards my bed.

I wanted to sit down, but Jasmine's scent still mingled in the sheets. A bolt of lust shot through me as an image of my face buried between her luscious legs played across my mind.

I closed my eyes, inhaling deeply. I couldn't get any part of Jasmine out of my mind even if I tried. I definitely couldn't deal with all of this right now.

Foregoing sitting on the bed, I turned towards my desk. I pulled out the chair and plopped down with a heavy sigh. "Kris, just get out of my room already. If you really feel it's necessary for us to talk, we can do it later. But not now, okay?"

"Well, seeing as how I'm technically not in your room, I don't really have to go anywhere, now do I?"

I looked up, ready to tear into her, only to realize the brat was right. Kris was standing just outside of my door waving and smiling at me. Seeing her there like that must have snapped something inside of me. I threw my head back and let out a loud bark of laughter.

This was Kris in all her glory. I should have known to expect this. I used to do the same shit to her all the time when we were kids. I would stand right in her doorway harassing her and there wasn't anything she could do about it. I wasn't in her room, so she couldn't tell me to get out. Payback was a bitch, huh?

Kris walked further into my room. "Well, look who finally put the sour puss away and laughed."

I scrubbed a hand across my face. "What do you want, Kris? If you're here to be a pain in my ass and drive me crazy, how about a rain check?"

She crossed her arms and looked around the room. I followed her eyes wondering what it was she was looking for.

## Chapter 5

In the process, I ended up actually taking a look at my room for the first time since I'd been home at seventeen. It amazed me how little nothing changed, but in a way it all did. I wasn't that same kid who left. I was a man now drowning in a bunch of shit I had no idea how to sift through.

"You know, bro, I think it's time you got your own place."

I cocked my eyebrow at her doing nothing to conceal the smirk on my lips. "You came in here to kick me out? Well shit, with a sister like you who needs any enemies?"

She rolled her eyes and scoffed. "I didn't mean it like that! I just think you need your own space. This room and house belong to a person who barely even exists anymore. Yes, people grow and change; that is the natural order of things. But it's different for you though, isn't it?"

I looked around the room trying to see exactly what she saw that made her make such a statement. The walls were painted a bland brown, a color that made me a little depressed now that I actually stared at it. The furniture was the same furniture I had since I was fifteen. I had picked it out then, and now, I had to wonder why? I mean, it served its purpose and I was use to having a hell of a lot less, but none of this stuff was really mine. Kris was right. I might be back, but I wasn't really home yet.

Kris cut into my thoughts. "I didn't come in here to give you shit about your living arrangements. You know, I'm glad you're back and whole."

"I came in here because dad seems to think you and Jas are going to destroy each other. Apparently, all that shit you've both gone through has killed who you use to be. He thinks that's what's going to hurt you both as a couple."

"Pops said all that, huh?"

I couldn't keep the surprise off my face. But now I was grateful my sister was standing here and not my pops. I wouldn't have been able to have a civil conversation with him telling me I should walk away from Jasmine. Especially when not so long ago he told me to go for it.

"Yeah, he did. It's funny because he and mom were your biggest fans. Now, it's almost like he's just given up. Though, given what he thinks he stands to lose if this relationship goes south, I can see why. Do you want my opinion?"

I chuckled despite myself. "If I say no, what are my chances of you not giving me your two cents on the matter?"

"Very slim, bro." She laughed before continuing. "Look, as hard as this is to say, I actually think you two have a shot at something real. Yes, I know, I've joined the dark side and I'm on Team Angel and Jasmine."

"I see the way you two look at each other when you think no one is paying attention. There's definitely something there. I think what you've both gone through is a good and bad thing. Ya suffered through a lot individually and it's changed you drastically but that change can give you something good. You and Jas have this chance to relearn each other, and that gives the relationship some excitement and, most importantly, growth. What's gonna kill you, though, is that neither one of you has complete trust in each other. Especially with your past."

## Chapter 5

She held up her hand cutting off the protest I had. "Yes, I know she told you about being raped. But I'm sure she spared you the gritty details and who was responsible for it. You also weren't here to see what burying her brother did to her. You left remember? And lets not forget the mountain of shit you're clinging to."

I spoke up. I was annoyed my sister was butting in on something she had no clue about. She wasn't in this relationship with us. She had no idea what was going on between Jasmine and me.

"We don't need to sit down and hash out our baggage, Kris. It's in the past for a reason, it can stay there."

Kris gave me a leveled look. "Spare me the bullshit, bro. Both of your issues can never stay hidden. They are so much a part of who you are now. There are too many triggers around you that can and will bring all that shit up."

"Perfect example: Look at what happened in the kitchen, Angel. You practically bit Jasmine's head off over a letter. A letter I can put money on had something to do with your past baggage. You gotta learn to have trust in each other with all your shit, or this is never going to work."

I had to stop myself from rolling my eyes. I hated to admit it but Kris was right. The trust was there, but it wasn't what it needed to be. There was too much shit between us though. It wasn't fair to burden someone else with all that. I was barely staying afloat; how was Jasmine ever going to be able to tread in the same water?

"It's not that simple, Kris. My demons barely play well with me. What makes you think they're not going to destroy her when I let her in?"

Kris came and pulled up a chair beside me. She turned to look at me. Her hazel eyes bored into me as if she was trying to see through me.

"You know, Angel. If I could I'd take all your pain and suffering away. It kills me that I can't. But I'm going to at least help you where I can. You gotta let her in, Angel. Don't worry about what she can handle. I don't think neither one of you gives each other enough credit on what they can and can't handle."

"Kris, it's not about what either one of us can handle. I don't want to be the one to weigh her down more. Jas got enough on her plate; she don't need to deal with my shit too."

The look on her face was utter disappointment. Surprisingly, it hurt a lot to know my little sister was disappointed in me. But again, she wasn't in our daily struggles. She had no clue what Jas and myself were doing as a couple. Kris let out an audible sigh and headed to the door.

"That's it, Kris? This is a little short, even for you."

Kris turned around. "What's the point, Angel? You clearly don't love her enough."

### *Kris*

If the situation weren't so dire, I'd laugh at Angel's facial expression: jaw on the floor eyes, popping out of his head. I

## CHAPTER 5

stood there waiting to see if he would respond, or if he was going to continue to look at me like a deer in headlights. If these two couldn't trust each other there was no point in continuing what they were doing.

I mean, sure they trusted each other enough to have sex, but that was the easy part. Getting naked physically and fucking were probably the easiest things to do. But getting naked emotionally and mentally took balls. Neither Jasmine nor Angel stripped themselves completely bare in front of each other, and that was going to continue to cause problems. They both wanted more from each other but did nothing to achieve it.

Angel was still staring at me like I had sprouted two heads. I giggled. "What's the matter, bro? Cat got your tongue?"

He shook his head. "What makes you think I don't love her enough?"

"That fight in the kitchen. You shut her out and pushed her away."

"She didn't have to run. She could have pushed back."

"You didn't have to be a dick. She asked you to let her in and you shut her out."

I let out a frustrated breath while pinching the bridge of my nose. I wasn't even in this relationship and they were driving me crazy.

"Look, let's put it this way, while you were gone and Jasmine went through what she did, everyone was treating her with kid gloves. Did you see how well that turned out? It wasn't until you came back that you pushed her the way she needed to be pushed. I'm by no means saying she's one hundred percent better or even completely past it. But, because of that push she's a lot closer to being okay then she was two months ago."

"Answer me this, do you see yourself with Jas in the long run?"

"That's a little too early to tell, sis."

"Dude, either you're in this for the long haul or you're not. Whatever this is, you need to decide quickly what it is you want. Don't drag this shit out any longer than necessary if you're not willing to put in the work to be with her. If you want this with her, stop being a sulky brat and put your big boy pants on. Go get her and let her in."

# Chapter 6

*Jasmine*

Oh, God, that voice; that fucking voice. No, this couldn't be happening; no, not now. Tony swore he wasn't here.

"Hi, Jasmine."

I was going to be sick. That voice, the way it said my name brought me right back to the night I lost everything.

*His hands were everywhere, marking me in places I've never been touched before.*

"Marcus, please."

*My plea was a broken whisper across my swollen lips. He confused my plea to stop for a plea to continue.*

"That's it, Jasmine. Keep begging me for more."

*I cried, not only from the physical pain but from the embarrassment it brought on as well. I fought as hard as I could, but I had no more fight left in me. I lay there broken, taking everything he was giving– just like he promised I would. Why didn't I fight harder? I should have been stronger than him, stronger than this.*

"Jasmine!"

That voice wasn't Marcus', this time. It was Tony's. What the hell was Tony doing here? Where was I? I felt hands on my arms gripping me hard. These hands were huge, they couldn't be Marcus' and they were shaking me hard.

"Jasmine, damn it!"

I let out a gasp of air that I wasn't aware I was holding. All too soon the images of the night I was raped faded and Tony's kitchen came into view.

Tony was staring at me like I lost my damn mind, which probably wasn't too far from the truth.

"You okay, Jas? Where'd you go?"

I nodded my head. I wasn't too sure I could trust my voice just yet. What had set me off again? A throat cleared and I turned around to find the source.

A very bored-looking Mr. Marcelo was standing by the kitchen door. Instant hatred laced right through me. As much as Mr. Marcelo helped, and I use that term loosely, I couldn't stand the sight or sound of him. He could never deny Marcus was his son. I don't know how we all missed it before. They were built the same, right down to the cold dead look in their brown eyes.

Before I met Marcus, I thought Mr. Marcelo appeared mean-natured because he was a lawyer, and I thought that's how he had to be so he could be the best. After his son raped me, I knew some people were just evil little shits.

Mr. Marcelo smiled in my direction, but it wasn't pleasant by any stretch. "Ms. Ortiz, to what do I owe this pleasure?"

"Mr. Marcelo, it's been a while."

## Chapter 6

"Clearly not long enough, Jasmine."

"Pops!"

Tony rustled behind me. I put my hand up to stop any comments he had on my behalf. It was moments like this I was amazed that Tony could possibly share the same DNA as Marcus and their father. Tony was a saint compared to the two of them.

"It's cool, Tony. Trust me the feeling is mutual. I gotta give you credit, though. How you maintained any shred of decency and goodness growing up with those two is beyond me."

Mr. Marcelo laughed but it held little humor. "Still so naïve, Jasmine. Trust me when I tell you, Tony is a lot more like myself and Marcus than he's led you to believe."

He titled his head, staring at me strangely. I started to feel a little uneasy. It was the same look Marcus had when he would look at me.

This had become incredibly uncomfortable too quickly. I tried to hide my discomfort. I didn't want to show any disadvantage to Mr. Marcelo. He'd pounce on it like the rabid dog he was.

Mr. Marcelo smiled and it wasn't friendly. "Is that the reason you're here, Jasmine? Is it to discuss Marcus? I guess my son was right, you would miss him."

A flash of red fell over my gaze. I saw myself launch into Mr. Marcelo and beat the shit out of him. I took a step forward only to be stopped by Tony's hand on my arm. I shook my head, trying to clear it of all the murderous thoughts I had. *Breathe, Jasmine. Just breathe.* Though the anger was a welcome change, it was still a waste.

Mr. Marcelo excelled at being a dickhead and was clearly trying to get under my skin. I was not going to give him the satisfaction by reacting to him. I refused to let him know that his sleazy son or himself had any affect on my life.

"Actually, Mr. Marcelo." I was able to portray a calm I wasn't sure I actually felt. "I was just reminding Tony here about the terms to our little agreement pertaining to your other offspring. I seem to recall he wasn't supposed to have any contact with me at all. Shit, as far as I remember, he wasn't supposed to know I existed anymore."

Mr. Marcelo was eyeing me like I wasn't the brightest crayon in the box. "Of course, I remember the agreement. I wrote it up. Are you here to renegotiate?"

I turned back to look at Tony and saw that he had this sickly look on his face. "Oh, so we haven't told your pops yet about the recent events?"

He shook his head, and I turned back to face his father. "Now, that's very odd that you don't know what your darling boy has been up to. He sent me a nice little care package a few weeks ago, and now I've been getting blocked texts from some anonymous person."

I watched as Mr. Marcelo took everything in. Something flashed in his eyes but it happened too quickly for me to catch it and in its place he slipped on his lawyer's mask. It was such a quick shift. I was sure I would have missed it if I wasn't watching him.

"I'm sorry to hear that, Ms. Ortiz. I will be sure to talk to his guards and get it handled at once. We wouldn't want to upset you further."

He opened the kitchen door; I guess I was getting dismissed. I wanted to be stubborn and press about this sudden discharge, but I had stuff to take care of.

"If you handled him in the beginning, I wouldn't be standing here having this conversation with you. He's your son." I looked back and Tony who was clearly fighting with something inside him going by the worry in his eyes. "And he's your brother. Put a fucking muzzle on him already."

I made my way towards the door when Tony reached out and grabbed my arm. "Jas, wait. Look, I'm sorry about everything. I'm sure my father and I will get everything straightened out. You won't have to worry about this or anything anymore. As a sign of good faith, how about you and the gang come over and we do a barbecue like old times?"

Tony decided now would be the perfect time to be Chatty Cathy? "Um, Tony. Is this the time or place for the invite?"

"No, it's not. But I can't let you leave like this. You're like family to me. Come on, I think it will be fun. Besides I'm cooking, I will even make your favorite, ribs."

I was a sucker for some barbecue food. Tony knew what to do to soften me up. "Fine, Tony. If Angel and I ever get back on speaking terms, I will let him and the rest of them know. I need to know when it is though; we have a wedding to go."

He's eyebrows shot up. "Who do you know that's getting married?"

"One of Angel's friends, though with recent events, it's very possible I'm no longer invited. But I will let you know okay, Tony?"

"So being your date is out the question then, huh?"

I shook my head, laughing at him. He grabbed me into a big bear hug, whispering in my ear. "It will all work out, you'll see."

"I know, Tony. I won't have it any other way."

\*\*

*Tony*

After Jasmine left, my pops and I sat at the kitchen table in silence, neither one of us willing to speak. The weight of the guilt was starting to wear me down. I was tired of lying to Jasmine; I was tired of covering for Marcus. Would this constantly be my life? Would I always be forced to clean up his mess?

I scrubbed a hand down my face trying to wash away some of the exhaustion I felt. This had to end; at this point in the game we had to do something about Marcus and quickly. My father made a move to get up and leave but I grabbed his arm, stopping him.

## Chapter 6

"Where are you going?"

He ripped his arm out of my grip. "Last I checked, I was the parent here not you."

"Really? I couldn't tell."

"What the fuck is that supposed to mean?"

I let out an annoyed breath. "You know, for a hotshot lawyer, you shouldn't be this dense or stupid. What are you going to do about Marcus?"

"There's nothing to be done. All he's doing is scaring her; he won't cause her any physical harm."

I couldn't help the laughter that bubbled up. My father really just said that? He already physically hurt her, and I was sure if he were given another chance, he'd do it again. You would think, even if he didn't give two shits about Jasmine or what happened to Marcus, the lawyer in him would care about the breach of agreement his son was causing.

"Hello, pops. If he continues to reach out to her and she can prove it's him, that's a total breach of the agreement you wrote up. You do know this right? If she wants to, she can ruin your precious career."

"She doesn't have the balls to do anything, Tony. If she did, we wouldn't be standing here having this conversation now. Your brother would be sitting in Rikers Island, probably being someone's bitch."

The cold words hit me harder than I expected. Did my father really not give a shit about Marcus? "Dad, she didn't say anything because you made me convince her not to. I'm not doing that shit again."

My father's expression was sheer boredom. "Any and all evidence proving she was raped has been destroyed. Even if she tried to make the speculation, no lawyer is going to go up against me and win. They also ruled Jay's death a vehicular accident. If he wasn't speeding and hadn't run that stop sign, Marcus never would have slammed his car into Jay's."

I sat in stunned in silence. How had my mom ever put up with this man? He couldn't be this heartless, could he?

The front door opened carrying heavy footsteps into the kitchen. "Honey, I'm home!"

I was out of my seat with my hands wrapped around Marcus' neck. "Where the fuck have you been?"

He laughed. The fucking bastard laughed and I squeezed harder. "I don't see what's funny about my question, Marcus. Where did you go?"

His cold stare held mine, daring me to squeeze even harder. And I did. What I wouldn't give to end his miserable life right now. I'd probably get away with it too. My father was, was a great lawyer after all.

Marcus smiled at me. "Look pops." He coughed as my hold tightened. "My brother is trying to be my keeper. Aren't you proud? Look at how far we've come." He wheezed out the rest.

## Chapter 6

My father spoke up. "Knock it off, you two. Tony, let go of your brother and let's talk this out."

Yes, because endless talking always fixed everything in this household. I squeezed a little harder just for good measure before I reluctantly let go of Marcus. I sat down at the kitchen table with my arms crossed. I couldn't wait for my pop's latest lecture on how we're family and blah, blah, blah. I really wanted to pick Marcus up and beat my father with him. Maybe then these two would grasp how serious this situation was.

Marcus went to the fridge to pull out a soda. "So, pops, bro, what's on the agenda for this family meeting?"

"Your brother wants you to leave Jasmine alone." Our pops told Marcus in a deadpan tone that meant he really didn't give a shit one way or the other. I really did come from a family of dickheads, which didn't bode well for me.

Marcus walked over to where I sat and put the soda down in front of me. He stayed behind me, his mouth close to my ear.

"What is it about Jasmine that you feel the need to protect so passionately? You've turned a blind eye for all the other girls, Tony. Shit, I've told you countless of times which girl I was going to have before I had her, and yet Jasmine was the only one you fought me on. She's the only one you still fight me on."

He stood up and walked to take the seat across from me. "You want to protect her so fiercely, and I can't seem to fathom why that is."

He sat quietly for a moment, seeming to collect his thoughts, and then a nasty smile broke out across his face. "I know your little secret, Tony." He laughed. "I figured you out, brother. There's only one reason you'd warn me away from her and not the other ones. You want her for yourself. Don't you, Tony?"

His cold brown eyes locked on mine as the smile disappeared and he grew serious. Marcus leaned across the table. "You won't scare me away from her just so you can have her all to yourself. You will never have a chance with her, Tony. I can promise you that."

He slowly leaned back, never taking his eyes off of mine. "But since you're my brother, I can be nice and throw you a bone. You want to know what she feels like when she's wrapped tight around your dick? Milking your cock—"

I didn't even bother to let him finish; I reached over the table and connected my fist to his jaw. I was able to hit him twice before our father tossed me off him.

"That's enough of this shit. What have I told you boys before?"

"Oh, shove it, pops. This is not the time for 'we protect family' bullshit. How about you be a father, and handle your son. Shit, better yet, how about you be the lawyer you swear you are and handle your client."

Marcus stayed on the floor laughing like the nut job he was. "We're all related, Tony. I'm as much a part of you as I am of him. But I won't share Jasmine with you if that's what's getting your panties in a bunch. Jasmine is mine."

## Chapter 6

I pinched the bridge of my nose. The headache I had been fighting since Jasmine's phone call threatened to make my head explode from the inside out. I was going to die at an early age either from an ulcer or an aneurism dealing with this sad excuse for a family. It was getting harder and harder to deal with Marcus and his delusional self.

"I don't know how else to make this clear for you, Marcus. Just leave Jasmine alone, already. She's not yours and she does not want you. She will not come to you. In fact, her and Angel are together now. They're going to a wedding together. They're doing couple shit together because, guess what? They are together."

I shouted at Marcus. Maybe, if I screamed it loud enough, he'd get through his thick skull that Jasmine did not belong to him.

"For the love of God, just leave it alone and get on with your life."

Whatever humor Marcus had disappeared the second I mentioned Angel's name. I saw his features change drastically as he slowly got up and wiped the blood from his mouth. Marcus had that same cold stare in his eyes our father got when he was about to destroy the prosecution. Oh no. Nothing good was going to come of this.

"Marcus, don't do anything stupid."

"I'm going to tell you this one last time, Tony. When this is all over, you will see how right I am. Jasmine is mine. One way or another, I will have her again."

INTO PIECES

# Chapter 7

*Jasmine*

I was sitting in the hotel room contemplating finding a bus or train to take my ass back home. I was still trying to figure out how I even got conned into coming up here. Angel and I hadn't spoken since our disagreement. So, it wasn't like we came together. Shit, if we were getting technical I was now a wedding crasher. Well, look at me being all badass and shit.

I chuckled to myself. Holy shit this was pitiful. Was it too much to ask for a little communication? Was it so hard to say, "Hey, Jasmine. How's it going?"

I ran my hands through my hair annoyed with how things turned out. Why couldn't Angel just say all is forgiven and forgotten and we'd go right back to how we were before our fight? The days we were holed up in his room were perfect. But I knew we couldn't stay like that. The real world had come knocking, begging for attention.

The real world sucked.

I let out a frustrated breath. It had been entirely too long since we'd spoken to one another. I made sure to hit up him about my number changing but other than a "K," he didn't respond further or hit me up after. And we all know what "K" means. That was the equivalent to a whatever.

I knew things between us wouldn't be easy, but this was bordering on a little ridiculous. What made this whole situation worse? I actually missed him. Which was strange considering he was gone most of my life. But even when he was a million miles away, we always managed to talk. He may not have been here physically, but I always felt him here the rare times we got a chance to speak.

Now that we lived in the same time zone and in the same neighborhood, there was never more distance between us. It was like we were in two different worlds, unable to speak the same language.

I was having a hard time believing we really weren't going to get past this. Did we hit a plateau already? Were we only going to have great sex and this push-and-pull bullshit? I really thought being with him would put a balm on the shit storm of my life not add to it.

A loud knocking interrupted my thoughts. "Open up, you sexy bitch. I forgot my key."

I smiled. Kris had been keyed up since we left, and her infectious attitude managed to make me feel a little better. "What if I don't want to?"

"Well, then, I guess you get to go to the wedding in your birthday suit."

I let out a laugh as I walked to let the little gremlin in. We were splitting a room, and she had left earlier to find some dresses for us. According to her, a wedding on short notice didn't give her much time to prepare. I thought three weeks was plenty of time, but Kris liked to go above and beyond sometimes and she needed ample time to prep.

## Chapter 7

I groaned inwardly. I hoped she picked out dresses one can actually wear to a wedding and not something you'd wear to a club.

I didn't have the door unlocked for more than two seconds before Kris came barging into the room. She had on a beautiful strapless lavender dress that fit her perfectly. It stopped just above her knee. It looked so soft and elegant and almost calming, which was a complete contrast to her personality. Her hair was up in a messy bun.

I smirked. "You know, Chase isn't going to like that your hair is up."

"I'm aware." She whirled around to face me and her smile was pure devious. "Hopefully, I can convince him to take it down for me."

"Dude! Really?"

Kris shrugged. "What?" She had this mock look of innocence. "I promise, I'm gonna behave tonight. Scouts honor."

I busted out laughing. "You were never a scout, Kris." I nodded towards the two dress bags in her hands. "You planning on a couple of outfit changes through the night?"

She shook her head. "As tempting as that sounds, nope. These dresses are both for you."

I cocked my eyebrow at her. "So, I have a dress for the wedding and the reception?"

"No, I saw these two and I knew you'd look good in both. I just couldn't decide which would look better, but now that I think about it you're wearing the blue one."

She shoved the bag in my hand and ushered me towards the bathroom. "You plan on dressing me too? What if I don't want to wear blue?"

"Ha ha, funny girl you are."

She pushed me forcefully into the bathroom closing the door. "The blue one is a killer, Jas. That's the one that's going to get my brother's attention."

I walked back out of the bathroom chucking the dress bag at her head. "What if I don't want his attention, Kris? Give me the other dress."

She crossed her arms over her chest "Excuse me?"

I let out a sigh. "I'm just saying, what if there is no me and your brother?"

Kris let out this full belly laugh that had her whole body shaking. I really needed to branch out and make new friends. The ones I had were all certifiable, especially Kris. I wasn't aware I had said anything remotely funny.

"I don't mean to laugh, Jas. Honestly I don't, but that's probably the funniest thing I've heard. There's always going to be a you and Angel."

Yep, definitely certifiable. "I'm gonna need you to lay off the drugs, Kris. Shit, or start sharing the ones you're on that make you this delusional to think me and your brother have

CHAPTER 7

something." If she knew something, she needed to enlighten me a little. I was truly at a loss here.

She sobered up. "You have no faith, do you? Angel came home for you, Jas, nobody else. That's proof enough."

I scoffed. Here we go with this bullshit. It was cute and endearing that people believed he upped and left the Marines to come home for me. That he had some uncontrollable need to be with me and that was what drove him back here.

I rolled my eyes. I knew the truth. This was Angel's home. Where else was he going to go? He really didn't have any other options when his enlistment was over.

"Look, Kris. As much as this will pain you to hear, the only thing we've been great at since he's come home is sex. And look how long it took us to get there."

Kris laughed. "You're right, that was painful to hear. But let me ask you, what is it that you want from him? Is this only about sex? Are you just trying to erase the guy who hurt you, or do you want more with Angel?"

"You really want to talk about this? He's your brother."

"And you're my best friend. That doesn't stop because of who you're dating. If you want to talk, I'm always going to be there to listen."

Kris smiled warmly at me and I instantly reached out grabbing her hand. In all our chaos, she never once judged me on anything and I always knew if I needed it, she'd always be there. It was moments like these I was truly grateful I had her in my life.

I dropped her hand and walked over to the bed. This conversation seemed to be better if I sat down so I could think. "To answer your question, Kris, I'm not entirely sure what it is I want with him. I had this amazing idea in my head and maybe that's what's fucking this up. The picture I created about relationships definitely does not match what Angel and I are doing." I laughed a little. "Sad part is, I don't know if what we have even constitutes as a relationship."

I looked at Kris who was listening intently; this girl had her fair share of relationships and heartbreaks. From the outside looking in, it looked intoxicating in the best way possible.

"Hey, you remember how Jay was like a walking fortune cookie?"

Kris smiled and then rolled her eyes. "Who could forget? He *always* had something to say."

I laughed; sometimes Jay's endless philosophies annoyed the shit out of everyone.

"You know, he use to tell me. 'Jas I can't stop you from having boyfriends. It's gonna happen, can't do much about it. Though I will kill any guy who hurts you.'

I couldn't fight the grin that appeared on my face as my brother's voice filtered through my head. 'Just make sure when you find someone worth your time; the relationship is anything but mediocre. Love, much like life, should be

## CHAPTER 7

intoxicating. When they look at you, the ground beneath you should shake as the earth around you stands still.'

I got up and started pacing as the words just spilled from my mouth. "You know, this may be my first relationship, if we're calling it that, but I just expected more. I expected to be on this exhilarating ride. I always thought, well, before I was raped, I always thought I'd be in this state of bliss fifty percent of the time."

"I thought everything would be new and exciting. I thought I'd miss him when he was gone and not want to let him go when he was near. I truly believed I would have this whirlwind romance. But that's not anywhere near what we have. At least not yet."

"You know, I want to believe that Angel came home for me. I know he didn't, but some hidden romantic side of me wants that to be true. I want to walk into a crowded room and be the only one he sees. I know we're going to fight, that's normal, but I want to be able to fix it as soon as it happens. Do you know we haven't spoken since our fight? Look how long ago that was. Neither one of us is bothering to budge. Something's wrong here, Kris. Why aren't we moving past all this already?"

I stopped pacing and looked at Kris who didn't budge from her seat. I didn't need her to respond or give me some false pleasantries. I needed her to listen while I vented. She understood that, and I couldn't be more grateful for it because honestly that's what I needed right now.

I let out a breath. "Maybe it's me, Kris. Maybe Angel thinks I'm too broken. And you know I wouldn't blame him if that were the case. Some guys, especially subconsciously never really learn to deal with a girl whose been raped."

### *Kristal*

And here I thought, Angel and Jas would be the ones to heal each other. Instead of them mending each other, they managed to continue to hurt one another. I couldn't decided if I wanted to grab them and bash their heads together, or fall back and stay out of it completely.

The latter was probably the safest and wisest choice. But they meant entirely too much to me to just watch them destroy themselves.

I sat watching Jasmine fiddle with the bottom of her T-shirt looking so unsure of herself. She was once this fierce strong-minded person and somewhere along the way she lost sight of her strengths. But I knew better. Jasmine was still strong, even more so now. There was no way someone went through the shit she went through and still had the ability to want to wake up everyday unless they were strong.

I stood up and walked over to Jasmine, pulling her into a massive bear hug. It was the only thing I could give her right now. I didn't have any answers for her. That was okay. Sometimes that silent comfort, a strong hug, or the knowledge that someone is standing beside you, is all you need to know that you're going to be okay.

Jasmine pulled back first, wiping away a few escaped tears. "You know, all I do is cry now, Kris? It's insane. The waterworks start and they don't seem to stop."

## Chapter 7

She chuckled weakly and stepped around me to get the dress. "I guess I should get ready, huh? Don't want them to come complain how long we women take to get ready."

She turned to leave for the bathroom when I reached out and grabbed her arm. "Jas, wait. Are you sure you're okay?"

Talk about a stupid question. Of course she wasn't okay. I shook my head, but before I could speak Jasmine responded. "Don't worry about it, Kris. I have no other choice than to be okay. I won't accept anything less. I'm sure things will work out the way they're supposed to."

Jas' eyes darted to the clock on the wall. "Shit. They're going to be here in about two seconds, let me run and put this on." I let her go and she mad dashed into the bathroom.

These two were going to give me an ulcer. Angel was busy moping around or snapping at everyone and everything that got too close to him. I knew he missed her, but he refused to get off his stubborn ass and talk to her.

Pride was a funny thing; for the most part it was good to have. But when it came to love and relationships? That shit could be deadly.

Angel claimed if Jasmine really wanted to talk to him she would have made the effort to come see him. I told him maybe he should make himself more approachable. His response? He grunted and walked away. I had been tempted to chuck a pointy shoe at his head; maybe that would have knocked some sense into his thick skull.

Hopefully this weekend would put them back on the same playing field. One way or another, they needed to decide what it was they wanted.

I glanced at the clock on the nightstand. Shit! Angel and Chase would be here any second. The whole point to the blue dress was to get my brother to trip over himself. I didn't want him to see her half done; it would ruin the effect.

I walked to the bathroom door, knocked and sent a silent prayer to the heavens. Please let this night go well, without any hiccups. "Hey, Jas. You good in there?"

*Jasmine*

I nodded my head, unable to speak while I looked at my reflection. It was stupid really, I knew Kris couldn't see me but I still did it anyway. My voice was too busy stuck in my throat to speak. I was in complete awe at the dress she found for me. It was gorgeous.

The dress was a royal blue full-length gown with a tasteful slit up the side that revealed my leg. It was a low-cut halter that had a silver chain, which fell straight down my back. It was the only thing connecting my dress together. Honestly, this dress should have freaked me out. But I couldn't get over how good I look in it. And the best part? This dress fit me like a glove. No part of the dress was too big or a too tight. It fell just right against my body. Almost like the dress was tailor-made for me.

I turned one more time, looking at myself. "Holy shit." The royal blue looked amazing against my tan skin.

## Chapter 7

There was another knock on the door. "Jas, sweetie, I look very pretty and I would hate to have to bust in there, drag you out and mess up my pretty. You know how much I hate when people ignore me. So if you don't respond or come out in the next second, I will bust this damn door down and beat you on principle."

I rolled my eyes as I rushed to open the door. "You are by far the biggest pain in the ass in existence. If you didn't take so long finding dresses to wear, I would have had more time to get ready. Stop rushing me!"

Kristal's jaw was on the floor and her eyes were full and wide. "Holy shit, Jasmine." I smiled. Kris was right, there was no way Angel would be able to ignore me tonight.

"Let me look at you. Come, come turn around."

I turned around, grumbling under my breath. Her mother hen was out. We were clearly pressed for time, but she was going to make sure she inspected every inch of me.

When I turned back to face her, Kris was sporting a huge grin. She clapped her hands excitedly. "Damn, I do some good work. The dress looks amazing on you, Jas. Though, I think we should put your hair up and touch up your face with a little bit of make up."

No sooner had she finished her sentence there was a knock on the hotel door. My stomach bottomed out. *Oy vey*, they were here already? A flutter of butterflies flapped their very large wings inside my stomach. I didn't care how good I knew I looked, I was still nervous to see Angel.

Kris snickered. "Hey, Jas, be a doll and answer that; I have to use the ladies room."

She tried to side-step past me, but I snatched her up by her arm. "Oh no, no you don't. You are not leaving me alone!" I hissed.

I needed the support. At the very least, I needed her and Chase to fill any awkward silences that Angel and I would no doubt lapse into.

Kristal rolled her eyes. "Unbelievable, Jas. Stop being such a chicken shit. You put your big girl panties on today, now go answer the door."

She tried to pry my fingers off her arm, but I just held on tighter. "Jasmine, I swear I will pee on you if you don't let me go."

"Dude, ew!" I wrinkled my nose. "You wouldn't dare ruin both these dresses."

Kristal let out a sigh. "You're right, Jasmine. I wouldn't do that. But, I would totally do this."

She launched herself at my mid-section, pinching my side and causing me to release her arm. I cradled my side as a massive giggle fit erupted from my lips. Kristal dashed into the bathroom and locked the door. "Hey." I said in between giggles. "That was such a low blow."

There was another knock on the door and Kristal sing-songed from the bathroom. "Looks like you better get

## Chapter 7

that, Jasmine, before they leave without us. I would be really upset if I missed the wedding on the account of your cold feet."

"Well, maybe you should have opened the door yourself. You little shit." I turned around grumbling, "Damn gremlin."

I sobered quickly, fixing my dress more out of jittery nerves than anything else. I walked towards the door and took a couple of deep breaths. *Come on, Jasmine. You can do this. It's just Angel.*

I conjured up whatever courage I could muster and placed a smile on my face. *Here goes.* I opened the hotel door and my smile instantly fell. "Oh, it's only you."

"Well, shit, Jasmine. I'm happy to see you too."

Whatever hope I had about Angel and me died when I saw only Chase standing at the door. Why did I expect him to come pick me up? This wasn't some stupid fairy tale where the prince was going to come and whisk me away.

I pinched the bridge of my nose. I knew I shouldn't have come here. "I'm sorry, Chase. I didn't mean it like that I just–I think I'm gonna go home."

I turned and headed for the dresser, pulling whatever belongings I had out and into my duffle bag.

Chase came up behind me and placed his hands on top of mine stopping my movements. "Jasmine."

"It's fine, Chase. It really is." I looked up to see him looking at me with pity in his eyes. I wanted to smack the look off his face. "Don't you dare look at me like that. You damn well know I don't want nor do I need your pity."

"Trust me, Jas, the last thing I will give you is pity."

I scoffed. "Please don't insult me by lying either. Just let me go home with my pride still intact. It's clear he doesn't want me here, and I damn sure don't need to be here."

His hands moved, sliding up my arms and squeezing gently as his eyes softened. "He's not here because he's already at the church with the groom."

Ah, so now I was getting an upgraded excuse from the other day when we drove up here without Angel. Chase had told Kris that Angel wanted to head up early; you know, spend some much needed bro time with the groom.

I called bullshit. Angel wasn't worried about seeing the groom; he didn't want to be in the same space as I was. It looked like the drive up here didn't change his mind in the slightest.

"Chase, look don't–"

He cut me off. "Jasmine, stop it. You came all the way up here with us; you might as well stay and enjoy yourself. If you haven't noticed, your friend Kris knows how to have a good time. I'm sure you and her can get into enough trouble to keep you busy for the night."

I couldn't help it. I cracked a very reluctant smile. "Ah, and she smiles." Chase chuckled. "So what do you say,

# Chapter 7

Jasmine? It would be a shame to waste such a pretty dress on a train ride home, alone."

I rolled my eyes, caving. Chase had a point. Whether or not Angel and I even spoke at this thing was irrelevant. It would suck, but it was still irrelevant. I knew how to enjoy myself without him. I also had Kristal and her crazy self to keep me company.

"Alright, Chase. I'll stay. But you and Kris can't go running off and leaving me by myself."

Chase laughed. His eyes were light with humor. "I don't know what you're talking about. I–" He sucked in a harsh breath as the bathroom door behind me opened. Even if there were a billion people behind me, I would have known by the look on his face that it was Kris he was looking at.

His hazel eyes flooded with lust and something close to awe as they locked on Kris. His throat worked like he was struggling to gulp down air. He looked like a man consumed by the very breath she breathed.

I felt like I was a massive roadblock standing in their way, so I stepped around Chase. The second I moved, his long legs ate up the steps between them. I half-expected Chase to devour her face in a passionate kiss but he held himself, back stopping a few inches short of her.

He lifted his hand, and I saw it tremble slightly as he caressed her face, "Just when I think you can't get any more beautiful, you manage to prove me wrong. You have this knack for taking my breath away every time I look at you, Beauty."

## Into Pieces

Kris was leaning into Chase's hand as she looked intimately up at him. "Maybe you should stop looking, then."

He cupped her face in both of his hands, smirking a little bit. "I couldn't do that. My eyes seem glued to you. I'd be a happy man to die at your feet." Chase leaned in, placing the sweetest kiss on her forehead.

I swooned right along with Kris, but my swooning was quickly replaced with a pang of envy. I was envious at how easy this was for them. Watching them was like watching two people dance; where one led, the other followed. There was no need to ask for permission or awkwardness; they just knew. Their bodies were so in tune with each other; I don't even think Kris realized how her body was slowly getting closer to Chase's.

Angel and I may have had the physical aspect down, but this was different. There was an understanding here between Kris and Chase. As cliché as it was, it was like they were two pieces to a very special puzzle and they clicked in the right places.

Seeing them in this moment made me wonder if Angel and I would ever have it this simple. Were we doomed to constantly walk on eggshells around each other? Would we only have great sex and then allow the outside world to set one of us off so we could push the other away?

I wanted something special with Angel. I mean, if Kris and Chase can have it together and they weren't officially together, surely we could have it too, right?

## CHAPTER 7

It dawned on me then, maybe that was our problem. We were both trying to define something that didn't need any definitions. I liked him, he liked me, and we were together. It sounded simple enough, why were we complicating things?

I was making myself crazy watching these two being swept away in their own world. I turned to give them some type of privacy, and my knee connected with the stupid bedside table. "Ouch!" I winced as I heard Kris chuckle. Way to go, Jas, talk about being a cock-blocker.

"You okay, klutz?" Chase asked, interrupting my thoughts.

I turned back to them, noticing they were standing side-by-side holding hands. And just like that, the pang of envy was back. When it mattered, everything was simple for them.

I let out a sigh. "Yeah, I'm fine. Good thing this is a long dress. This is definitely going to leave a nice-sized bruise."

Chase checked the clock on the table that hit my knee. "I think it's time we head out. We don't need you attacking any more furniture. You ready?"

No, of course not. "Do I have a choice?"

They both walked up to me. Chase grabbed my chin, forcing me to look up at him. "Relax, Jas. It will be fun. No worries, okay?"

No worries? That was easy for him to say. I rolled my eyes. I needed to man up already. It was one night. I was here, might as well enjoy it. "Yeah, no worries. Let's go guys."

INTO PIECES

# CHAPTER 8

*Angel*

The wedding ceremony overall was nice. The wedding set up was the usual; priest, bride, groom and wedding party. A bunch of I dos and the "you may now kiss the bride." Don't ask me about anything specific because I couldn't tell you. I wasn't even sure if they wrote their own vows are not. My attention wasn't on the wedding. My attention was on Jasmine from the moment I saw her walk through those church doors.

Jasmine was breathtaking. Hands down the most beautiful female in this room. The royal blue dress, my sister had no doubt picked out, hugged every inch of Jasmine's lean body. The top was a halter encasing her perfect perky tits, making my hands itch to touch them. The back was open except for a silver chain that ran down the middle of her back and ended just above the curve of her ass. I wanted nothing more than to run my tongue and lips down her back following the length of the chain. There was a tasteful slit up her right leg. Every time she moved, I was afforded a glimpse of her mile-long legs–a place I desperately missed being in between.

Seeing Jasmine all dressed up made me kind of glad we didn't come down here together. There was no way we would have made it out of the room. I wanted to lock her away for a couple of days and devour every inch of her. I was having a difficult time wondering why I decided to stay away from her in the first place.

I was watching her now at the reception, talking amongst the guest. She fit in wonderfully; you would think she knew these people most of her life. It made me want to stand by her side like every other couple here. But as much as my dick wanted to be inside her, my feet couldn't find it in them to go and stand next to her. We hadn't talked since our fight. I guess there wasn't much to say.

Jasmine was gracious enough to text me however, and let me know she changed her number. Well, good for her, neither one of us made any effort to speak to each other after that. It kind of made you wonder what that said about us individually and our future together.

I spent entirely too much time without her to think about that future and to be honest, I wasn't sure there would be one. We continuously danced around any and all our issues. When something happened that let our demons come out and play; one pushed and the other one ran away, always.

The day in her kitchen with that damn package she pushed me away hard, and instead of pushing back, I walked away. It happened again in my kitchen. I pushed her away and she ran. That seemed to be our vicious cycle. We'd have great sex and then the real world would come barreling in like a freight train, knocking one of us down and causing the other to run. I hoped that cycle wasn't all we were going to be. If it was, there really wasn't a reason to continue on with this.

John, the groom, was sneaking up behind me. He walked with a heavy limp, no doubt the results from when we were attacked. His nickname had been Ghost when I meet him. No one ever heard him come or go. A six-foot-six, two-hundred-and-fifty pound man, one would think he made a lot of noise when he moved, but not John. If he didn't want to

## Chapter 8

be seen or heard, he wouldn't let his presences be known till it was too late.

"I know you can hear me, Torres. You don't have to pretend you don't."

His hand clasped my shoulder before coming to stand beside me. I looked in his direction; he definitely didn't look like the kid I met when I first went overseas. Back then he had a baby face with not a mark or blemish on him. Now he had a nasty scar that ran diagonal from his ear to his bottom lip. His eyes back then were still full of light and hope. It was a rare thing to see that in a warzone, but it was also what helped a lot of us through our time there.

Now his carefree look was gone. John was only a couple of years older than me but his eyes made him seem ancient. Like a kid who has seen exactly how cruel the world really was.

Looking at the man John became made me wonder, if I had been at my post that day, would things have been different? Would Tommy still be alive? Would John still be the baby face he was? In many ways I was responsible for so much loss. These guys had become brothers I wasn't granted at birth, and I let every single one of them down one way or another.

I laughed to myself. It's no wonder Jasmine and I were having problems. Of course she was going to run. I had a tendency to let those around me down, so why bother sticking around only to be disappointed in the end?

We both stood for a second not saying a word. John and I never had to speak when we were together. We enjoyed the quiet we were able to grant each other.

I followed John's line of sight, of course his eyes would be on his bride. The second she walked down that aisle, his eyes never left her. It was clear he was counting down the minutes before he kicked us all out.

"You know, John, if you want us gone just say the word. I'm sure even a bunch of drunk Marines can get out of here in two minutes tops."

He laughed. "Still a clown, I see. As much as I would love that, Brooke wanted this. Certain things, especially the little things, you just have to give to them."

"So that's the girl you came all the way home for, huh?"

He smirked; the intensity in his eyes went up as he watched Brooke laugh about something. Then a goofy grin splayed across his face. It was clear how much he adored her.

Brooke must have sensed John watching her. Her whole body shifted towards his direction. The second her eyes fell on him, she completely light up. There was so much love and adoration on her face when she looked back at him. She wasn't guarded and she hid nothing from her expression. They both looked so in love with each other. The whole room probably disappeared for them.

I felt like an intruder standing in with them on this stolen moment. I turned my attention to where Jasmine was. She was making small talk with one of the bridesmaids.

I watched her, willing her to sense me the way Brooke did with John. But she continued talking to the girl, none the wiser that I was here watching her, wanting her to feel something.

## CHAPTER 8

I heard John clear his throat. Did he start speaking? My head seemed to be more in clouds then in any present situation lately. "I'm sorry, you were saying something, John?"

He chuckled. "I was telling you how Brooke and I got together."

I pulled my attention away from Jasmine to face John eyeing me. "What?"

"Are you gonna pay attention to me or space out again?"

"Married all of a couple of hours and you're already acting like an old maid." I turned directly towards him. "You have my full attention, sweetheart. You may continue."

John laughed. "You can be a real schmuck sometimes, you know that?"

I shrugged. "Yeah, shit happens. Now back to this glorious story of you and your blushing bride."

I paused for a second trying to recall any and all our conversations. Only I couldn't find any detail of John saying he was with someone. "Um, my memory is usually spot on. I don't remember you saying you were with anyone when we met."

John shook his head. "That's because I wasn't. I knew I was going overseas; I didn't want to start something I wasn't sure I was going to be able to give my all or even part of me. We've been best friends since grade school. And it was always clear that we liked each other. But our timing always sucked. Brooke always had a boyfriend, and I was off being a douche. It kind of made you think it wasn't meant to be."

INTO PIECES

His eyes zeroed in on his bride before continuing. "I always knew I loved her, but it wasn't until I got hurt that I realized how deep that love was. You never know how much you truly need something or someone till the second it's about to be taken away from you."

He smiled. "It's funny how life works sometimes. Back when we were kids the most important things were Saturday morning cartoons. Now? I can't sleep unless she's in my arms. I don't understand how I survived all this time without her."

"You know, now that I've had time to think about it; if I didn't join the Marines, Brooke wouldn't be standing here as my bride. So in hindsight, I can put what happened to us at rest and be grateful for it. If I never got hurt like that, we'd still be out there and she probably would have run off and married some random dude." He laughed a little and his voice grew serious as he watched Brooke move around the hall. "On my hands and knees, Torres, I would go to hell and back for her."

Even if I didn't know John as well as I did, the conviction in his voice told me how serious he was. Anything Brooke wanted he would fight like hell to give it to her.

Brooke was a lucky girl to have John by her side. The truth though—John was even luckier to find someone to love the damaged man he came home to be. I couldn't help but envy what John was able to find with Brooke. I could only hope to be that lucky.

I turned back to face the crowd, my eyes seeming to instinctively seek out Jasmine. I really couldn't keep my eyes off of her tonight, or any night since I came home. I could admit it now, she was the reason I came back here. I needed

## Chapter 8

the calmness and stillness I found when I read her letters. Being near her now though, and knowing her intimately, she invoked anything but stillness. Jasmine created a certain type of chaos inside me. It was a chaos I found myself hungering for constantly.

I saw the punch coming a second too late and barely had time to dodge it. I guess John could still get the drop on someone if he wanted to.

"Ah, I see you still have your instincts, Torres. I never could get the drop on you."

I shook my head. Seriously? That was why he took a swing at me? The damn fool was trying to see if I was getting rusty?

"Bro? Is there a reason why you're testing my skills at your wedding? You know I like that rough shit but, come on, not in front of your bride."

"Well, if you'd paid a little more attention to me when I spoke, I wouldn't have to beat you. I don't like being ignored, you fuck." He grumbled.

"Wow, someone's a little needy today." I chuckled and placed my hands over my heart. "I'm so sorry, sweet pea. What can I ever do to make it up to you?"

John grinned. "Rub my feet and tell me I'm pretty."

We both laughed loudly enough to catch a few stares from the people who were closer to us. I missed this, the bullshitting and heckling back and forth with my brothers.

I sobered first. "So, what were you really talking about?"

John mocked offense. "How can you tell me you love me and never pay attention to me?"

"Maybe you should try harder to keep my attention."

He chuckled. "I can't even be mad you're ignoring me. Tommy was right about you. You zone out any time Jasmine is mentioned or crosses your mind. I never thought I'd see it, but, dude, you've had a one track mind since she got here."

My head whipped around to face him. The ass shit had a big shit-eating grin on his face. "How do you know she's even here?"

"Because, Torres, I see your eyes, and they've been tracking her ever since she walked through the church."

I gave him a stupid look. "That's bullshit, John. I'm staring at your ugly puss right now."

John laughed harder. "You maybe looking at my pretty face, but as I said, you've been tracking her movements. I can bet my left nut you know exactly where she is right now. I gotta tell you, Torres." He whistled. "She is a beauty. That blue dress fits her like a glove. If I wasn't married–"

I growled cutting him off. "Yeah, but you are, so back off, John. Now."

He threw his hands up laughing in earnest now. "Temper, temper, Torres. Relax, bro, I don't want her. Every other single Marine in here might, though."

"Yeah, well, they can't fucking have her." I threw my hands up in frustration. Unbelievable! The words slipped out

## Chapter 8

of my mouth before I thought better of it. John was right about one thing: when it came to Jasmine, my brain seemed to shut down. Any intelligent response or thought I had was gone. I had no claim to her, and yet here I was acting like a damn caveman.

John sobered and eyed me curiously before speaking. "You two haven't said two words to each other since you've gotten here though. What's going on?"

If I knew the answer to that question, I'd be over there with her and not talking to this pain in the ass. I wished this wedding were a few weeks earlier when I had an answer to his question. If this wedding was a few weeks ago, no one would question who Jasmine belonged to. But this wasn't a few weeks ago, this was today, and in all honesty, I wasn't a hundred percent sure what my answer was.

I wanted her, that much was clear. Physically we had this crazy combustible chemistry. The sex got better every time I was inside her or any time I got to taste her. But beyond that, that's where we were struggling. We had a history because we've always been in each other's life, but that's where it ended.

I thought back to the conversation Kris and I had. We were different people now. We had no clue who we were as adults. Who knew if the people we were now could even tolerate each other outside of the sex?

I saw the way Jasmine looked at me sometimes. She was still searching for the old Angel. It was too bad that kid wasn't coming back. He might make an appearance here or there but nothing permanent. I had been through too much to hold on to him.

Maybe that was where our real issues stemmed from. It wasn't that we were being suffocated by our demons. It was the fact we were operating on this false idea that we were still those same kids we use to be.

I watched as Jasmine got dragged to the dance floor by the tiny flower girl. The little girl couldn't have been more than three years old but she was a demanding little thing, telling Jasmine to dance with her.

The flower girl made Jasmine spin her around and kept yelling, "Like a princess, like a princess. Are you a princess like the other girls?" Jasmine laughed. I didn't make out what she was saying, but the little girl stuck out her tongue in response. This little girl was a brat to say the least, but Jasmine indulged her and continued to laugh.

I was struck by how unguarded Jasmine looked right in that moment. She was so open and genuinely happy. How many times since the rape and Jay's death did she have these moments? Did she ever really have them with me?

She looked up then, directly at me. Her smile was brighter now. I felt like I was sucker punched in the gut. I couldn't get my lungs to work properly. My heart sped up a little faster and I couldn't move. I couldn't do anything but stare at her. She was always beautiful, but nothing compared to when she genuinely smiled at me like that.

Her smile began to die. The very demanding flower girl dragged her off the dance floor and to the cake table. Why the hell didn't I do or say anything? What the hell was wrong with me? I felt John's hands on my shoulder, urging me to turn around, but my feet were rooted in place.

"Come on, Torres. If you're not going to talk to her, let's go for a walk."

"I'm good right here. Besides, I know you don't want to be away from Brooke."

"You're right, but I don't know when's the next time I'm going to see or talk to your ass. So the least you can do is humor me and go for a walk."

I winced. John was right. I ended up cutting everyone off after the attack happened. I thought it was better that way; easy to forget. I thought if I stayed in touch with everyone, all it would do was bring up unnecessary shit and emotions. Which is why I couldn't figure out how I was so gung-ho about coming up here.

I had every intention of bailing, especially after my fight with Jasmine. Chase and my sis strong-armed me into coming up here. They thought it would be a good idea. They ended up being right, of course, something I would never tell them out loud. I could only hope this meant more face time with my brothers after this.

## Into Pieces

# Chapter 9

*Jasmine*

Boy was that little girl a handful. I had to get one of the bridesmaids to take her off my hands. I finally made it to my table without the flower girl demanding something else from me. She was a cute bossy little thing but she tired me out.

The second I sat down, my eyes instinctively sought out Angel. I saw him still standing at the entranceway with John.

He looked so handsome in his dress blues. My brain was having a hard time functioning when I looked at him. I couldn't do anything but stare. As stupid as it sounded even in my own head, he simply took my breath away.

Angel looked every bit the solider he was. And the few times he smiled, my knees went weak. A few of the girls here couldn't keep their eyes off him either. Though I had no claim to him, the little green monster showed up anyway wanting to pluck their eyes out.

Both John and Angel were turning to leave; they probably had a lot of catching up to do. Before Angel completely walked out of the hall, he turned back looking directly at me. Something passed in his eyes that I couldn't decipher. Why didn't he just say something to me already?

I couldn't take the staring contest anymore, so I quickly looked away. Maybe that look on his face was annoyance. Angel probably didn't like the fact that I showed up and was interloping on his friends. I knew I shouldn't have let Chase talk me into staying. I should have just gone home.

Kris plopped down in the seat across from me giggling. "Jasmine, Jasmine, Jasmine. There are so many gorgeous men here tonight. Have you picked one yet? Why are you sitting down? You need to be out mingling."

I narrowed my eyes. "Are you drunk?"

She giggled again. "Nope, not even tipsy." She leaned in a little to whisper like she had some juicy secret. "They're giving out champagne like it's candy. It's delicious. You should have some."

I groaned. Kris could handle the hardest liquor out there. She wouldn't even get a buzz from it or have a hangover; girl had the tolerance of an Irishman. But give her a little champagne and she was a mass of uncontrollable giggles.

Chase started walking over to our table, and as soon as Kris spotted him, her giggles stopped. Her eyes got huge and her mouth formed an "O" shape.

I started laughing. "Hey, Kris. You might want to close your mouth, you're drooling."

"Come on, Jasmine. Chase cleans up very nice. He's completely lickable in his suit."

I shook my head as Chase approached the table with what I hoped was a glass filled with water.

"Here, Kris. Think it's time we switched you to water."

## Chapter 9

He sat down in the chair next to hers, pulling her closer to him. Chase's arm draped across the back of her chair and his hand barely touched her shoulder. I saw Kris visibly relax into him as she tried to wedge herself closer.

There was that envious pang again. Here Kristal and Chase sat, *together*, barely touching each other, not even in a relationship and yet anyone watching them could feel their connection.

This was ridiculous. Watching them made me want to march right outside and demand some type of answer from Angel. I hated this limbo phase we were in. Here I was at a wedding he invited me to and, other than a couple of stare downs, he didn't acknowledge me at all. If he couldn't get past what happened in his kitchen, then he needed to speak up and end things already. If it wasn't over, then he needed to cut the silent treatment already.

"Hey, grumpy." Chase said interrupting my thoughts.

"I'm not grumpy." I snapped.

"Whatever you say." Chase chuckled. "I'm guessing by your temperament you and Angel haven't spoken yet?" I gave him a no shit look. "Well, have you seen him at all?"

"Yeah, he just stepped out with the groom. Why?"

"Some chick keeps looking for him. Somehow they keep missing each other. I think she's the flower girl's mom. She said it was important."

INTO PIECES

She was going to have to get in line. Angel and I had too much to discuss, and it needed to happen sooner rather than later.

"Hey, Jasmine." Kris piped up after finishing her water. "You remember that hot Marine with the grey eyes?"

I chuckled. "You've pointed out a lot of hot Marines today, Kris. Little hard to keep track."

She wasn't looking at me anymore. She was drooling on herself as a tall brute of a man with incredible eyes made his way towards our table. Kris gave him a toothy grin once he got close enough.

"Hi, sexy." Kris said at the same time Chase growled and put his hand on the back of her neck. I cracked a smile. This was about to get entertaining. Chase was totally going to get into a pissing match.

Mister sexy eyes looked at Chase and his lips split into this devilish grin. I would have to be dead not to notice how hot he was. At least six-foot-five and built like a truck. His eyes and smile invited nothing but fun and mischief.

"Easy, bro. Everyone in here knows she's yours. I'm not here for her." He turned his smile and eyes in my direction. "I'm actually here for you."

### *Kristal*

Chase and I both laughed as Jasmine's entire face fell. Her eyes and mouth both dropped to the floor. She fell over her words. "Me?" she squeaked out.

## Chapter 9

Mister sexy eyes chuckled. "Yes you, sweetheart." He purred the words, and even though he wasn't speaking to me, it made my toes curl. Damn, this guy was good. Not only did he have the look, but his voice oozed sex.

Jasmine still looked baffled. This girl didn't know how many single men in here had been eyeing her since she walked through the door, including my dipshit brother.

I was so annoyed with him tonight. I thought for sure once he saw her in the dress it would kick his ass in motion. All he did was stay as far away from her as possible.

Well, you know what? His loss. I loved him to death, but you snooze, you lose. Clearly mister sexy eyes wanted her attention and she deserved it. I was over the whole "males keeping females in limbo" business.

I was ready to punch Chase in his throat. All night when someone made an attempt to talk to me, he was by my side being a possessive little shit head.

But let me try and push up on him or go in for a little kiss, he wasn't having it. 'It's not the right time, Kris,' and blah, blah, blah. I tuned him out after the first million times he repeated himself. It was always the same shit different day with him.

I must be a glutton for punishment. I continued to put up with it. I didn't hold out entirely for him, but I wanted to be with him. I knew Chase felt the same way, I just didn't know what the real reason was that had him holding back.

Mister sexy eyes introduced himself as Damien as he took Jas' hand in his and kissed it. A little pride surged through me as I watched her melt a little at the gesture. If this Damien dude had tried that a few months ago, Jasmine would have flinched and ran out of here.

She was learning to trust being in her own skin again; it was a good thing. She came a long way in such a short time.

Jasmine said something smart, and Damien smiled a smile that had sin written all over it. This guy had trouble oozing out of his pores; the good kind though. It was the kind of trouble I wanted with Chase, but he didn't want to play along. He would push me away until someone else came sniffing around, and it was only then that he wanted to act like I belonged to him.

I shook off his hold, annoyed with him and how the night was turning out. He growled, and I growled right back at his ass. I was through with him and his shit.

Damien and Jas both looked at us. Jasmine didn't bother to hide her chuckle as Damien turned to speak to Jas. "How about we leave these two love birds alone and you let me entertain you on the dance floor?"

I saw Jasmine visibly pull back a little bit, unsure of the request. Oh no, not tonight. She wasn't backing out of this. One of us was going to enjoy this weekend with a hot sexy man.

"I think she'd be happy to join you on the dance floor, Damien."

## Chapter 9

I pinned Jasmine with a hard stare telling her I'd beat her senseless if she declined. I turned my attention to Chase as I continued. "One of us should be having a good time tonight, and clearly it's looking like it won't be me."

## Into Pieces

# Chapter 10

### *Angel*

We walked out on to a huge balcony. I closed my eyes, inhaling the smells around me. It still amazed me the things you managed to miss when you no longer had access to them. I could count the number of nights I woke up missing the smell of the trees in bloom and the not-so-clean air of New York. As odd as it was, I was glad I had the opportunity to enjoy the little things again.

I opened my eyes, taking in the amazing view. There were weeping willows and flowers everywhere. I looked down noticing one flower in particular, the White Violet. It was Jasmine's favorite.

I glanced back to the hall, wondering if she even had the chance to come out here yet. She would have loved this view. Between the stillness and the unexpected calmness it offered, Jas would have enjoyed getting lost in her thoughts out here.

"It's beautiful out here, no? I think all this was the main reason Brooke picked this location."

I smirked. "It is beautiful, but you didn't bring me out here to look at the view. Unless of course you're trying to seduce me."

"I don't have to try. All I have to do is bat my pretty eyelashes and you'd throw the panties at me."

"Oh, baby! I love it when you talk dirty to me."

We both laughed good heartily. John clapped me on the shoulder. "I've missed you, Torres."

That statement took me by surprise. I always thought the guys didn't think about me too much. You know, because it would hurt too much to remember what we all lost out there.

I cleared my throat, trying to drive the tight emotions I was feeling out of my voice. "So what's up, John? What was so important you had to drag me all the way out here?"

He finally sobered and let out a breath that sounded like he had the weight of the world on his shoulders. "Time."

I looked at him confused. He wasn't looking at me, though. His gaze was fixed on something in the distance. "You brought me all the way out here to tell me about time?" I turned leaning against the railing.

"Time is a funny thing, Angel. It's something that isn't guaranteed to be long enough and once it's gone, we can never get it back."

I eyed him curiously. Yes, he made a valid point. But what did that have to do with us being out here?

John turned and looked at me, smirking. "There's a point I promise. I'm getting to it now." He leaned his forearms on the railing before he continued. "You know, it's funny, Torres. As kids growing up, we have this sense of invincibility. We think nothing at all can touch us. It makes us fearless and careless. It's a belief we tend to carry into our teenage years and even in early adulthood. In our mind's, we're Thor or Superman. Nothing can stop us."

## CHAPTER 10

He let out a ragged breath. "You know, I don't think I've ever gotten rid of that feeling? Even after I joined the Marines, I still thought I was fucking invincible."

He chuckled weakly. "A limp and a scar down my face later, I can be honest with myself and say I may not be as untouchable as my mind led me to believe. I mean, even Superman had his kryptonite."

I clapped him on his back. "War tends to do a lot of things to you." Shit, I knew first hand exactly what he felt. That feeling of invincibility was knocked out of me the day we put Jay in the ground. When I went overseas, any shred of invincibility I was trying to hold on to disappeared; guys I talked to one day would be gone the next.

John turned then, mimicking my pose against the railing. "No, you're not listening. I remember the feeling of invincibility, and I remember the exact moment that feeling disappeared." He turned, looking me dead in the eyes. "Oddly enough, it wasn't the day I joined the Marines or the day I got hurt and Tommy died."

John walked towards one of the windows that allowed us a view inside. He put his hand to the glass and titled his head. "The day I lost the feeling of invincibility was the same day I found out I won't live long enough to see my one year anniversary with Brooke."

I stood stunned. I was too baffled and furious to speak. What the fuck? We were Marines, we went to war; we barely came back alive and unscathed. John was going to sit here and tell me he survived all that only to fucking come home and die?

I took short breaths trying to calm myself. I didn't know the whole story; I actually had no idea what was going on. I tried clearing my throat; I needed to remove any type of heat from my words.

When I spoke I didn't manage much. "Are you sure, John?" He chuckled; the bastard had the nerve to chuckle like this was some kind of comedy.

He turned to face me and crossed his arms over his chest. He leaned against the window. "Oh, I'm very much sure, Angel. I have cancer. Very soon my organs will shut down one by one, and then I will cease to exist."

I was taken aback by how matter-of-fact he was about all of this. Was he just going to sit back and let it happen to him? Surely there was something that could be done to prolong his time; shit, maybe there was something he could do to beat this. He didn't survive what we survived only to get killed by a disease from the inside out.

"What about chemo?"

"I don't want it."

"Why the hell not?" I demanded. Like I really had any say in this.

He shrugged. "It's simple. There's no guarantee it's going to work. I'd much rather spend my days living and making love to Brooke. I can't do that if the chemo is knocking me on my ass more often than not."

"But–"

## Chapter 10

He cut me off. "It's my decision, Torres. I don't want to be bedridden the whole time. Brooke and I already discussed this. Look, Angel." He let out a tired breath and pinched the bridge of his nose. "I didn't tell you this so we can hash it out about my options. I wasn't even going to tell you till I saw the way you were watching Jas."

I threw my hands up and began to pace. "What the hell does you being sick have to do with Jas and myself?"

"Everything."

I stopped pacing and looked at him. He didn't elaborate. He just stared back at me. Oh, okay, so he was going to drop a bomb like that and then be mister vague.

"Bro, I want nothing more than to punch you in that ugly pus of yours and pray I knock some sense into you and hopefully bring your speech back. This way you can explain to me how you dying is connected to my relationship with Jas or lack thereof."

"If you'd calm your overdramatic ass down already. I'd have no problem telling you." I went to say some slick shit but John cut me off. "Stop, Torres. You want me to explain myself, how about you shut up and listen?"

I went back to my original post—leaned up against the railing, arms crossed, trying my best to keep my grumbling under control. "I'm listening."

John chuckled. "Good. Like I said, I had no intentions of telling anyone I was sick until the time got closer. The only reason I'm telling you is so you can wake up and stop wasting time."

"As humans, especially males, we waste so much time with the wrong one because it's easy. Little boys don't like to work for anything until we get some sense knocked into us and become men. Trust me when I tell you, knowing what I know now, I would go back in a heartbeat and get more time with Brooke. My heart hurts knowing I will never see her pregnant or watch our kids grow or be able to grow old with her. If you didn't learn this being a Marine, I hope to hell you learn it now. Nothing in life is promised. Stop being a stubborn jackass. You almost lost your opportunity to be with Jasmine once. Don't fuck up and let her slip through your hands again."

# Chapter 11

*Chase*

Kris moved to sit in the chair that Jas just vacated. Twice now Kris tried to get up and get away from me but I kept reaching out, halting her movement. I couldn't let her go, not tonight. I was being a selfish bastard, and judging by the daggers Kris was currently throwing at me, she knew it too.

I chuckled and I swear I heard her growl. I couldn't give her what she wanted, not yet anyway. But I'll be damned if I let someone else touch what was mine.

"You know, Chase."

Kris started. Those three words held every ounce of venom she possessed. She was getting ready to tear me a new asshole. I was terrified and turned on all at the same time. There was nothing sexier than a hot Spanish girl's temper directed at you. All that passion was honed in on you; it gave you a tiny glimpse of what she would be like when it was different kind of passion burning through her.

"You may cock block me all you want tonight. But I'm gonna let you in on a little secret. You damn sure can't do that shit forever." She let out a breath. "Something's gotta give already. I won't wait for you, and you damn sure know how unfair it is to expect me to."

She sat back in her chair crossing her arms over her chest. My eyes zeroed in on the action as it pushed her breast higher over her dress. I licked my lips as she continued to speak.

## Into Pieces

"I see it as something simple, Chase. Either you want me or—"

I didn't give her time to finish. I was up and out of my chair practically looming over her as our lips locked. She didn't kiss me back right away, probably trying to hold on to whatever resolve she thought she had left.

Yeah, that wouldn't do; I slipped my tongue out across her luscious lips and I felt the hitch in her breath. Kris had the most amazing lips I've ever had the pleasure of tasting. It made me burn with desire wondering if her other lips were just as appetizing.

She finally started kissing me back. Her tongue darted out to meet mine and I couldn't hold back my groan. This girl was going to be the death of me, and with her lips on me like this, it was a death I was glad to meet.

I was lost to this kiss, to her. The way her body naturally leaned into mine, seeking more of me. She couldn't resist me anymore than I could resist her, which made me feel even worse for keeping her hanging. I–Ouch!

I pulled back swearing. "You bit me?" I heard the shock in my own voice. This wasn't a-little-pain-a-little-pleasure kinky shit. She was trying to break skin; it hurt.

Kris had a nasty smile on her face and stood up. "What's the matter, Chase? You can't handle a little bite? Here's an idea, maybe you should keep your lips to yourself since it's not the right time and all."

## CHAPTER 11

She turned and stomped away. I let her go this time. She was right. I was being an extra special dickhead tonight. I scrubbed a hand down my face and sat down. I was tired. This back and forth was starting to wear on me too.

I shook my head; maybe I should have let Jasmine leave. We could have left together. We both seemed to be batting a hundred tonight. At least I was. Jas looked like she was moving on just fine with Damien.

"Oh, shoot, you sat down already."

I looked up into the face of the bride—Brooke, I think her name was. I wasn't paying much attention to anything other than Kris tonight. "Can I help you with something?"

She beamed. "Actually, yes you can. I was told you know where my husband is. Do you mind getting him for me, please?"

I let out a breath; I couldn't exactly turn her down. She was after all the bride and this was her day. "He's outside with Angel. I'll get him for you and congrats again."

I made my way out to the balcony where Angel and John were embraced in a hug. There was something heavy in the air, and I instantly felt like a dick for intruding on it. Looks like I was zero for two tonight.

I cleared my throat twice before they broke apart. Both John and Angel sniffed and their eyes were watery. Shit, what did I interrupt?

"I'm sorry to intrude, but your bride is asking for you."

John chuckled weakly. "Demanding little thing, isn't she?"

He clapped Angel on the shoulder. "Remember what I told you. Time is anything but your friend."

He walked past me while Angel walked towards the railing. I tried to think back to a time when I had seen him cry and I couldn't. Angel always held it together. He was the solid while everyone else around him broke apart.

I walked up, throwing my arm around his shoulder. "You good?"

Angel let out a breath, and I noticed his white-knuckle grip on the railing. "Not in the slightest, Chase. I some how keep fucking things up."

"Yeah? I guess that makes two of us man."

### *Jasmine*

I laughed as Damien led me off the dance floor and back to my table. He was even gentlemen enough to hold out my seat for me. He took the seat across from me and kept staring at me with humor in his eyes.

"See something that amuses you, Damien?"

"Nope. I'm just impressed and surprised you were able to keep up with me on the dance floor."

I let out a loud laugh. I was rusty, I knew that, but no one could touch me when it came it dancing; especially with salsa.

## Chapter 11

"What are you talking about, Damien? I ran circles around you on that last song. I didn't even break a sweat." I cocked my eyebrow at him as he took a napkin to wipe the sweat from his face.

"Hey! These dress blues don't come with any ventilation. Don't let a little sweat fool you. I'm not tired. I could always go another round with a pretty girl like you." Damien winked.

I chuckled. This guy was good. I was surprised he didn't have a harem of females waiting in the wings for him. He was at least six-foot-five, cock diesel with these smoky grey eyes that seemed to have a delicious heat to them. Add that to the fact that he was a Marine, and the panties were definitely getting thrown at him on the regular. Yet here he was sitting with me.

What seemed to surprise me even more was how easy this was for me. Had this been a couple of months ago, I would have been stuck in a corner bored out of my mind and too scared to have any fun. I would have flinched and panicked the second Damien showed any interest in me. But that was then and this was now, and I had to say I was actually enjoying myself.

"Hey, sweetheart, am I boring you?" Damien asked, interrupting my thoughts. I chuckled but didn't respond to him. "Oh, so I am, huh?" He moved and pulled out the seat next to me to sit. "Looks like I'm going to have to find a way to keep you entertained and engaged."

He draped an arm across the back of my chair. "So let me ask you a question. How is it someone as beautiful as you is single?"

"Who says I'm single?"

It was Damien's turn to chuckle. "Sweetheart, sweetheart. If you do have a man, I think you need to drop him. He should never leave something as precious as you alone. There's a high possibility someone might come and snatch you up."

I threw my head back, laughing and letting out a very un-lady like snort. Wow, was this guy serious? "Please, please tell me you have more game than that, Damien. Or are you not used to stringing sentences together because that pretty face of yours is what gets you all the girls?"

He smiled, his whole face lighting up. "You really think I'm pretty?" he said while batting his eyelashes at me. We both fell into a fit of laughter while the DJ called the attention of the hall.

"If I can get everyone off the dance floor, please. Thank you! It is now time once again to join Mr. and Mrs. Arroyo in a dance. Hey, John, buddy, where are you? Your beautiful bride is waiting."

John came limping into the hall making a beeline for Brooke. I expected Angel to be behind him, but he hadn't come in yet.

I turned my face from the exit. Clearly Angel made up his mind about us already. I was done looking for him, done waiting for him to acknowledge my presence. I was here to enjoy myself and that's exactly what I intended to do.

## CHAPTER 11

John hit the dance floor and practically devoured his wife's face. He kissed her so deeply you had to be dead not to feel what he was feeling.

The DJ cleared his throat. "Hey, kids, save it for the honeymoon. This is family night." That earned a couple of chuckles from the guest. "Okay, guys, this one's for you."

Kait Weston's "Till Death Do Us Part" began to play. And the water works were about to start. It was such a beautiful song. The way John looked at Brooke while she sang the lyrics stole my breath away. Watching them made me think of Angel. This whole wedding somehow made me question the relationship we had. Better, yet it made me question if we would ever have a relationship.

Were we ever going to find a way past all our demons and make this work? I wanted nothing more than to have Angel look at me the way John looked at Brooke. He looked at her like she was the only one in this room that mattered.

The DJ spoke again asking all the other couples to join the bride and groom on the dance floor. Little by little couples started making their way towards the dance floor. Damien got up holding out his hand to me. I looked up at him in confusion.

He let out a breath. "Come on, Jasmine. Let's dance."

"We're not a couple."

He laughed. "It's okay. I won't tell anyone. Come on, what's the harm in one more dance, sweetheart?"

I relented and took his hand as he led me to the dance floor. He put my arms around his neck as his hands went to my waist pulling me closer to him, and we began swaying to the song.

I could feel Damien's eyes on my face, but I refused to look directly at him. With the lyrics of the song ringing in my head and the surrounding atmosphere, it felt too intimate to gaze into his eyes. It would feel like we were a real couple, and I didn't want to be that with him.

Damien's hand left my waist to cup my face. "I don't think I've told you yet how beautiful you are, Jasmine."

He leaned in before I could get my brain to function correctly and respond. I leaned back and my eyes shifted to movement behind Damien.

"Oh, shit." I gasped and immediately stepped away from him. Angel was making a beeline for us and he looked pissed.

"Hey. What's wrong?" Damien asked concern lacing his voice. I shook my head as Angel's hand came down hard on Damien's shoulder.

"She's spoken for." Angel growled.

Damien chuckled. "Ah, say no more, Torres. My apologies. Jasmine, it's been a pleasure."

He leaned in, placing a kiss on my cheek entirely too close to my lips causing Angel to growl low in his chest. Damien laughed and winked at me before walking away.

## CHAPTER 11

This was the closest Angel and I had been in weeks. My whole body was yearning to reach out and touch him, but something kept me rooted in place. I couldn't find any strength to walk the two steps it would take to throw myself in his arms. I also couldn't find the strength to say anything to him, and judging by his silence, I guess he couldn't either.

"Forget this." I turned to get off the dance floor and away from him. I couldn't deal with the stare down we were giving each other. It was too much.

A hand reached out and grabbed my wrist. My body instantly melted at the touch. He spun me around into his waiting body, and just like Damien, he wrapped my hands around his neck while his hands were tight on my waist.

This time, the dance was different and not just because I was with a different person. Damien didn't hold me as close as Angel did. He was pressed so close barely a breath could pass between us. He still didn't say anything, though, he just swayed to the new song playing; John Legend's "All of Me." As the first lyrics began to play, I lifted my eyes to his, refusing to look or be anywhere else but here.

As we began to dance, it felt like the night at the seaport. The world faded away and there was only us. I found myself smiling and I saw the glint in Angel's eyes as well; he knew it too.

Here and now is what we excelled at. When everything faded away; there was no wedding, no Marcus and none of Angel's demons invading this moment. There was no need to speak. I heard his words.

It was this moment that I wanted. This undeniable connection I was feeling with him. It was in the quiet moments that I allowed myself to be open to him and believe we actually had a shot at a future together.

This was simple and we handled simple well. But there was this thing called life and it enjoyed un-simplifying things. We needed to find a way to survive the shit that life threw at us. It was easy to be okay in the quiet. The trouble we had was being okay in the chaos.

As the song ended, we continued to sway to some unspoken tempo only we could hear. It was too bad we couldn't stay like this. I wanted to lock out everyone and everything that threatened to break us.

Unfortunately, there was no way to keep the world out. That shit came barreling through any and all barricades you could set up.

I heard some female call Angel's last name. He seemed to ignore it or he hadn't heard it yet, which was fine with me. I could continue to pretend the world out there didn't exist. But the voice seemed to get louder or maybe closer, and I felt Angel's whole body tense.

"Hey, you okay?" His response was a low growl and he gripped my waist tighter.

"Hey, Angel. What's going on? Talk to me."

He let out a breath leaning his head against mine. "I'm so sorry, Love."

## Chapter 11

He placed a sweet kiss on my forehead and turned around to face the intrusion. I went to step beside him to see who caused the shift in Angel's mood, but he pushed me back behind him. I went to move again and he threw me behind him, blocking my view. Unbelievable! What the hell was he trying to shield me from?

INTO PIECES

# Chapter 12

***Angel***

It was only a matter of time before I ran into her. I made it my business to avoid her ever since John told me she was here. She was one of the main reasons why I wasn't so keen on the idea to come. I couldn't face her.

I couldn't handle seeing the accusations and hurt on her face. I knew I'd be crippled by it. I couldn't look her in the eyes and see her disappointment in me, knowing I failed her. I wasn't ready to face that. If I was being honest, I don't think that was something I'd ever be ready for.

As much as I wanted to dodge this yet again, I knew I couldn't. I had no choice but to deal with this confrontation because she definitely wasn't going anywhere now.

I wished this wasn't happening, though, especially in front of Jasmine who kept insisting on standing beside me. She wasn't trying to have me protect her from this.

I gripped her wrist unsuccessfully trying to hold her still. She made some un-ladylike noise before renewing her struggles. God, she was so stubborn.

I turned toward her. "Please, Jasmine."

It was all I could mange. My voice was thick with emotion. Somehow my plea was more than just a plea for her to be still. I saw it in her eyes the second she caught on to exactly what I was asking her. I let out a small breath, thankful that she understood. She relented her struggles, but that didn't stop her from asking questions.

"What's wrong, Angel?"

I shook my head. "Please, Jasmine."

That seemed to be the only two words my brain would let me speak. I guess it knew if I said more than that, I would continue to talk until I poured everything out to her. There was too much I needed to say to her and too much we needed to talk about. I guess, though, it would just have to wait.

I heard the angry clips of a pair of heels getting closer. I closed my eyes willing whatever strength I had left in me to surface so I could face her–Bella, Tommy's wife. Between the shit John told me about his health and the shit going on with Jasmine, I wasn't sure how much more I could handle tonight.

I turned to face Bella and watched as her steps faltered a little bit, causing the small hand she was holding on to trip.

"Oh no, mommy." The little girl gasped.

"I'm sorry, sweetheart." She whispered, refusing to take her eyes off me.

We both stood rooted in place. Neither one of us was capable of doing anything but stare at each other. I watched as Bella's emotions splayed across her face. Utter sadness to hurt and then finally anger.

"Hey, mommy, why we stop?" My eyes darted to the little girl standing beside her. It was the flower girl I saw dancing with Jasmine earlier.

## CHAPTER 12

When she finally looked in my direction, I felt like I'd been hit by a semitruck. Everything around me came to a screeching halt. "Holy shit." I choked out. Everything I was running from came rushing to the forefront. The wall I so expertly built around my emotions came crumbling down.

"Sadie."

I whispered her name and the little girl's face lit up in the same exact way Tommy's did when he smiled. And just like that I was brought back to the night Bella made me promise to bring her husband home and right back to the fateful night I broke that promise.

I couldn't get enough air in my lungs. This was too much. Seeing this little girl who was the spitting image of Tommy broke every and any defenses I thought I had. I was drowning; everything I was running from, every single demon I had, came rushing through, the wall no longer there to hold them at bay.

The weight of them caused my knees to buckle. I was sure I'd hit the ground hard, walling in the pain I thought I could outrun. I couldn't figure out how I was still standing.

That's when I felt her. Through my emotional haze, Jasmine was standing right there. I didn't remember letting go of her or hearing her move from around me. But there she was, slowly anchoring me, bringing me back to the surface. She always seemed to ground me when I needed it the most.

Her lips were moving but I couldn't make out what she was saying. I wasn't focused on her words; they didn't seem important. I was focused on her presence. She was here and she was trying to ease my hurt.

I heard my name in the distance as soft hands caressed my face wiping away tears I wasn't aware I had spilled. This was all such a mess.

I heard my name again. She was slowly breaking through the heavy fog my emotions held me in.

"That's it," she crooned, "my strong warrior."

I blinked a couple of times. Slowly, everything was centering itself. I remembered where I was as my eyes finally focused and zeroed in on Jasmine.

She was as beautiful as ever and her eyes were laced with concern. "Hey," I croaked. Holy shit, was that my voice?

"Hey," she repeated, but I heard her question. I shook my head, not trusting my voice yet. I leaned my head against hers, closing my eyes and inhaling her raspberry scent.

It was in this moment where my life and my emotions were chaotic that I realized how vital she was to me, to my sanity. She didn't necessarily quiet the storm raging inside of me. Oh no, that storm still beat loudly. Just now, in her presence, that storm was no longer deafening nor threatening to swallow me whole.

It looked like my little sis was right. There was no way we gave each other enough credit. I was sure Jasmine would have tucked tail and run. But my demons were out and about and here she was standing strong with me, beside me. It looked like our demons might just get along after all.

## Chapter 12

A throat cleared somewhere in the distance and just like earlier, I did not want this moment, albeit an emotional one, to end. I somehow found a glimmer of peace and all I wanted to do was hold on to it for a little while longer.

The throat cleared again and I reluctantly pulled back from Jasmine, immediately missing her warmth. I moved in front of her and she didn't protest this time. She laid a hand on my back letting me know she was still there if I needed her.

She had called me a strong warrior? Please. She was the warrior, she always had been. I wasn't her strong warrior; she was mine.

I turned around facing an angry Bella. I guess it was now or never. I really had no choice in the matter. I had nowhere to run. And honestly, I was to tired too anyway.

"Torres."

My name was like a whip being cracked. I had to stop myself from flinching at her tone. This was going to hurt. Bella was going to make sure she ripped me open and stripped me bare. To be fair, she had every fucking right to lay into me.

I caused her to hurt; I caused her beautiful little girl to grow up without knowing her father. Her pain was my fault and if she needed to hurt me to feel even an ounce better, I would gladly grin it and bear it.

She didn't utter another word yet. We both were stuck staring at each other. Bella looked like she was sizing me up, getting ready to attack. I faced countless deaths and nothing scared me more than the look in Bella's eyes.

I wanted to speak, to tell her something, but I still didn't trust my voice. Besides, what exactly could I say to her?

Bella cleared her throat. "I hate you." The words were just above a whisper but I felt each one with as much force as a blow to the skull.

She let her head fall into her hand before taking a deep breath and facing me. "I had this whole speech planned out. I've been waiting since the day I found out about Tommy."

Her voice broke and I saw the tears begin to form in her eyes. "Excuse me." She cleared her throat, again trying to find her resolve. "You never reached out to me. Not once, Torres. I thought Tommy was your friend. How could you? You promised."

The last word was spoken on a sob. I reached for her, only to have her step back like I had an infectious disease.

"Don't you dare touch me. Don't you dare offer your concern, especially after all this time!"

"Bella."

My voice cracked. I cleared it, trying desperately to hold my shit together. "Bella." My voice sounded steadier than I felt. "I'm sorry."

Those two little words seemed inadequate but they were all I had to offer her. They weren't any empty sentiment that really didn't mean much. I truly was sorry.

I was sorry I took away her chance to grow old with the love of her life. I was sorry I took a father away from his child. I

## CHAPTER 12

was sorry I couldn't protect him the way Marines should protect each other. I was sorry I didn't bring him home, alive.

Mostly, I was sorry for causing the deep pain Bella dealt with day in and day out. I couldn't even begin to understand how her heart survived it. The worse thing about all of this? I couldn't do anything to fix it.

"You're sorry?" she whispered it. I registered the shock in her barely audible tone before she laughed humorlessly.

"You're really going to sit here after all this time and tell me you're sorry?" Bella stepped closer to me. "You can take your sorry and shove it, Torres."

Her hand came up in a tight fist and she swung it down at my chest. "Your sorry won't bring Tommy back." Another hit. "Your sorry won't take away this crushing pain I have. I'm suffocated by it everyday." Another hit. "Your sorry won't help me explain to this beautiful little girl why her father isn't here."

Her fist kept coming, each hit harder than the last. "Your sorry doesn't mean shit to me, Torres." Another hit. "I just want Tommy home."

She collapsed into my chest sobbing, the hits no longer able to hold back her sorrow. Bella openly cried as her daughter clutched her legs, begging her not to be sad anymore.

I couldn't do anything but engulf her in my arms. She didn't try to push me away this time. Instead she held on tighter as her sobs wracked her entire body.

## Into Pieces

How long did she have to hold on to all this? I felt my own tears trickle down my face as I squeezed Bella tighter. I should have reached out to her sooner. All those years she was left alone with her pain. I messed up so much in my life. I needed to find a way to fix it all.

# CHAPTER 13

*Jasmine*

I was off in the corner pacing and chewing my nail beds to shreds. My perfect manicure was now nonexistent. The polish was stuck between my lips and littered the length of my dress. I was stressed, to say the least. How long had Angel been out there? I mean seriously?

After Bella's nice little breakdown, she handed him an envelope with his name scribbled on it. He took it and excused himself. That seemed like forever ago. What was he reading, a thesaurus?

"You're going to drive yourself crazy, Jas. Why don't you sit down already?" Chase mused.

Chase, the groom, Bella, and myself had a table off in the farthest corner of the room. Bella placed herself as far away from us as she could get. Her eyes were still watery and bloodshot red from the heavy crying she did earlier.

There was a huge part of me that felt sorry for her. Well no. I wasn't sorry for her. If I was, that would mean I'd pitted her and I didn't. What I felt towards her was sympathy.

I understood loss, especially her kind of loss. What I went through might have been different. Jay was only my brother, after all. But I knew and understood all too well what it felt like to lose a part of you. Honestly, I had to give her credit. I had no idea where she found the strength to wake up and face the world everyday.

## Into Pieces

I saw a flash of movement in the corner of my eye. I turned and spotted Angel walk into the hall. He scanned the room, probably looking for Bella.

The instant his eyes fell on me, a gasp escaped my lips. His beautiful green eyes were a turbulent sea of emotions.

Just looking into them told me exactly how much pain he was in. No matter how fine he may have said he was, he couldn't hide from me with his eyes. Not now, anyway.

They looked more haunted now than they did the night he finally came home. I wanted nothing more than to go to him, but something had my feet still rooted in their place.

I didn't want to rush over to him and overwhelm him only to have him shut me out. I continued to hold his gaze, silently letting him know I was here for him.

Angel closed his eyes and I saw his chest repeatedly rise and fall with each deep breath he took. When his eyes opened again, they seemed different. They softened and looked almost pleading. It was that pleading look that made my feet move to get him.

I took a step and Chase reached out grabbing my arm. I turned a questioning look at him, but he shook his head.

"What's the problem, Chase?"

"I don't think you should go to him just yet, Jas."

"Why the hell not?"

## CHAPTER 13

"I can't gauge his mood. I don't think it would be a good idea to approach him yet. I think we've had enough attention on us tonight."

I opened my mouth to say something but quickly snapped it shut. Chase, unfortunately, had a valid point but it wasn't one that mattered. Something inside me knew Angel was done with the scenes for the night.

I tried to tug myself out of his grasp but Chase squeezed my arm tighter and I winced.

"Jasmine."

"Stop trying to manhandle me, Chase. Look, I know you're coming from a good place. I get it. I really do. But let me go."

As soon as I spoke the last word, a hush that fell over the party. The atmosphere changed and I heard Chase swallow loudly. I felt Angel behind me. He was close enough that I felt each exhale he took against my ear, but he wasn't close enough to touch.

The growl that emanated from his chest was loud enough that I felt the vibrations from it against my back. Chase immediately released my arm and backed up. I had to bite my lip to keep from smiling. The look of a little fear on Chase's face was priceless. Served him right for keeping me from Angel.

I turned and came face-to-face with my beautiful warrior. His eyes were still a turbulent sea that bored into mine. It felt like he was forcing me to see everything he was feeling. Everything he kept bottled up was bleeding through those eyes of his, and I refused to look away or be scared by it. He wanted me to see? Fine. I'd stand here all night taking it all in and show him I wasn't going anywhere, not this time.

He reached into his pocket and pulled out the envelope with his name on it. His eyes never left mine as he spoke to Bella.

"I read it. Did you ever get her baptized?"

Bella came over and took the envelope. "No."

He nodded his head. "Good. My number's on the back."

It was then that he looked directly at her. His piercing green eyes leveled with hers. "When you're ready, call me. I'll be there this time." He absently reached out grabbing my wrist. He made lazy circles with his thumb across my erratic pulse.

"Jasmine," he said my name in a pained whisper. He turned back to face me. "Come take a walk with me. I think it's about time we talked."

Angel turned, threading his fingers through mine as we walked the length of the reception hall. All eyes were glued to us. No doubt people were curious to see what other form of entertainment we would provide for the evening. I couldn't wait for this night to be over.

He finally led me outside to an empty balcony. I was thankful for the much-needed privacy it would give us. It was the first time I had the chance to come out here and the view was truly breathtaking. The way the moon and the stars

## CHAPTER 13

reflected against the stillness of the water offered a sense of peace I hadn't felt in a very long time.

I felt Angel move behind me. Every nerve in my body went on high alert. His chest was to my back, barely touching but close enough to make me feel every single firm inch of him. His arms and hands caged me in against the railing as his lips came down against my ear. His breath was warm and it caused goose bumps to spread across my exposed skin.

It was taking everything in me not to push myself back and rub against him like a starved cat craving his affection. We were supposed to be out here talking nothing else. Yet, I couldn't summon the energy to push him away. I wanted this. I wanted his hands and his lips on me, stroking me to a desire only he could satisfy.

"My sweetest sin," he whispered in my ear, and my head dropped back on his shoulder. "I was out here earlier with John and I thought of you. It's beautiful out here no?"

I nodded. I couldn't trust my voice to not sound needy.

"But now that I see you out here with this as a backdrop; it's just simply..."

His words fell away as he took one of his hands and ran it from my neck down the middle of my back, following the same path as the silver chain on my dress. He barely touched me. His fingers were light like a feather, barely there but enough to ignite a fire deep inside me.

## Into Pieces

"Have I told you how beautiful you look tonight? I haven't been able to keep my eyes off you since you walked through those church doors, Jasmine."

Angel's hands stopped right where the silver chain ended at the curve between my lower back and the top of my ass. He placed a light kiss below my ear and my knees buckled. I was sure I would have hit the floor if not for the death grip I had on the railing.

"I love how responsive you are to me, Jasmine. I can't decide if I want to worship you like this or peel this dress off that delectable body of yours."

His hand dipped lower, caressing my ass. He hummed low in his throat and the sound caused a rush of liquid to dampen my already soaked g-string. I wanted him. My body craved him.

Angel chuckled. "You know, it's been driving me crazy all night wondering if you wore anything underneath this." His hand moved across my ass again and he groaned. "What am I going to do with you, Love?"

Angel whipped me around and his lips came crashing down hard against mine. This wasn't a slow soothing kiss meant to seduce. No, this was a hard lip-biting I-need-to-consume-all-of-you kiss. And it had me groaning and going limp in his hold.

His body was flush against mine as his hands tightened around my wrist. He effectively caged me in and held my body in a way that allowed him to continue to devour me.

CHAPTER 13

This was exactly what I wanted, what I yearned for all those weeks without him. I was hungry for him and everything he had to offer. I was dizzy and light-headed from his intoxicating taste and touch. He was the best kind of drug I've had the pleasure of consuming.

Somewhere in the rational part of my mind I knew I should stop this. This was doing nothing to help our current issues, but I just couldn't get enough of him.

He groaned into my mouth as he pushed his erection into me. My body responded back desperately trying to get as close to him as possible. He wanted me with just as much force as I wanted him. He couldn't fight the chemistry anymore than I could.

All too soon he tore his mouth from mine as he stepped as far back as possible. I had to swallow my whimper of frustration as I struggled to keep myself steady. I didn't realize how much I was using his body for support until he stepped away and I almost went with him.

Angel's eyes were now mossy green; he was aroused. He licked his lips as I watched him drink in the sight of me. I was sure with my swollen lips and my erratic breathing I looked as sexualy frustrated as I felt.

Angel took a deep breath and adjusted himself. Good. I smirked. It was nice to see I wasn't the only one affected. All that control he possessed and I was able to get him to lose it almost every single time.

"I didn't ask you out here for this, Jas. It's just every time I get within an inch of you, I have this desire to consume and devour you." He chuckled while running a hand down his face. "But we do need to talk. I think it's long overdue."

That was a pity. Our chemistry seemed to be the only thing we excelled at and something I thoroughly enjoyed. I wanted to close the distance between us and finish what he started. My libido had fully taken over and it wanted to be satisfied.

But that wasn't going to solve anything. I took a deep breath, desperately trying to get my hormones under control. We did need to talk. We had a lot of shit to put on the table and raging hormones were just going to prolong this.

"I'm all ears. Though I can't imagine what you'd have to say now. You were quiet for weeks."

I winced. I heard the bitchiness in my own tone. That was my frustration speaking, every time he kissed me it ignited a deep hunger. I wanted him to slack the lust he caused, but that wasn't going to happen. We had too much to discuss.

Angel scowled and crossed his arms. "That works both ways, Love. I didn't see you reaching out to me these past weeks either."

"That's bullshit and you know it. I told you I changed my number and you didn't even respond. You saw me millions of times and you walked on by. You shut me out, Angel. You always shut me out."

His voice softened. "And you continue to push me away, Jas." He dropped his arms. "We used to talk about everything

## CHAPTER 13

and anything. Now it's like pulling teeth with you. What the hell happened to us?"

I shrugged. "I wish I knew. Things were a lot simpler back then. Maybe life got a little too complicated for us."

"I don't think it's that."

Angel walked back over to me. He brought his hands up to cup my face. With heels on I was at eye level with him. "You know, I like you at this height." He brought his thumb over my bottom lip and my breath hitched.

"Always so responsive to me. You really do make it hard to stay away or focus on anything but you." Angel leaned in like he was going to kiss me again but abruptly pulled back. "You see, every time I get too close I have to touch and taste you. I don't think I would even know how to resist you."

He let out a breath. "But regretfully, now is not the time for that. I want this Jas. I want you; us. But if we can't find a way to fix our issues, we're not going to make it as a couple."

My stomach bottomed out. Whatever arousal I was feeling completely died out as he dumped this cold bucket of water on me.

This was it. It looked like these weeks without each other put things in perspective for him. We were going to end before we ever really had a chance to begin.

My mind began to race at all the possibilities. Did he even want to fix us? Did he find these quiet weeks without me had been easier than struggling through our issues? It made complete sense now why he kept pulling away. The sexual chemistry might have been there, but it wasn't enough for him.

Angel turned and headed back towards the entranceway. He faced the window that allowed you a look into the reception hall. I noticed then how relaxed he looked. His posture no longer held the tension he had from earlier. It looked like whatever was weighing him down he no longer cared about.

"Did you want to participate in the bouquet throwing, Jas?"

What? How did this even matter? Talk about whiplash. I thought we were out here to talk or end whatever this was between us. What was with the small talk?

"I wasn't all that eager to catch the bouquet. Why are you asking?"

"They're doing it now and Kris is front and center." He chuckled a little bit. "I almost feel bad for everyone in there."

I smiled despite myself, picturing Kris' short self in front and throwing elbows. Odds were, she was going home with the bouquet even if it meant she took out a few people along the way. Kris was a little monster.

As much as I would have paid to see Kris in action, I wasn't sure what that bit of information had to do with anything. I thought we were out here to discuss us, not engage in this pointless talk.

## Chapter 13

Angel still stood looking at the window. I guess whatever was happening inside was more important than the here and now.

I saw Angel let out a breath and he finally turned around to face me. Neither his face nor his eyes gave anything away. *And here we go.*

"Jasmine."

He said my name in a whisper that felt like an intimate caress. He may have been able to keep his emotions off his face, but he couldn't hide them in his voice.

"My sweetest sin. What am I going to do with you? Do you think you're ever going to let me truly love you?"

## Into Pieces

# Chapter 14

*Kris*

Of course this son of a bitch would catch the garter belt. All the single Marines in here and not one of them bothered to step up or fight him on catching the damn thing. Thanks to Chase who all but clubbed me and dragged me away, every hot male in here completely backed off because they thought we were together. Idiots.

I had half a mind to pass the bouquet off to some other chick just to wipe that smug little smile off his stupid face. But, when I actually thought about it, I wasn't too pleased with the idea of his hands on some other chick. So here we were, sitting in the middle of the dance floor waiting for Chase to put the garter belt on me. I just had to go and catch the bouquet.

The DJ stood next to Chase trying to grab his attention, but he wasn't paying him any mind. His eyes stayed locked on mine. His hazel eyes darkened as he drank me in. There was a fire there. A fire I knew burned solely for me. It was too bad I never experienced that fire fully unleashed. No matter how hard I pushed, Chase always held on to his control.

The DJ spoke into the mic. "You ready for this, man? I saw her catch the bouquet; she's a feisty one."

Chase's lips pulled into a knowing smirk that had my toes curling. He knew exactly how feisty I could get and no matter what he said, I knew how much he relished it. "No worries. I can handle her just fine." He winked at me as the guys in the audience erupted into a chorus of cheers.

Handle me? Yeah aight. He couldn't handle me even on my worst day. I raised a questioning eyebrow at him and he chuckled in response.

The DJ spoke again. "Alright, alright. This should definitely get interesting. Just try to keep it PG, that's all I ask."

Chase licked his lips and it sent a shot of heat straight to my core. I had to bite back my groan of anticipation. I might be pissed at him, but my body clearly still liked him. I could feel my arousal growing at the prospect of Chase's hands on me.

Chase knew it too, going by the flare of his nostrils. He knew all he had to do was look at me with those eyes and my body would respond. This wasn't going to be over quick. Nope, he was going to make sure he dragged this out to drive me crazy.

The DJ walked away as the lights dimmed and the music began to play. It was a slow sensual song that oozed sex. The temperature in the room instantly shot up a few degrees as Chase stalked towards me. He looked like a jungle cat, smooth, sleek and powerful.

I wasn't going to survive this. There was no way I was going to walk away unscathed from this menial task. Chase would no doubt turn this into something; something that was going to leave me in a pool of my own desire desperately seeking more from him.

I tried to think about something dull and uninteresting. I tried to look away but I couldn't. Chase's eyes were locked on mine holding me captive. The promise was clear he was going

## Chapter 14

to devour every single inch of me. The only thing I could do was sit here and let it happen.

He licked his lips as his eyes finally left my face to travel the length of my body. My breath hitched and my legs opened on their own accord, willingly inviting him in. I saw his nostrils flare as he watched my body's response to him.

When he finally reached me, he stepped in between my legs, widening them to fit his size. He brought his lips down to my ear, groaning my name. I had to bite back my answering whimper.

Chase's hands shot into my hair snapping the hair tie that held my bun in place. I winced at the pain, but it was quickly forgotten as his hands massaged my scalp soothing the ache.

"Shh, Kris, a little pain for a little pleasure. I told you before you need to wear your hair loose. How many times do I need to remind you how much I like to run my hands through your hair?"

I didn't respond. I could barely get my head to nod let alone form a coherent sentence. His hands in my hair felt amazing. I titled my head back, trying to get closer to his touch, and purred.

Purred? Seriously, who was I? I was supposed to be mad at him, right? Yeah, when he rubbed my head like this, I couldn't summon the strength to bring my defensives back up.

All too soon his hands were out of my hair and gripping my hips hard. My eyes flew open to his and his lips were turned into a devious smile.

"I think it's time for a little payback, Kris. I need you as crazy as you've been making me all night."

"Give it your best shot."

I tried to sound challenging, but I heard the huskiness in my voice. His nearness was turning me on more than I cared to admit.

His eyes darkened, and on a growl, his hands went back into my hair forcing me to stare directly into his heated gaze.

"I know what my hands on your body do to you, Beauty. Once I'm done, you'll be begging me to take you. Now, try and keep that sexy little mouth of yours quiet while I touch you. We do have an audience."

Chase dropped to his knees in front of me. I felt my core throb with anticipation. I wanted us alone. I wanted him, as he was, fully clothed and head in between my legs licking me till I screamed my pleasures. The thought and visual sent another rush of wetness to my core. My thong was soaked with my own juices.

Chase pulled my legs open wider to accommodate his width. His hands massaged my calves as they traveled up and down the length of my legs. I loved the roughness of his hands against my body. His delicious smile was still in place as he watched me closely, gauging my reactions.

His hands went higher up my legs, but nowhere near where I wanted him. I tried to scoot down a little. I wanted to get closer to his touch, but he held my knees tight, shaking his head.

## CHAPTER 14

"Stay put, Kris, or I'll stop." He leaned in closer and hummed. "I can smell how wet you are for me. You're hot for me aren't you, Beauty?" I nodded my head in response. "Do you ache for me, Beauty?"

"Yes," I whispered.

Chase bit his bottom lip and a small whimper escaped mine. God, what was he doing to me? He shot up abruptly his lips to my ear. "Good. I want you to ache for me, Kris. I want you to be so consumed with desire that not even your best vibrator can relieve your ache. I want your body to crave mine, Beauty. I want you helpless to your desire for me."

He adjusted himself as he stood beside me. An eruption of applauds broke me out of my trance. The DJ came into view his hand stretched out in front of me. I stared at it for a second. I couldn't get my brain to pull itself out of the lust haze I was practically drowning in. The DJ chuckled while he pulled me up, and I completely stumbled into his hold.

The DJ spoke into his microphone. "Now, that was just hot. Can we get another round of applause for these two?"

All I heard were the males hollering and cheering. I looked down and noticed the garter belt was wrapped around my leg. When the hell did he slip it on? I looked over at Chase who had a huge shit eating grin on his face. Well-played, Chase.

**

***Chase***

We were back at the hotel, heading to her room. I was still trying to figure out how I even allowed myself to be alone with her. With barely enough blood sitting in my upper region, I knew heading back here was a big mistake. Somehow my dick was in charge of my body now, forcing my feet to follow wherever Kris led. I chuckled to myself. I was honest enough to know that, even if I wasn't thinking with my dick, I'd follow her anywhere.

She was walking a little ahead of me. Her hair was a mess down her back from my hands, which itched to touch those luscious strands again.

She was deliberately walking with an extra switch in her hips. Every step exaggerated her curves, and my dick was ready to break out of my slacks just to get a simple touch against her skin.

I had to stop twice to adjust myself. Kris was slowly succeeding in driving me past my breaking point. Whatever control I thought I had disappeared whenever Kris was around and the little minx knew it. She pushed every chance she got, testing the waters to see how far she could get me to go.

Some sick part of me enjoyed watching her push me because I always pushed back. It made me harder knowing how badly she wanted me to sink into her. I knew when we finally did have sex it was going to be explosive.

She stopped at the front of her door and I let out a long and suffering breath. Okay this was it. The plan was to get her

## CHAPTER 14

to her room and leave. *Just make sure she's in the door and turn and walk away.*

That was the plan. A plan I really needed to follow thoroughly. I knew Kris was waiting for the perfect opportunity to get revenge on me for the stunt I pulled down at the reception hall. I saw it in her eyes the second the DJ stopped us and as we made our way back to the hotel; she was concocting her plan of attack. I was thrilled and scared. At this point in the night, I didn't think I had the strength to turn her down and that was dangerous.

I cleared my throat. "Um, well, goodnight, Kris. I'll see you in the morning." I turned to walk away when she grabbed my wrist slipping her hand into mine.

"You're gonna give me a complex, Chase. You're always running from me," she purred.

Oh, yeah, she was laying the charm on thick. I knew what she was doing and it shouldn't have worked. But it did; it always did.

She squeezed my hand. "Come on, Chase. Where are you gonna go? You know damn well Jas and Angel have a lot of talking to do, and if they're not talking, they're fucking. It's gonna get a little crowded in that room you and my brother share."

Kris was good, I'd give her that. I actually thought of that when we first drove down here and split the rooms. I assumed I would have crashed with someone else or booked another room for the night. I had no intentions of spending the night with Kris. I knew what would happen if I did.

## INTO PIECES

I heard the click of the lock on the hotel door and Kris' hand slipped from mine. I instantly missed her touch and turned around to face her. She walked through the door holding it open. I couldn't get my feet to move in either direction.

"I don't bite. I mean, only if you want me to."

That sexy mouth of hers turned into a smile so devious I knew walking into this hotel room was going to make me hurt. But that didn't make my feet move in the opposite direction. Nope, my feet took me right to the front of the door. I held my hands on either side of the doorframe, my one last pathetic attempt at not going through with this.

I was breathing heavy, trying to get some much-needed oxygen into my brain. But the air around me only held Kris' familiar sent and it made me harder than I thought possible.

"Kristal."

I said her name in a pained groan. She stepped close to me, running a hand down my chest and my body tightened in response. She smirked.

"Now what was it you told me? Oh yeah— I know what my touch does to you, Chase. Once I'm done, you'll be begging me to put you out of your misery." She grabbed hold of my belt pulling me farther into the room and closer to her. My head was on her head and my lips were a breath away from hers. She licked her lips, and I had to force myself to stay still and not dive right into that luscious mouth of hers.

## CHAPTER 14

"And when you think you can't take anymore, I'm going to continue to give it to you until you can't breathe or taste anything but me. And when you're at your breaking point, I still won't put you out of your misery, Chase."

She dropped her hold and walked further into the room slowly undressing. "If you're not going to stay, be a doll and close the door on your way out."

I was in the room slamming the door before she got the last word out. I picked her up and hauled her little ass up against the nearest wall. She was in a strapless bra and a red thong.

That color–red–was everything it represented on Kris skin: passion, fire and desire. It was like waving a flag in a bull's face, and it was enticing all sorts of naughty images, mainly Kris on her back with me balls deep inside her.

She wrapped her fuck-me heels around my waist, squeezing me tight with her legs, insuring I wouldn't go anywhere–as if I wanted to.

I trailed my index finger down the column of her throat loving the way her breath hitched and her pulse sped up. It was quiet except for our heavy breathing. It would be so easy to slip her thong to the side and sink myself deep inside of her.

This wasn't right though. If I took her now, there was no way I'd be able to stop myself from taking her over and over again. One taste would not satisfy my hunger for her.

Though fucking her over and over again had its merits, I wanted more with her. I wanted more than sweaty nights in between the sheets. I wanted to claim her and consume her. I wanted her to belong to me and me alone, but there was no way that was happening.

I laughed to myself. Timing was a bitch. It was something that never worked in our favor. First there was Jay and then there was school and now work was threatening to get in the way. I should take this as a hint, right? There had to be a reason we never had our moment. It looked like all we'd ever be was a missed opportunity.

"Chase."

She whispered my name and it brought me out of my internal musing. I loved the way my name came off her lips. Usually it was said in frustration, but right now it was a lusty plea.

She might have come up here with the intent to have me by the balls in a painful way, but she couldn't deny how much I affected her.

"What do you need, Kristal?"

Her eyes were heavy and clouded with pure lust. "You, Chase."

That statement alone had the ability to bring me to my knees. I was a bastard. I knew I should have walked away, but I was here now and I couldn't stop myself from continuing to touch her.

I ran a finger down between her perky breasts and her breath faltered. I smiled. I loved how responsive she was. Kris

## CHAPTER 14

starred in every single one of my naughty daydreams since we were younger. Her hair, her eyes and that sexy little mouth of hers, even her size was perfect for me.

"You're so little, Kris. Do you know how easy I could break you?"

Her chin titled higher and her lust-filled eyes locked on mine now with a hint of challenging amusement. God, I loved how she always found a way to push me.

"Oh no, Chase. You can't break me. Not in the way I could break you." She leaned in getting closer to my touch. "I think that's why you keep running."

"You're wrong."

I scooped her up, by her ass backing up towards the bed. I fell back on to it with her on top of me. She immediately sat up, grinding herself against my cock. I moaned loudly gripping her hips hard to stop her before I made a fool out of myself.

"Chase, please."

She sounded so sexy with my name on her lips. I cupped her face running a finger over her lips and the little minx bit it before sucking it into her mouth. My dick was throbbing and I pushed into her, causing her whole body to arch and we groaned in unison.

I sat up, pulling her body close to mine. I pulled her hair back harder than I intended to, forcing her to look directly into my eyes.

Kris was magnificent any and everyday of the week but right now? She was perfection. She was open and vulnerable waiting patiently for me to give her, what she needed. What she craved.

"You got it all wrong." I placed small kisses on her cheek, then her chin and neck. I couldn't help from touching her in someway. "You're not going to break me, Beauty."

Her pupils were dilated. She was close. I knew if I slipped my finger inside her thong I'd find her wet and willing. "Chase." She moaned my name again across those lips that could drive a man insane.

My lips hovered above hers. "You have the power to bring me to my knees. All I want to do is dive into you, but I know the second that I do, I will drown."

"So why is that such a bad thing?" She placed a hand on top of the hand I had cupping her cheek. "You know I want you, Chase." It took every single ounce of control I possessed not to kiss her right then and there.

This sucked. I wanted her more than I wanted my next breath but I couldn't give her what she wanted. I knew she'd be okay with just sex but she deserved more and I wanted to be the one to give it to her.

Kris saw my hesitation. She started pushing off of me. "Unbelievable, Chase. One night. That's all I'm asking for and you can't even give me that."

## Chapter 14

She pushed at my chest and I let her go. She stormed to the other side of the bed towards the bathroom throwing on a big T-shirt to hide herself from me.

"I can't keep doing this with you, Chase. Either we give this a go or we don't. I'm tired of the whiplash. I can't do it anymore."

Her voice broke towards the end and it made me feel like the biggest asshole on the planet.

"Kris."

"Don't, Chase. Don't give me the same song and dance. Are you holding back because of Jay? Does this have anything to do with him?"

I blinked in surprise. "Why would this have to do with him?"

Kris rolled her eyes. "Guy code. You guys were boys, best friends. I did sleep with him. Shit, he was my first and I did have real feelings for him."

I wish things were that simple and that relationship with Jay was the only thing holding me back. Truth was, there was so much more to it. There was stuff I didn't exactly know how to explain to her fully. So I pushed her away. Even though the only thing I wanted was to keep her close.

Kris came back to sit down next to me. "What are you so scared of, Chase?"

"You."

## Into Pieces

I cupped her face, forcing her to look at me so she could see the truth in my eyes even if she didn't believe my words.

"You're going to destroy me, Kris. I've only had a small taste of you and I'm already drowning. Could you imagine if I let myself go completely? You'd own me."

Kris cupped my face, bringing me closer to her. "I still don't see the problem. I want you."

I closed my eyes, allowing myself to get lost in her scent. I kissed her nose and forehead, savoring this small intimate moment between us, knowing full well it might be our last.

"I can't, Kris. I'm sorry."

She dropped her hold on me and abruptly got up and headed for the bathroom. I felt the air around us shift from hot sex and lust to an arctic chill. Kris paused when she got to the bathroom door. Her back was still towards me. She refused to even spare me a glance as she spoke.

"If this is what you think you want, that's fine. I'm done fighting. I'm too exhausted to keep playing this game, and honestly, it doesn't get me anywhere. So if this is the way you want it," she shrugged, "who am I to fight it? Oh, and you can crash here if you have nowhere to go tonight. I know Angel and Jas have a long night ahead of them."

She walked fully into the bathroom, shutting the door with a soft click. The sound was deafening in the silence that remained. Kris was fire and passion and everything she did was explosive. This quiet exit wasn't what I expected. Kris didn't gracefully bow out of anything. She fought tooth and nail till she got what she wanted.

I got up, intent on barging into the bathroom and demand she fight back. But when I reached the bathroom door I reminded myself that this was what I wanted. I wanted her to understand that we couldn't be together, and judging from the closed door in my face, she finally understood that.

So why did it feel like not only did I lose something precious but I just made the biggest mistake of my life?

INTO PIECES

# Chapter 15

***Angel***

Jasmine didn't answer right away, if anything, she looked confused by my question. I let out a resigned sigh; this wasn't how I wanted this to go. I actually had a whole speech planned out. I had so much to say to her, and the second I got her out here alone, my brain completely short-circuited. I was hungry for her. I had this all-consuming need to touch and taste her. I knew kissing her would be a mistake, it would only lead to sex–something I craved with her.

Sex didn't solve anything, though, and we desperately needed to figure out our relationship. There was no way we'd survive this if we continued with the same push-and-pull cycle. As much as I wanted to fuck her, I wanted what we had to mean more. If we couldn't fix us, we were going to end up hurting each other worse than either one of us would ever imagine.

I had to force myself to pull back from her. I needed to physically put some space between us so I could concentrate on the task at hand. I couldn't focus on how erratic her breathing was as her eyes traveled the length of my body.

She was just as hungry for me as I was for her. I saw it in her eyes, and as much as this pained me too, she was going to have to wait until we came to some type of consensus.

Jas cleared her voice. "I'm sorry, Angel. I don't really understand what it is you're trying to ask."

"It's a very simple question, Jas. Girls want a guy to love them but rarely are we ever gifted with the privilege to do so."

She rolled her eyes. "I can't stop you from loving me. Why'd you really bring me out here, Angel?"

I let out a sigh and looked to the sky, praying for patience. This whole situation seemed to get more frustrating by the minute. Our communication was horrible. I wasn't sure how else to get my point across to her.

I looked back at her and watched as impatience filtered through her eyes. She was getting as annoyed with all this as I was. For some strange reason, that caused me to laugh. There was a time when I could tell this girl anything. We had always been able to talk to each other, and now it almost felt like we didn't *want* to speak to each other.

I couldn't understand how we went from speaking every day—while I was gone, no less—to staring at each other all night. John had definitely been right about one thing: you go around thinking nothing is changing, and then one day you finally look up and everything is different.

"Look, Angel I'm not sure why you brought me out here but–."

I cut her off. "Because we need to talk, Jas. You know this."

She let out a frustrated breath and tried to move past me. I moved with her to block her path. "Why do you insist on running from me?"

## CHAPTER 15

Jas threw her hands up and let out a ridiculous sound. She jabbed a finger at my chest as she spoke. "I'm not going to stand here and wait for you to let me in, Angel. You want to talk, then talk to me."

I grabbed hold of her wrist, stopping the assault on my chest. "Are you willing to listen?" That took her by surprise and she tugged her hand trying to force me to release her. I didn't. I thoroughly enjoyed the feel of her skin against mine too much to let her go right away.

I drew lazy circles against her pulse and relished the way it sped up. When she spoke, her voice had a husky undertone to it and it caused me to curse under my breath.

"Why would you think I wouldn't listen to you?"

*My demons could destroy you. I don't want my pain to break you. There's a part of me that's okay with you not wanting to be there for me. I don't want to shatter the illusion you still have of me.*

I didn't say those words out loud. I should have, but I was holding back. I was still struggling with letting her in. I didn't trust her to completely understand and accept the man I was now.

I knew she loved the kid I was before I left to the Marines, and I knew she continued to love that kid who wrote her all those letters. But I was a different person now. That kid she new barely existed anymore. He died a slow death everyday he spent overseas. She didn't know the man I was becoming. Just like I didn't know the woman she was becoming.

I genuinely wanted to know her though, as intimately as I could outside of sex. I wanted to get inside her mentally and emotionally. I wanted her to lay all her walls down and not hide anything from me. I wanted the privilege to love all of her, even the ugly parts.

I was man enough to admit that it was a little unfair of me to ask her to open up when I could barely let my guard down around her. I wanted her to accept the man I was, to love all of who I was. I knew there couldn't be a chance for those things to ever happen until I took that risk with her.

I watched as Jasmine anxiously shifted her weight from one foot to the next before visibly trying to relax. She leaned against the railing, crossing her arms, clearly waiting for me to continue.

I chuckled despite myself. I was surprised at how well she held herself together tonight. She was amazing. No matter how hard I pushed, she stood her ground and remained beside me, forcing me to accept the comfort and support she was offering. She didn't crack or fold under the pressure or run in the other direction. Shit, if anything, she was ready to attack the hurdle that was barreling straight towards me.

If I learned anything tonight, it showed me what a force Jasmine would be by my side if I let her. But, tonight was just one night. There would be others and some were guaranteed to be way worse than tonight.

Did Jasmine have the strength to do this all the time? Loving a battered man wasn't easy. Shit, this whole relationship wouldn't be easy with all our baggage. But we'd never know if we could survive it unless we took that risk with each other.

I thought back to the conversation with John. He told me he always knew Brooke was the one for him. He knew she would always accept him no matter the circumstances. And he was right, given that she agreed to marry him knowing the uphill battle they had.

I told John I was amazed she stood by him through it all. His response was, *'That's what you do when you love someone. You accept their baggage and deal with the shit life throws at you along the way. You just learn to become a team and deal with it together. That's the only way you're going to survive it.'*

I wondered if we would ever be able to get to that level. In such a short time we've come a long way, and in the same breath we've managed to push ourselves backwards.

I looked back towards the window that led into the entranceway. John and Brooke where dancing again, they both had goofy grins on their faces.

I admired them and had the upmost respect for them both, Brooke especially. They didn't know how long they had with each other and they made damn sure to seize any and every opportunity they had. They figured out what was important early enough and pushed all that other bullshit aside.

In my mind, I replaced Jasmine and myself where John and Brooke stood. The second the picture took form, everything came to a standstill and sped up at the same time.

## INTO PIECES

My heart exploded out of my chest and my lungs couldn't get enough air in them as a surge of pure happiness washed over me. I couldn't hold back my own goofy grin.

I wanted what John had and I wanted it with Jasmine. Tommy's death may have gotten my feet moving in her direction. But it was John's take on his life that put everything in perspective for me.

It's funny how life worked. The world around you had to crumble and fall before you took notice and care of the things that were important.

Each day's a blessing we're given an opportunity to live, and most of us never really do. We're always lying and hiding with a false hope that tomorrow's going to come and we can fix it or make it better. The truth is, we never really get tomorrow. Each day is just a step closer to the grave. And each day above it, I wanted to spend with Jasmine.

I was done fighting this. Too much time was wasted running around in circles. She wanted me to let her in? Fine, I'd find a way to let her in. I'd make a conscious effort to chip away at my own walls to give her glimpse of what was on the inside. I had so many regrets already. I didn't want her to be one of them. Jasmine was worth the risk. I loved her, and I was going to open myself up to her and pray we'd make it through this.

With my mind made up, I had renewed energy. We had something worth fighting for. Now, I had to convince Jasmine's stubborn ass to fight with me instead of against me.

## Chapter 15

I turned, looking back at a very quiet Jasmine. I smirked. She really hadn't said much since she came out here. Was she expecting me to do all the talking along with all the decision-making about us? That wasn't going to cut it. *We* were in this together, so *we* were going to figure this shit out.

I stalked towards her and her eyes widened. When I was close enough, I pressed into her, pushing her back against the railing. I saw the sharp inhale she took, and I swear I could hear her pulse jackhammer against her neck.

I noticed it now that I was actually paying attention; this was easy for her. She was able to open up to me sexually. She let her guard down and showed me how vulnerable she was even after everything she'd been through.

Jasmine trusted me with her body. She knew I wouldn't hurt her here. I helped her erase a painful memory by creating new ones, and for that, she willingly gave herself to me. Jas was perfect here. I wanted her to be as open as she was now outside of sex with me and me alone.

Breathless she stammered over her words. "Wha–what are you doing? I–." She cleared her throat. "I thought you wanted to talk, Angel."

I cupped her face, making sure her eyes never left mine. "And yet you haven't really said anything have you, Jasmine? We *both* need to talk, not just me. Stop running already. I'm here trying to let you in. Open up to me, Jasmine, and tell me what it is you want."

INTO PIECES

# CHAPTER 16

### *Jasmine*

I couldn't think straight with him this close. My brain was clouded by his scent. All I could think about was his pressing erection against my stomach. He wanted me sexually but he wasn't pressing the issue. I knew he brought me out here to talk, but with him this close, I really didn't understand why talking was important.

I heard his deep inhale before he spoke again. "It's amazing how open you are right now. Yet you run every time things get serious. Why is that, Jasmine? What are you running from?"`

I blinked, trying to get my mind out of the lust haze Angel's close proximity caused. I licked my lips and watched how his green eyes darkened. "Angel." Oh, there was no way I could concentrate enough to string coherent words together.

Thankfully he stepped back chuckling. "It's nice to know I have that affect on your body. I want that affect on your mind as well. I want the mere mention of my name to arouse you physically, mentally, and emotionally."

"But I need you to open up to me and trust me unconditionally. I'm not here to judge or hurt you. I want to be everything you want and need. You gotta let me in. Let me love you, Jasmine."

He was saying all the right things and a normal girl would have heard him utter those words and ran straight into his open arms. Me? I had this insane urge to run in the opposite direction. I wanted to get as far away as possible from him and all of this.

The air around us was thick with emotions I couldn't deal with right now. Some sick part of me wished he brought me out here to end us just so I wouldn't be stuck in the position I was in now.

I wanted to let him in. I wanted to show him all of my troubles and have him take them away. But I couldn't trust that the dark parts inside of me wouldn't scare him off. I know he believed he wanted to be what I needed, but I wasn't confident he could truly accept all of me and still want me to be his.

I didn't care what he or anyone else said. There was no way any man would want to invest their time and love with a girl who had been raped. That's an experience that truly damages us. We never get over that feeling of being violated or the feeling of worthlessness. It kind of makes it a little difficult to believe someone could love you unconditionally.

I mean, sure, we learn to have sex. Sex, essentially, is easy. You don't need to have a connection with the person to partake in it. It could very well be about seeking pleasure or scratching an itch.

Angel and I excelled at sex because that's what we focused on. We weren't looking past that moment. But in doing so, it lead us to this push-and-pull cycle we were constantly in. I begged him to let me in, because maybe I saw us being more than just sex. Maybe, deep down, I wanted a little more from him.

## Chapter 16

But since he's been home, all he's done is push me away. Now, he was standing here asking me to let him in and bare my soul to him? I wasn't sure I was ready for all that just yet. I didn't know if I was capable of fully opening up to him.

After I was raped, I kept everyone at an arm's length. I was constantly on guard. It was the whole reason I found myself training in Uncle Luke's gym. I didn't trust myself anymore with the decision to trust those around me. How could I ever be sure those I surrounded myself with wouldn't hurt me?

It sucked that I put Angel in that category. I did, however, trust him more than I trusted anyone but was it enough to fully let my guard down? Especially since he constantly pushed me away and shut me out?

That wasn't the case tonight, though. We didn't get stuck in our usual push-and-pull cycle. After the whole confrontation between him and Bella, I thought for sure he'd push me away. I thought he'd find a way to be an asshole and force me in the opposite direction so he could deal with it on his own. But he didn't, he sought me out, made sure I was still standing by him. Even when he wasn't strong enough to stand on his own, he didn't hide from me. Instead, he leaned on me for support.

I was finally allowed a glimpse behind the walls and the mask he always had up. All night he continued to leave himself open for me, showing me exactly what demons he was dealing with daily. He didn't push and I didn't run. Maybe there was hope for us after all.

If tonight was the worst it got for us and we somehow managed to get through it, then we'd be okay to handle everything else that came our way.

INTO PIECES

I cleared my throat. "Angel?"

"Yes, Love?"

"What is it that you want?"

His eyes immediately darkened. "You, Jasmine. *All* of you."

Five words, they were five simple words. Angel didn't utter some profound answer. He didn't recite some rehearsed poem. They were just five words put together, and they were loaded with so many possibilities.

The conviction behind those words made my stomach bottom out. I swore I swallowed a million butterflies whose wings insisted on flapping around like crazy. His answer managed to leave me speechless. All I could do was nod and lick my suddenly dry lips.

I heard myself whisper out loud the first thing my mind could come up with. "Okay."

Angel took one step forward and was in my face, surrounding me again. My body instinctively leaned into his. His big hands skimmed my shoulders to cup the back of my neck forcing me to look into his eyes and bringing me closer to his face.

"Oh no, Love. You don't get to say okay. You've already had one decision taken away from you. I won't be an asshole and take this one away too. If you want this the way I want it, then you need to be real clear about it. I won't fight for this alone, Jasmine."

## Chapter 16

I didn't have time to respond. A throat cleared behind us. We both looked in the direction of the intrusion. It was one of the groomsmen. "Um, sorry to interrupt, but we're starting to shut down."

I let out a tiny breath a little grateful for the intrusion because I still couldn't find my voice. I tried to step around Angel when his head whipped around to face me. His lips were turned into a smirk. "Still trying to run, Love?" He chuckled. "We're not finished. You can't escape me just yet."

\*\*

We went back inside to say our goodbyes. Angel's hands were constantly on me as we made our way through the throng of people. Either his arm was draped over my shoulder or his hand was placed firmly on my lower back or holding my hand. I couldn't tell if he was holding on because he needed to touch me or because he feared I was going to disappear.

When we stopped by John and Brooke, John pulled me into an unexpected bear hug that made me yelp my surprise. He and Angel chuckled before he set me down.

John's goofy grin turned serious as he began to speak low enough for only me to hear. "Be good to him, Jasmine. He's been through hell and back. And you're the only reason he made it through that hell alive. Whatever you two decide, make sure you give it your all." He chucked me under my chin. "You'll be good for him, just like Brooke's good for me."

He kissed me on the cheek and grabbed his bride's hand and hauled ass out of the hall. I smiled as I watched them depart and sent a silent prayer up for them to have a long and happy marriage.

Angel was behind me. His hand trailed down the exposed skin at my back. I shuddered and leaned in closer, relishing his touch. He whispered in my ear, "You ready to go?"

I nodded my head as he turned me around to lead me out of the hall. Bella and her daughter Sadie were waiting for us at the entrance.

I cringed, bracing myself for yet another confrontation. I held my breath as Angel bent down to get eye level with Sadie. He leaned in and whispered something only she could hear.

After Angel finished speaking, the little girl nodded her head and threw herself in his arms. It was then I found myself visibly relaxing, even though Sadie outpour of affection momentarily stunned me.

Angel was literally a stranger to her and yet here she was hugging him fiercely. I guess it's true what they say: kids always know who the good souls are.

He stood up with Sadie still latched tightly in his arms. He took one look at Bella and with his free arm engulfed her in a makeshift hug. He was whispering something to her and she nodded in return. They stood embraced for what seemed like an eternity. I was content to let them have that moment, it seemed long overdue.

Eventually, a teary-eyed Bella pulled away. Sadie looked at her and reached out to her. "Oh no, mommy. No more crying, everything is going to be okay."

## Chapter 16

"I know, baby," she whispered.

Angel instantly reached out, grabbing my hand tight. I squeezed back. Bella went to walk away when Angel grabbed hold of her.

"I was serious about what I said, Bella. You need anything at all, you call me. I know you have no right to believe me considering I wasn't there for you before. It's different this time. Don't hesitate to reach out to me, please. I really would like the opportunity to get to know my goddaughter."

Bella was quiet for a moment. Her eyes seemed to get even more watery as she stood silently watching Angel. When I thought she wasn't going to say anything, she reached her hand out to cup Angel's cheek. "Okay."

Angel questioned, "Okay?"

"You're a good man, Angel. It's not going to be easy, but I think we can figure a friendship out."

Angel placed his hand on top of hers. "Thank you, Bella." And with that, she walked off.

I watched Angel's whole body relax as he let out a long breath. I squeezed the hand I was holding and his eyes shot to mine. "You're still here, Jasmine?"

I smiled. I threw my arms around his shoulders and hugged him close to me. "There's nowhere else I'd rather be. Come on, let's get out of here."

INTO PIECES

# Chapter 17

### *Angel*

We were back in my hotel room. Jasmine walked in ahead of me and I didn't go much further than standing against the door. I was exhausted. Tonight had mentally and emotionally taken a lot out of me and the night still wasn't over. Jasmine and I still needed to talk. The "okay" that she gave me really didn't say much.

We were in an enclosed space, now. No more interruptions for the remainder of the night. I knew Chase was crashing somewhere else, so he wasn't going to barge in on us. We had all the time in the world now to get to the bottom of what we were going to be to each other.

Jasmine looked around the hotel room before making her way to a chair in the far corner. As she sat, her brown eyes were locked on my face searching.

A small smile spread across her kissable lips before she whispered, "Thank you."

"For what?" I asked, confused.

"All of this. You didn't have to let me in, tonight. I honestly didn't expect you to. I know how hard that must have been for you."

Something in her voice changed along with the look in her eyes. She seemed almost regretful. Oh shit. Did I completely

## INTO PIECES

misread her? Was she really going to walk away after the shit storm that happened tonight?

I let out a resigned sigh. I couldn't blame her if she decided to walk away from us, well me. My playground of demons wasn't the most pleasant place to be. I could barely handle it on some days I couldn't expect her to volunteer to be there with me. It wasn't her baggage to deal with.

We both started to speak at the same time. Jasmine blushed as she giggled. The sound of her giggles hit me hard and low in my sternum. I was amazed how her soft laughter had the ability to warm me from the inside out.

I had it bad, didn't I? Every sound she made, the way she moved, made my body respond to her. Even now as she sat in that chair doing nothing but twirling a strand of hair, my dick was hardening for her.

And it wasn't so much that I was ready and wanting to have sex with her. I mean, hell yeah, I wanted to fuck the shit out of her, but what I was feeling was a different sensation altogether.

I wasn't looking for just a good time or to scratch an itch. No. I wanted to consume every single inch of her. I want to touch and taste and savor every move her body made underneath mine, along with the sounds I knew would escape those sensual lips of hers.

I wanted to brand her, and not in some douche bag way. I wanted to brand her in the way she branded me. I wanted to be inside her, I wanted to be in her veins, in her heart, and in her

## Chapter 17

mind. I wanted her just as lost in me as I was in her every time she was near me.

But, going by the look on her face, that was never going to happen. It looked like she was throwing in the towel.

Well, at least she realized early on she wasn't cut out for this. I would have hated to invest more time in this to have it tarnished and destroyed at the end.

Jasmine chewed on her bottom lip before speaking. "Did you want to say something? I didn't mean to talk over you before."

"I think I did enough talking for the night, Jasmine." My voice was even and void of the whirlwind of emotions I was feeling inside.

Jasmine started to stand. I guess this was it. Time to say goodbye and cut our losses.

"Um, Angel. Were you serious about what you told me earlier? You know, when I asked you about what you wanted?"

"Yes. I want you, Jasmine, and not just in the 'we're only having sex' kind of way. I want everything with you. The good the bad and the ugly, I just want you."

She let out a breath and her hand reached behind her. "Good. I was hoping you were serious."

As she spoke the last word her dress fell to the floor, baring her beautiful body to me. I sucked in a sharp breath. My hand braced against the hotel door was the only thing keeping me from falling on my face. I knew she wasn't wearing anything under that dress but to have it confirmed? I groaned out loud, scrubbing a hand down my face.

"What–" I croaked. I cleared my throat hoping my voice would come out steadier this time. "What are you doing, Jasmine?"

She shrugged. "You want me, I want you."

I shook my head, hopefully clearing some of the arousal that was threatening to take over. "I think you miss understood me. I want more than sex with you, Jasmine."

She stepped out of the pool the dress had made down by her feet. She went to bend at the waist to remove her heels and I heard my own voice sharpen as I told her. "Keep the shoes on, Jasmine."

She snapped back up. Her brown eyes went heavy as her nipples bedded from the sharp tone of my command. Her tongue jutted out, licking her lips and making them moist.

I had to hold on to the doorknob–shit was the only thing keeping me upright. All I wanted to do was get on my hands and knees and crawl over to her, kissing, sucking and nibbling my way up her gorgeous body. I could feast on her for days. I was losing this battle. I saw it clear as day: this wasn't going to end any other way but with me inside her.

I shook my head again, trying desperately to get the blood back into my brain and out of my dick. I cleared my throat. "Jasmine," was the only thing I could groan out, and the little minx took it as her cue to move.

## Chapter 17

She started walking towards me and every step she took made my dick swell bigger than I thought was possible. He was dying to get inside her too. I couldn't concentrate on anything but the sexy-as-sin female walking towards me in those godforsaken fuck me heels. This honestly wasn't fair. A man could only take so much.

She stopped so close to me, barely a feather could pass between us. She didn't reach out to touch me or fidget with her hands. She was confident as she stood before me, her brown eyes heavy with arousal locked on mine. Jasmine licked her lips. "I know you want more than sex, Angel."

"Jasmine." I groaned. Some tiny part of me, way deep down inside was going for self-preservation. I held on to that bastard trying very hard to stop the direction this night was heading in.

"Jasmine, please. I want more. I'm not going to fuck you."

She smiled a sweet smile at me. "That's fine, Angel. I want you to make love to me instead."

And there it went. The last strand of my sanity snapped into itty bitty little pieces. Here was Jasmine standing vulnerable and naked both physically and emotionally. She was asking me to make love to her? I remember the first time she ever uttered those words to me. I wanted to weep with joy. They had been music to my ears. But she wasn't ready then. She was skittish and fearful and so unsure of herself. Now she stood before me the confident woman I always knew she was.

Uttering those words now, I knew this was it. There was no way I could turn her down tonight, or ever. I wouldn't be able to walk away from her now even if I wanted to. This was that exact moment I knew everything would finally fall into place for us.

**_Jasmine_**

I stood still, waiting for Angel to respond. The second we got to his room, I made up my mind about us. I didn't know how to string the words together, though. I couldn't find the right way to tell him I wanted what he wanted.

I thought of the next best thing. I loved him and I wanted him to make love to me. I knew, this time it would bring us together. Sometimes words weren't really needed to convey what you wanted to say.

It took a lot of false bravado to strip myself bare in front of him. I didn't know where the strength came from, but I knew if I didn't take this step now, I would regret it later. I was tired of the 'what ifs' and the what 'could have beens'. I wanted this and I was going to act on it to get it.

I stood waiting in all my naked glory, barely containing my rapid heartbeat. I wished he would move, respond, shit, even a blink I'd be happy with. Angel just continued into stare in my eyes.

"Angel?" My voice was a whisper. Maybe he needed a push? Before I even thought to do something else, a painful groan tore from somewhere deep inside him. Angel moved quickly wrapping his arms around me, bringing me even closer to him.

## Chapter 17

His lips crashed hard against mine. His hands were fisted in my hair holding me perfectly still against him while he took my mouth. There was something delicious about the feel of his uniform against my bare skin. It caused just the right amount of friction to make my need for him grow.

He nipped at my bottom lip before pulling back to look at me. His hands came down to cup my face. "My sweetest sin." His thumbs swiped under my eyes. "This is what you want?" I could only nodded my response. The raw emotion in his green eyes left me speechless.

"That's not good enough, Love. You should know by now I need to hear you say it. I need you to voice what it is you want."

"You." I took a breath. "I want you, all of you, even the bad. I want you to make love to me, Angel."

"Always, Jasmine."

INTO PIECES

# CHAPTER 18

*Jasmine*

His lips were on mine again. But there was no urgency in his touch. There was no overexcitement to quickly get inside each other. The hunger was there but it was on a slow sensual boil. Each touch, each sensation, felt like I was experiencing Angel for the first time again.

I was relearning how his lips tasted against mine. The way his body moved and felt beside me, on top of me and inside me. Each slow stroke I felt someplace new, and it brought on different sensations I've never experienced before. This was how Angel planned to consume me, and I was too caught up in him to do anything else but enjoy it.

Angel's lips moved down to my neck. He bit down softly as he angled his hips to thrust deep inside me. His pelvic bone brushed against my clit. The pressure wasn't enough to throw me over the edge like I desperately wanted, but it continued to give me this delicious torture I found myself enjoying despite the release I craved.

He seemed to enjoy this slow pace he set for us as well. Each prolonged stroke, each slow touch, pushed the worries I had outside of my head. He was doing a fine job of keeping me focused on only him.

Even though we weren't hurriedly tearing into each other, Angel knew exactly how to give me what I yearned for and needed. He was methodical. He instinctively knew all the right spots to hit to get my body to respond the way he wanted it to.

He brought his lips back to my ear biting the lobe and eliciting a deep moan out of me. He growled slow and deep in his chest. His voice dropped to this sensual drawl that had my body opening up more for him on its own.

"You see how I can make you feel, my love?"

He moved to look at me but I closed my eyes, the emotions had become too much, threatening to spill over. We made it this far without words as we gazed deeply into each other's eyes; there was no need for it now.

He pulled my hair back tight, but I kept my eyes shut. I couldn't look at him, not right now. I couldn't handle seeing the depth of emotion lying bare in Angel's eyes. If I did, I'd begin to crack and he'd see all of me.

"Look at me, Jasmine." His voice had my eyes opening on their own accord. "No more hiding from me, Love. You can trust me."

It was almost a plea. His mossy green eyes were boring into mine daring me to look away. As much as I wanted it, I couldn't. Not right now.

And that's when it happened. Every wall I had perfectly placed around my heart and emotions began to crack. Little by little, the walls started to crumble and the tears began to fall from my eyes. Angel completely stopped moving and cupped my face. "Tears? I'm not hurting you, am I?"

I shook my head. "No, Angel."

"So, the tears?"

## Chapter 18

"I'm overwhelmed by everything I see and feel with you right now."

His face took on a confused and hurt look. "They're happy tears." I spoke quickly, trying to tell him as best I could how happy I was with him being here, now. I was scared shitless about how I felt. But the joy I was currently feeling was overwhelming and overshadowing that fear.

I cupped his face with my own hands. "You've managed to make everything perfect, even the bad stuff. How did I ever get so lucky?"

Angel smiled and I swear it caused me to cry a little more. "I'm the lucky one, Jasmine. You've given me more than I ever thought I deserved. But I'm a selfish bastard. I want your heart, Jasmine. I told you on the balcony this was more than sex and I mean that. The good, the bad and the ugly, I want us to have it and face it together. I want you to be mine in all ways there is."

Angel pushed slowly back into me, our eyes never leaving each other's. It was the most intimate and open we'd been with one another. This was more than us having sex. We were both being emotionally stripped naked. I felt his heart beat in tune with mine. I felt completely connected with him. I was an extension of him.

He pushed into me again and I lifted my hips to meet him halfway. He chuckled and gripped my hips, keeping me in place.

"Always so impatient."

I smiled. "Not impatient, Angel. I want you to make love to me."

He kissed me slow and deep, and I wept a little more from the emotion he poured into it. Angel may never say the actual words but I felt it. Every single time he kissed me or touched me like this, I knew he loved me. I just prayed that our love would be enough to hold us together through all the hard times life would no doubt throw at us.

# Chapter 19

*Chase*

Light was starting to break into the windows and the warm body next to me began to stir. "Shh." I kissed the top of her head and waited for her to settle back into sleep.

Once I was sure she was knocked out, I quietly removed myself from the bed. I knew if I stayed curled up next to her any longer, I'd never be able to leave. I threw my shirt back on, not bothering to button it or put my tie and jacket on.

I knew I was an ass for leaving like this, but I would have been an even bigger ass if I stayed longer. Our boundaries had finally been drawn out last night. We knew exactly where things stood between us. I felt hollow after that conversation. It wasn't what I wanted, but it was the right thing to do.

I was shocked and even grateful she let me spend the night here, especially with her tucked in my arms. I guess she needed it as much as I did. It was the most intimate I've been with her and the closest we've ever actually been. It felt right having her there, and it was the most torturous experience I've had.

All night all I could think about was how much I wanted Kris like this in my arms for the long haul. It was a dangerous thought, considering I wasn't sure that far into the future would ever exist for us.

With a resigned sigh, I headed for the door. It was too early in the morning to think about all this heavy shit. This wedding had done nothing but bring up things I've never allowed myself to think about.

I laughed at myself; look at who was in touch with his emotions. Angel would have a field day if he knew how much of an emotional sap I turned into in the course of twenty-four hours.

I opened the door and Jasmine tumbled in. I caught her arms, steadying her and noticing that her hair was a mess and she was carrying her shoes.

I grinned wide. I guess someone worked out their issues. All night long too, going by the tired look on her face. I couldn't help myself from needling her about it either. "Doing the walk a shame, are we, Jasmine?"

She flustered as she hit me with one of her shoes. "I'd have to be ashamed of what I did for it be a walk of shame, Chase. And you should be one to talk. Sneaking out in the wee hours of the morning."

"I'm not sneaking out, brat. I just wasn't trying to wake up Kris."

"Right." She patted me on the chest. "If you two are looking for round two." The brat winked. "I'll be more than happy to go get breakfast downstairs," Jasmine said with a crooked smile.

I laughed. Jas wanted me and Kris together just as much as I was pushing her and Angel together. As of last night, at least one of us was getting their way. "It's not even like that, Jas. Nothing of significance happened last night."

## Chapter 19

"Why not?"

I looked back into the room at Kris' sleeping form. Timing. It was never the right time for us, and it looked like it never would be. I turned back to Jasmine, giving her a kiss on the cheek. "I'm happy for you and Angel. It was about time the two of you guys figured shit out. Lord knows I was getting tired of Angel sulking."

Jas went to speak up but I cut her off with a shake of my head. "You're wasting your breath. I don't think me and Kris are meant to be."

I walked past Jasmine and headed off to the room I shared with Angel. With any luck, Jas wore his ass out and he'd still be sleeping. And if not? Hopefully he was downstairs at the gym. I wasn't in the mood for his inquisitions today either.

\*\*

I put my key into the lock of the hotel door only to have it swing open before I could turn the handle. Angel stood in his towel with a look of utter disappointment. "Oh, it's you."

I pushed past him. "Well, shit, fuck you too."

He closed the door. "What are you doing here?"

I went to sit down on the chair, but looking at the disarray the room was in, I thought better of it. Didn't know what I'd be sitting in if I sat down anywhere. I turned back to look at Angel who was pacing the length of the room. "You okay, bro?"

He looked up and nodded but continued to pace. It hit me then: the disappointed look on his face when I walked in, his abruptness and now the pacing. Angel was nervous and that shit had me belly over and laughing hard. I couldn't remember a time when Angel was this nervous about anything, especially a girl. This motherfucker had balls the size of Texas. There wasn't much that could rattle his cage. I guess Jas was the exception.

"What the hell is wrong with you? Why are you laughing like that?"

"Dude, you gotta relax a little. Jasmine didn't run off anywhere. She'll be back, I promise."

Angel stopped pacing and he crossed his arms over his chest. "What are you talking about?"

I shook my head. "You got it bad, bro. I gotta admit it, looks quite good on you. Nice to see you aren't Superman all the time."

Angel grunted before sitting on the bed. I didn't expect him to speak about it further. We were boys; we didn't have to speak. We understood each other, even in the silence. But he still spoke up.

"I know you might find this hard to believe, but, I'm worried, Chase. We finally had some type of breakthrough last night. I know we did. I felt that shit down to my soul. And I know she did too."

"That's a good thing, right? What are you biting your nails about?"

## CHAPTER 19

He looked up at me. His green eyes were filled with worry. "What if it's not enough, Chase? What if whatever we feel towards each other isn't enough to get us through anything?"

"And what if it is?"

Angel smirked. "Always answer a question with a question? You really have this Doctor Phil shit down pat."

I laughed. "Don't be a dick."

"Speaking of, how did last night go for you? You found a place to crash?"

"Why don't you just ask what you really want to know?"

Angel chuckled at me as he got up and walked towards the bathroom. "See? That Doc Phil shit is out again. How'd it go with my sister? I was kind of occupied most of the night, so I didn't see much of you two."

I rolled my eyes. I had no intention of getting into the dynamics of my non-relationship, especially with him. "Nothing out of the ordinary happened. At this rate, you have nothing to worry about."

Angel looked at me. His green eyes seemed to be weighing me out. "You know, I think it's funny how much you're pushing me and Jas together. Yet, you're sitting on your ass with my sister. Trust me, no man will ever be good enough for my baby sister. But I like you, Chase. I respect you. If you think Kris is someone you can see yourself with long term, then go for it."

## Into Pieces

"The only thing wasting time is going to get you is regret. I think it's time you man up, chump. I can't have a little bitch pining away at my baby sis."

The bastard had the nerve to laugh before closing the bathroom door. I let out a frustrated breath and scrubbed a hand down my face. I was exhausted. Probably the most exhausted I've been in a long time. Being an adult and making adult decisions sucked. Angel was a dick for what he said. Unfortunately, he was right.

# Chapter 20

*Marcus*

Tony didn't bullshit when he said Jasmine and Angel were spending some fun-filled weekend together. He refused to tell me exactly where they were going. Apparently, he didn't think that tidbit of information was important enough to find out. The shit forced me to spend the better part of Friday night trying to follow behind her.

She drove up with Chase and that pain in the ass Kris. I couldn't stand that loudmouthed bitch. I couldn't wait for the day when someone put her in place. I would have loved to do it myself, but I had other pressing issues.

I was able to follow Jasmine outside of the city. It wasn't until then that Chase caught on to *someone* tailing him. He actually did a pretty good job at losing me. For a split second he managed to gain some of my respect, but that did nothing to soften how infuriated I was.

Jasmine insisted on playing this stupid game with me, and my patience was wearing thin. Some small part of me knew I should give her time to come to back me on her own. Under normal circumstances, I might have even enjoyed this little cat-and-mouse game. But at the rate this stupid cunt was going, she'd likely forget whom she belonged to. I'll be damned if I lost her to Angel. In the end, she was mine and no one else was allowed to have her.

If she needed a bigger push in the right direction, I had no problem forcefully guiding her back to me. My plan B was fool proof as long as the pieces fell into place accordingly, and I knew they would.

Honestly, I was happy Jasmine was forcing my hand. This plan had been my favorite. Anything that would destroy Angel and permanently get him out of the picture made all this shit worth it.

The car door swung open and a nice little redhead stepped into the passenger seat. It was such a shame she wasn't a real redhead; I've never had a ginger before. I've always wondered how they'd taste.

Vivian had doused herself with that nasty perfume she always wore. It was a nauseating scent that permeated the whole car every time she got in it. I hated that scent; it was suffocating and took days to clear.

How the hell Angel ever touched this bitch was beyond me. She was nothing like Jasmine or any of his other little flings, for that matter. She was easy. Easy to manipulate, easy to control and that was something that was going to come in handy soon enough.

"I don't understand, Marcus," her voice came out whiney. Every time she opened her fucking mouth she whined, even when she moaned.

"You said if we fucked around, it would make Angel jealous and he'd want me back. It's been weeks and he's still sitting there with that bitch. You know, I heard from a friend he took her away for the weekend. How am I supposed to get him back if he's constantly with her?"

## Chapter 20

I grinded my teeth. She was annoying. She never stood a damn chance. Anyone with eyes could see why he'd want Jasmine over her. Shit, I didn't want to touch her but I was forced to. She was the only one who had been willing to play my little game.

The second she'd seen me walk into Uncle Luke's gym she threw herself at me. She didn't even bother to play hard to get. She pulled me to the lockers in the back room and went down on me.

Angel always went for the girls who had some fight in them. This pretty little redhead Vivian had none what's so ever. She really wasn't much fun. I broke her that first night easily enough. She let me do anything I wanted without so much as a peep. Where's the fun in that?

"Marcus, hello, are you even listening?" She tapped me repeatedly. "Did you hear what I said? When are you going to do what you promised and get me Angel back?"

I reached out smacking her across her face before wrapping my hand around her slim throat. I applied just enough pressure to block off some of her air. Her eyes enlarged and she tried to scratch at my arm. I could have ended her right now. I desperately wanted to. She'd proven to be a lousy fuck and a major headache. Unfortunately, I needed Angel and his little posse back in Long Island before I could set the rest of the plan in motion.

"What is it about Angel you stupid cunts seem to fall so hard for? He discarded you as soon as he got what he wanted from you, and here you are scheming with me–a better fuck, no doubt–trying to get him back. You know, he's only going to use and discard you again, Vivian."

She tried to speak but I squeezed her neck tighter. Her eyes got wider as she franticly scratched at my arms.

"Give it a rest already, Vivian. I'm not going to kill you. I need you, remember? But you don't get to speak until I tell you to okay? Nod your head if you understand."

She nodded and a few tears ran down her face. A huge grin split across my lips. "Ah, good, you're crying. I honestly thought you wouldn't be smart enough to be scared. Now I'm going to tell you exactly what it is I need you to do."

I relayed all the information not releasing my hold around her neck. "Do you understand exactly what you need to do, Vivian?" She nodded frantically. "That's a good girl. I think it's better if you sleep now."

With my hold tightening around her neck, I smacked her head hard against the passenger window. Between the pressure on her neck and the smack against the window, it was lights out for Vivian. I put the car in drive and headed home. It was time to get ready.

# Chapter 21

## Jasmine

Angel insisted we ride back home together, alone. Kris practically had a meltdown about it. She didn't take too kindly to the idea that she'd be stuck in the car for the three- hours with Chase by herself. I thought for sure they spent a semi-good night together. I didn't get all the details from her. All Kris said was that they spent the night in each other's arms. I guess it was something I would have to grill her about later.

We rode in comfortable silence. I watched as the sun lit up the entire sky, shining brightly against the buildings of the city. I had my window rolled all the way down, enjoying the summer breeze that whipped through my hair.

I didn't feel weighed down like I normally did. I was light. I felt like I was floating on a cloud that was encased in comfort, security and happiness. Surprisingly, throughout all the chaos and all the high emotions that ran wild this weekend, I found a certain kind of calmness.

It was there as I stood by Angel's side as he faced just a fraction of the baggage he had. I knew this was where I belonged, by his side. I felt connected to him in a way that wasn't there before. It went beyond the fact that we've known each other forever. It was something different, like the pieces were starting to fit together. The feeling magnified as we made love.

## Into Pieces

I had given Angel a little bit of my heart as well as my body back in that hotel room. I had no regrets. Everything felt right this weekend with him. We finally found our own little rhyme and reason.

I would be lying if I said I wasn't scared by all the possibilities. We may have survived–shit, even–thrived despite the chaos that happened over the weekend. But that was just one night and it was only Angel's demons that were out to play. What would happen when my demons came out? I was sure they'd come out soon, too. I felt them lurking in the corner, waiting for the perfect opportunity to strike.

We stopped at a red light. The song on the radio changed to Ellie Goulding's "Dead in the Water." Angel squeezed my leg, trying to get my attention. I looked over into his green eyes and smiled. I visibly saw him trying to let his guard down and remain as open as possible to me. I returned his smile, once again finding the calm I felt with him before.

The song was the only sound in the car. The beat and the words surrounded us, drowning out the rest of the world. I listened to her sing as I continued to stare into those beautiful green eyes of his. I was suddenly hit with an overwhelming sense of emotions I had a hard time holding back. This was where I always wanted to be, standing beside him and staring into those eyes that were filled with so much love for me.

"Thanks for showing up, Jas. Even after our argument. I don't think I could have done this weekend without you being there."

I felt myself smile at him. "That makes me happy. I'm glad I could be there for you. Thank you for letting me in, Angel."

## Chapter 21

Angel smiled as he leaned in and placed a small kiss on my lips. It was so simple and so sweet. His kisses always had the power to bring me to my knees. Now they had the power to rip me wide open and completely bare myself to him.

A car horn honked behind us and we both pulled away from each other laughing. He kissed my nose and pulled away completely focusing on the road ahead. "I guess we better get going. You ready to step back into reality, Love?"

Pssh, no. I didn't even want to. In our own world, everything was simple and almost perfect. I would love to stay wrapped in our own little cocoon, focused only on each other.

I wasn't ready for what the real world would bring. I wasn't ready for all the things that were going to get thrown at us once we stepped out of our comfort zone. There was a very rational fear in the back of mind, that we wouldn't survive it.

"If I tell you no, will you turn around and drive us off into the sunset?"

Angel's deep chuckle sent a blanket of warmth around me. "If I could, I would. But life doesn't work that way."

I let out a sigh and chewed on my bottom lip. I was extremely nervous about what was going to come next for us. Our track record proved to be unkind to the both of us. We'd take one step forward and something would set us a million steps back.

"Stop worrying, Jas." He laughed to himself. "I cannot believe I'm even going to quote this but…." Angel stopped at a stop sign and turned in his seat to face me. His green eyes, seeming so much lighter after this weekend, bored into mine as he cupped my face in his hands.

"Only those couples meant to be together go through everything that's meant to tear them apart. But don't worry so much, Love." He chucked me under the chin. "We will always come out on top."

He stared at me intently, trying to get me to believe what he was saying. "I'm not going anywhere, Jasmine. It's you and me now. Whatever the world throws at us, we face it and survive it together. Got it?"

He kissed my nose. "Let's see what this big bad world has in store for us." He winked before rewarding me with one of his beautiful smiles.

It was that smile that made me believe I could conquer the world and we'd get through anything.

\*\*

We pulled up in front of my house and there were a load of cops in and around my home. I jumped out of the car before Angel completely pulled to a stop. I heard Angel scream my name in the distance but I didn't bother responding.

What the hell was going on? I knew my mom wasn't home, yet but could they be here for her? Did something happen? I took in the front of the house and sniffed the air. I didn't smell smoke or gas, so I ruled that out.

I walked up my walkway and an officer tried to cut me off. "Excuse me, miss, you can't go in there."

## Chapter 21

"I live here."

"You have ID?"

I let out an annoyed breath as I reached for my wallet. "Officer Santos, she's good, she lives here."

"Chase? How the hell did you beat me here? What are you even doing here? Do you know what's going on?"

I was hysterical. I heard each word I spoke get louder as I was pressed with more questions. I walked up the front steps and Chase stepped aside to let me into my home. What I saw completely took me by surprise.

My home, the place I rested my head at night, was completely flipped upside down and ransacked. It looked like someone let a Tasmanian devil loose on my poor home.

The couch and love seat were cut up and sliced wide open. Its stuffing littered the floor everywhere. The dishes that had been in the cabinets were all out and smashed into pieces. There was glass everywhere. I looked at Chase, waiting for some type of confirmation or explanation. Shit, anything.

"Do you know if anything was taken?" My voice was unsteady. My nerves were officially shot. What else could possibly go wrong?

"Oh shit, Jay's room."

I sprinted across the hall and glass crunched underneath my feet. Jay's door was still closed and a part of me couldn't bring myself to open it. I feared the pictures my mother left up in his room and the furniture he owned would be destroyed.

## Into Pieces

I didn't want to lose another piece of my brother. These were materialistic things. They shouldn't hold any value, but to me they did. They belonged to my big brother. They were the few things that were his and that he had touched daily. I silently prayed that whoever destroyed my home didn't ruin the only thing I had left of Jay.

"Please still be in one piece. Please don't let him be violated too."

I took a deep breath, steadying myself for what was to come. I turned the knob but didn't get much further than that. Two warm hands were on my shoulders spinning me around and into an embrace. I inhaled the familiar scent that was associated with Angel, and my body instinctively relaxed into his hold.

"Whatever this is, I promise you we will deal with it together. Whatever you need from me, it's yours, Jas."

I hugged Angel tighter as he continued to whisper reassuring words to me. Here we were not even an hour into our regular lives and a shit storm was already brewing. What I wouldn't give to have stayed locked up in that hotel room for just a little while longer.

# Chapter 22

*Angel*

I stood back, watching as Jasmine answered the officer's questions. I looked at the mess that was now her home. I was baffled that someone would even do this to her. That bafflement quickly turned into anger when I realized this wasn't some random break in. This vandalism was a personal attack. We did a walk through twice, and Jasmine was certain nothing was missing in this chaos.

Someone had been watching her entirely too closely for my liking. They knew her schedule well enough to know when to wait to destroy her home. This was clearly meant to send a message, but why? What could this person possibly gain from destroying her home? I had to wonder if this vandalism had anything to do with that package she received in the beginning of the summer.

Chase approached me. He looked as exhausted as I felt. After the emotional weekend we had, to come home to this? It was too much to take. I had no idea how Jas was still standing on her feet. If I was being honest, I was ready to drop too. The only thing keeping me up right was the need to protect Jasmine from all the bad shit that kept happening to us.

"What's up, Chase?"

He scrubbed a hand down his face. "Bro, I don't know how to tell you this."

"Spitting it out quickly is best."

He let out a breath. "There was a note."

"Excuse me?"

Chase's face looked stricken with disgust. "The cops, they found a note. But it was ripped up like someone came in and tried to get rid of it. Or, the person who did this." He waved a hand around the destruction that was left. "Decided against the note at the last second and tried to tear it from where it was stashed."

A red haze fell over my eyes. I felt my temperature rise. I knew this shit was a personal attack and every instinct in me wanted to grab Jasmine, throw her over my shoulder and lock her ass away tight. This way I would have no distractions when I handled the son of a bitch. He was dead, him and that asshole who raped her.

That's when it hit me. "We still don't know who raped her, right? You think this could be the same person? You think maybe he's feeling a certain type of way since she's with me now?"

Chase looked around the house again. "Given the vandalism and how bad her room was trashed, it would make sense, especially with the note that was left. Though, I gotta tell you, Angel. If it's the same person, we need to find out who this is ASAP. If he did this, that means that bastard is entirely too close, watching her. He just trashed her house, what if he goes after her again?"

Those were my thoughts exactly. That bastard was out there probably in plain sight, and it pissed me off that we had

## Chapter 22

no idea who it was. And why the hell wasn't this guy locked up in some jail cell being someone's bitch?

Once all this madness and police questioning ended, I'd find a way to ask Jas who it was that raped her. I know essentially it wasn't any of my business, but if that guy and the person who trashed her house were one in the same, then I needed all the information I could get.

Jas probably wouldn't be ready to tell me just yet, especially with all that was going on. I'd do my own research first just incase she wasn't too open to the idea of telling me. She'd hate me for invading but her safety came first, always.

"Yo, Chase. Let me see the note."

"You know I can't do that, Angel. It's against policy."

I turned to look at him with a questioning eyebrow. "No way in hell, are you a good ol' boy in blue."

The bastard smirked. "Never said I was."

I growled, grabbing him by his already wrinkled shirt. "Today really isn't the day to fuck with me on this, Chase. We boys and all, but I will fucking kill you for trying to stop me from protecting what's mine. Now show me the note."

"Is there a problem, gentlemen?"

A uniformed officer approached us with his hand on his gun. My eyes never left Chase's. I wanted him to see exactly how serious I was. I wasn't there to protect her when she got raped, but I'll be damn if I sat back and watched her get violated anymore. Jasmine was mine and I would protect her at all costs.

Chase chuckled as he addressed the cop. "No problem here, officer. It's just a little disagreement between friends. We've settled it now."

"We have?"

"Soon as you get your hands off of me."

I dropped my hold and stepped back. Chase addressed the cop who I noticed was the one who had been questioning Jas. I turned, looking for her, and saw her bolt into her room.

"Hold that thought, Chase."

I ran after her, following her to her room. She slammed the door behind her, a clear indication that she was done talking to everyone right now. I grabbed the doorknob, intent on barging in behind her. We just had this conversation about shutting each other out and running away. Why was she doing this again? Didn't we just let each other know how important facing our problems together was? Why was she still running from me?

I let out a breath and stepped away from her door. My emotions were a little all over the place, even more so now that we came home to this intrusion. I had to believe Jas wasn't completely shutting me out. This was a lot for her to deal with. If she needed time to collect herself, get her mind right, then I was going to back up a little and give her some breathing room. When she was ready she'd come to me and we'd deal with this together.

## Chapter 22

The door swung open and Jas stood there with her gym shorts, a tank and her gym bag slung over her shoulder. She stopped short when she saw me standing in front of her.

"Angel? You're still here?"

I pulled her close to me, the need to touch her growing stronger by the second. "I'm always going to be here, Love. I told you that." I cupped her face tilting her head up so her pretty brown eyes were locked on mine. It felt good when she reached out and wrapped her arms around my waist pulling me even closer. Slow progress was still progress. Jas wasn't pushing me away entirely, yet.

"I'm okay, Angel. I'm just going to get out of here for a few to clear my head."

"I know, Love."

Jas leaned in, shocking me with a kiss. I'm sure, for her, it was supposed to be a kiss of reassurance, but it turned into hot and desperate as soon as our lips touched. My dick was jumping out of my sweats to get closer to her.

A simple taste and Jas always brought my body to life. I was on fire for her. This girl had me by the balls and I fucking loved it.

I pulled back quickly before I did something rash, like push her back into her destroyed room and consume her in the middle of all this chaos. I'd make her forget about all the bullshit we kept landing in.

"You keep that up, Love, and I damn sure can find better ways to clear your mind."

I flashed her my wolfish grin and was rewarded with a smile. I dropped my hold on her and stepped back so she could leave.

She started to walk away. I reached out without even thinking about it and grabbed her arm, stopping her from leaving. I couldn't help myself. I was a junkie strung out on my sweet addiction, and I had no intentions of getting help for it. I wanted as much of her as she was willing to give. I was hooked from that very first kiss we had my first night back home.

I went in, my lips desperate for hers. I loved how Jasmine's body automatically leaned into mine. She was just as strung out as I was. I pulled back, enjoying the whimper that escaped her gorgeous lips.

Jas looked up at me. Her plump lips formed such a sweet smile, it made me ache a little. "You're totally trying to distract me, Angel."

I chuckled. "That's the plan."

I cupped her face in my hands, stroking her cheek with my thumb. I stared into those brown eyes of hers that had quickly become my greatest weakness. "I'll come by the gym later to pick you up." I reluctantly dropped my hold on her and stepped back to give her and myself some breathing room.

"I'd like that." She leaned in to kiss me again, but pulled back shaking her head. She started laughing. "I kiss you again, and I might not be able to leave."

## Chapter 22

My body hummed in anticipation as I felt my lips split into a wide grin.

"Angel."

I'm sure my name was supposed to come off as a warning. It would have been more believable if her eyes didn't dilate and her voice wasn't breathless when she spoke.

"Angel, you better put that smile away. And stop looking at me like I'm good enough to eat."

She had no idea. I grabbed her by the chin, pulling her face close to mine. I hummed when I got a whiff of her raspberry scent. "Love, I've been inside you so deep and often enough to know just how delicious you taste. I'd say you're good enough to devour."

Jasmine's mouth formed an "O" shape. I dropped my hold on her. I knew right then and there that, if I pushed a little bit more, she'd willing let me have her on her back with her legs wrapped around me.

Jas shook her head a little before a cheeky grin spread across her face. She threw her head back and laughed loudly. Okay, so not the reaction I thought she'd have, but hearing her genuine laughter in the midst of all this chaos truly was something special. The fact that I was the one who made her laugh like this, I felt like a fucking king.

"You're incorrigible, Angel." She giggled. "Save some of that stuff for later when we don't have an audience."

Her hand reached up to caress my face. I turned, kissing her palm. I watched as her eyes grew heavy and her breath hitched. Yeah, I think my earlier idea to take her was growing on Jas.

I groaned, leaning in to give her a kiss on her forehead. I pulled back quickly and practically threw her out the front door. If she stayed any longer and kept looking at me like she wanted to mount me, I could not be held accountable for my actions.

Chase approached me with a grin on his face. "I know I've said this to you already, but you really do have it bad."

I laughed. "And I'm man enough to admit you're right. I'm glad it's her who has me like this, you know? Anyway, don't try and change the subject. You have the note?"

"It's only part of it and it's whatever I could snap a picture of before the officers came to collect it."

"Stop stalling. I want to read it and then you're going to use your secret connections to help me figure out who it is."

He was chuckled. "Yes, master. Anything else?"

I shook my head. "Chase, that devil-may-care attitude is going to get you into trouble one day. You know that, right?"

"Pot calling the kettle there."

Chase pulled out his phone to open his photos. He eyed me wearily before letting out a breath. "You know, I really shouldn't be showing you this. But you and Jas are the closest thing to family I have. I want to protect her as much as you do.

## CHAPTER 22

And after reading this note, I promise I will do what I can to put this bastard down."

Chase turned his phone over to me and I grabbed it, zooming in on the words in the picture. It was a little blurry and the handwriting was barely legible but the message had been clear. This dick, whoever he was thought Jas was his and she would pay for forgetting who she belonged to. Not if I find you first, asshole.

# INTO PIECES

# Chapter 23

*Jasmine*

I walked into the gym, inhaling smell of sweat and rubber mats. I used it to try and center myself before I made my way over to the nearest punching bag. I came here with the intention of running the track or lifting something heavy. But I knew no matter how much I exhausted my body with that, I'd still want to put my fist through a wall. And since I wasn't in mood to have to pay for a repair job, I set myself up in front of a sturdy punching bag.

I was angry. I tried really hard to hide it at the house. I barely kept myself composed but here, here I was letting it all out. Not even back a day and already the world was conspiring against me being happy. Really, Universe? You really think it's necessary to throw some shit my way so soon? I mean, it's not like I haven't dealt with enough already.

Fuck it. If this was something that was going to happen, no problem. I wasn't the meek and helpless child I once was. I wasn't a victim, and I'd be damned if I was ever made to feel like that again. I wasn't scared by any of this. Hell no, I was plain old pissed off by it.

My anger grew as I stood here and thought about the person who had the audacity to come into my home. The place I rested my head. The place that housed all of my fondest memories of my brother and thought it was okay to destroy it. What? Were they trying to break me? Aw, so sad that was never going to happen again. I wasn't going to sit in the corner crying my eyes out wallowing in self-pity. That wasn't who I was.

I plugged in my headphones and put my iPod on shuffle. The first song that came on was AFI's "Prelude." I closed my eyes, letting the beat drown out all the unnecessary noise that surrounded me.

This was a short song; a minute and thirty-five seconds. I was going to use that minute and half to zone in on everything. Everything I'd been through and everything I was feeling, that's what I was focusing on.

After this session, all of the negative shit that was swimming around in my head would be gone. I'd be damned if I let my demons win this time.

The next song that filtered through my headphones was AFI's "I Hope You Suffer." My iPod knew exactly what kind of mood I was in. Good.

I squared off with the punching bag. I bounced lightly on my feet and threw a few light jabs looking for my rhythm. All too soon, every wrong ever done to me appeared on the bag.

The day I was raped replayed in my mind like it had a hundred times over. Only this time it didn't make me flinch or cower. It made me swing, harder then I intended to. The bag shook a little too wildly with the force of my punch. I steadied the bag, noticing how light I instantly felt. As soon as I let that lightness wash over me, other things began to pop into my mind.

## Chapter 23

I cracked a smile that was anything but friendly. So this was how it was going to be? I'd experience a little happiness and the bad would worm its way in? Yeah, I don't think so.

I swung again, just as hard as the first time. Each swing was a hit at the past and everything that held me back, that made me a victim. I was no longer that scared broken little girl. I was taking my life back. I was going to fight and continue to fight till there was nothing left to fight.

Jay's death popped in my mind next and I swung. I swung hard at the loss of his vibrant life. I swung at Jay for dying while trying to protect and avenge me. My blows kept landing harder and harder, jarring my entire body.

Marcus' face appeared. The bastard's cold dead eyes flashed in my mind, and I swung with everything I had. He tried to take everything from me. He almost succeeded too, but I was done. That little package and text he sent? I swung, destroying its hold on me.

Marcus no longer controlled my life. I was the only person who could control it. I knew shit was going to happen, but I had control on how I reacted to it. No one else got to tell me how I would live my life.

I was breaking free of all the bullshit that surrounded me. This break in, it was just another violation. I swung, letting the anger of it all travel through my body and into that punch. The universe wanted to keep throwing shit my way. Cool. I wasn't going to sit here and cry about it, asking the universe why me? Nope, I was going to scream right back at it, try me. I was going to be happy and that was the end of it. I refused to live any other way anymore.

I sagged against the punching bag. My head rested against it as I fought to get my breathing under control. I was worn out. My physical strength long since left me. But with each inhale and exhale came a renewed inner strength. I couldn't keep the smile off my face.

It was there, deep inside me. I felt the shift; everything began to click. I knew a couple of swings at a punching bag didn't magically fix anything, but it was one hell of a start. I was going to be okay. And for the first time in a long time I believed that.

A pair of hands grabbed my shoulders, and more out of habit and the buzz I was already on, I turned around swinging.

Angel caught my wrist, hauling me up against his body. He chuckled as he released his hold on my wrist. His hands traveled down the length of my body causing goose bumps to appear.

Angel's hands landed on my ass, and he cupped me right under my cheeks pulling me closer to his body. "How is it we keep meeting like this?" Angel smiled as he leaned in. His lips barely touched my own, but he was close enough that our breath mingled with each other's.

"What are you talking about?" My voice came out like a needy moan. It awed me that, no matter the circumstances, Angel always got my body to respond to him.

"This." Angel groaned. "I must be a masochist to enjoy the way you like abusing me." He leaned his lower body into mine, forcing me to feel how hard he was. I had to bite my lip to hold back my own groan.

## Chapter 23

"Yeah, definitely a masochist."

Angel leaned the rest of the way, our lips still barely touching when a throat cleared behind us. Inwardly I cursed and plotted the death of the intruder until he spoke.

"Angel, this is a gym, not your home." Uncle Luke laughed. "I swear it's like you haven't grown up at all."

My face flamed as Uncle Luke's voice filtered through my haze. I completely forgot I was at the gym. Being with Angel was always like that. I zeroed in on him and what we were doing, always forgetting about the rest of the world.

***Angel***

I cursed under my breath as I reluctantly pulled back a little from Jas. I still held her, though. My hands moved from her delectable ass to rest on her hips. And so that Uncle Luke didn't throw me out on my ass, there was now some space between us.

"Come on, Uncle Luke. We were just talking."

"Son, that excuse didn't work for you then and it won't work for you now. Unhand the lady and let her get back to her work out."

Jasmine's head fell back as she laughed out loud and did a very un-ladylike snort. "Looks like some things never change. Huh, Angel?"

I laughed with her despite myself. I looked at her and now that I wasn't looking at her with lust, I saw it. There was something different about her; in her eyes. They weren't as guarded as they had been when I first came home. The shadows were still there but they weren't as overpowering as they once were. She looked less weighed down and more playful. This was the good I wanted to see and desperately be apart of, just like I wanted to be apart of the bad with her.

I swatted her ass. "Don't be a brat. You're supposed to be on my side."

"Always will be. Except when it comes to the person who just so happens to be my trainer." She seemed to think about it for a second. "I don't know, man, run laps or be on your side. Umm. It's a tough choice honestly it is, but I'm not running laps for you. Now, do what he said and unhand me before you get me into trouble."

I laughed loudly gaining some looks from the other guys in the gym. "Damn, Love. You wouldn't run laps for me? Okay, I see how it is. I will unhand you, but first a kiss.

Jasmine put her hand on my chest pushing me away. "Oh no you don't. Don't start something you can't finish."

I pulled Jasmine in close, leaning like I was before Uncle Luke interrupted us. My lips were barely touching hers. But if I licked my own lips I was sure I'd be able to taste hers too.

"Angel?"

My name was a breathless whisper. It made my dick harder knowing I was the one who could turn her inside out just by being near her. "You and I both know just how well I can finish anything I start." I nuzzled my nose against hers,

## Chapter 23

denying us both the need to taste each other. "Go finish your workout. I'll wait for you."

I released her and stepped back. I waited for Jasmine to get going but she just stood there. Her brown eyes filled with lust, her breathing heavy and her face had a nice flush to it that had very little to do with her workout and everything to do with me. Pure male satisfaction slid through me. I loved having this affect on her.

I chuckled. "Jasmine?"

She shook her head. "How do you always do that?"

I smiled. I already knew what she was asking, but I still wanted to hear her say it. "Do what, Love?"

"Never mind." She glanced at the clock on the wall. "You're a little early. Did something happen?"

Jasmine looked more annoyed than worried that something might have happened. This was a massive improvement from the girl I found when I came home. Jasmine was slowly reacquainting herself with the girl she used to be. And while I loved the woman she was becoming; I hoped the girl she used to be reminded her that she was stronger than she thought and nothing could break her.

"I just came by to tell you, Tony stopped by. He said something about a barbecue? He wanted it to happen today, but given the events…"

I trailed off, purposely trying to gauge her reactions. There was a touch of sadness there, but she quickly replaced it with annoyance. There was a fire in her eyes I hadn't seen in a long time. I almost felt bad for the guy once he was caught. Jasmine was going to bury him if she got her hands on him first.

Jas put her head in her hands and groaned. "I have so much shit to clean up. This asshole caused me a huge inconvenience. I still have to call my mom."

I pulled her back into my arms; the need to keep her there was overwhelming, to say the least. I put my hand under her chin, forcing her eyes to meet mine.

"No worries, Love. I'll help you clean up, and as my reward..." I let my words die out as I leaned in closer, desperate for just one taste.

"Angel Torres! I banned you once, don't think I won't do it again. Hands off the girl."

I leaned my head against Jas. We were both snickering like a couple of school kids who got caught making out. She pushed me away. "You're totally going to get me into so much trouble, Angel. I swear."

"Only the good kind, promise." I winked.

She chuckled. "You know, you could have waited to tell me about the barbecue. You didn't have to come now and get yelled at twice."

"What can I say? I can't stay away."

"I bet," Jas said with a cheeky grin.

## CHAPTER 23

I gave her a quick kiss on her forehead, not daring to go any further than that with Uncle Luke breathing down my neck. "Go. I'll be by the front when you're done."

I walked away, knowing if I stood there any longer, Uncle Luke was going to throw me out on my ass and really never let me back in. Besides, I was sure Jasmine wasn't done dishing out her physical abuse on the punching bag. It didn't take a genius to figure out what she was swinging at. That girl had a lot of things go wrong in her life and I was sure most of that resurfaced after seeing her home in shambles.

I was pissed she ever had to go through what she went through, especially alone. I was annoyed, that after the weekend we had, Jasmine had to walk into her home and see it destroyed. I had Chase using his *secret* connections to look into some things for me. I still had no clue what it was he did for a living, but whatever it was, I was grateful it would get me the answers I sought.

I even got Tony to lend a helping hand and use whatever connections he had to get to the bottom of this. He said he might have some leads and I prayed they panned out. By the end of the week, hopefully, I'd have everything I needed to end this threat against Jasmine.

Some sick part of me prayed the scumbag who broke into her home was the same asshole that raped her. I wanted to meet that son of a bitch who thought he could ever touch what was mine. I was going to enjoy killing the bastard.

## Into Pieces

# Chapter 24

***Angel***

I leaned up against the front desk. Whatever receptionist they had on duty today wasn't there, so I wasn't invading or hindering anyone's work environment. I wasn't trying to give Uncle Luke more of a reason to kick me out on my ass. The man may be old, but he'd still whip my ass and send me home to my parents to finish the job.

I made sure I was out of the way so I could watch Jasmine finish her workout. Though, watching her sweat in her spandex shorts and T-shirt was a special kind of torture. My dick throbbed painfully when I walked in and saw her take one powerful swing after another. I was violently turned on watching her exude all that power. I was dying to have it unleashed on me, specifically beneath me and with her long legs wrapped around my waist while I pounded into her.

I couldn't wait to get her out of here. I had a desperate need to consume her that seemed to grow by the second. I had this feeling in my gut that some shit was about to blow and it was making me crazy. I felt like there wasn't enough time. I felt desperate, almost, to spend as much time with her and inside her as possible. I tried to shake it off, but it was still there. It probably had to do with all the shit that happened this past weekend. I wasn't a fool to dismiss my gut completely. I just hoped I was wrong.

The front door to the gym swung open and a gust of wind blew in a scent that I unfortunately knew well.

## Into Pieces

"Angel?"

The voice purred and I cringed. How I ever thought sleeping with her would be beneficial was beyond me. She turned out to be a lousy lay. She didn't have the fire and passion that Jasmine had. Hell, she had no fire period. She just laid there most of the time, and to top this all off, Vivian was bat shit crazy.

She couldn't take my subtle hints or my blunt words telling her I was no longer interested and that this was only a one-time thing. I always made sure any chick I fucked with knew the score before they got involved with me. I let them know as clear as day what this was, what it wasn't and what it would never be.

Any sign of crazy eyes and I was out. I had reading crazy down to a science. Though, clearly, I must have missed something with Vivian. She would not leave me alone, especially after my sister decked her.

I had no time or patience to get wrapped up with needy or insecure chicks. I was young, hung and in love with the female body. Every female was built differently. They tasted differently and I wanted to explore them all.

I was a cocky son of a bitch back then. I can admit it. Janet was the only girl then, who made me want to be in a relationship. She was just one of those girls. Janet had been the first girl I wanted more than sex with. She even had me talking about our future together.

## Chapter 24

But that didn't last long. I went to join the Marines to escape the shit storm between Jay and myself. I told Janet not to wait for me. I didn't think it was fair of me to ask her to.

When I left to boot camp, I thought for sure I'd miss her. I even wrote her a couple of times. But the letters stopped and I wasn't sad or disappointed by it. I was okay with us not being in contact. She didn't invade my thoughts the way I thought she would. She wasn't the girl that I missed or the girl I thought about constantly. She wasn't the one I wanted to come home to.

There was only one girl on my mind who I missed daily and that was Jasmine. I guess my subconscious figured things out a lot sooner than I wanted to admit to myself.

I never understood how important Jasmine was to my life until I no longer had her physically there. Looking back now, I truly understood the connection we had. I was always drawn to her and had a need to be near her. She was also the reason I was able to survive overseas. I sent a silent thank you to whoever was listening for bringing me back home alive and to her.

It amazed me the things that had to happen sometimes to get you to where you needed to be in life. My place was with Jasmine at my side, and until she told me otherwise, I was going to fight like hell to keep standing there. It wasn't like I wanted to be anywhere else anyway.

I turned, facing one of our collective problems. Vivian had become a problem because she couldn't understand my 'I'm not interested' terms no matter how I spelled it out. That was all about to change though, even if I had to be a dick about it.

Vivian smiled as she devoured me with her eyes. "Oh my God, Angel!" She threw herself at me, wrapping her arms and legs tightly around me.

The sound of a punching bag being hit completely stopped. Oh shit! I quickly pried Vivian off me and set her down and away from me. I felt Jasmine's eyes burning a hole in my back. If I didn't diffuse the situation quickly, I knew Jasmine was going to march herself over this way and physically tell Vivian I wasn't interested in her.

Jasmine wasn't a hothead by nature, but I remembered the barbecue my parents threw for me. My sister might have been the one hit Vivian, but I was sure had we not broken it up, Jasmine would have finished her off. And with all the shit going on surrounding Jasmine, she'd take out all her aggression on Vivian without thinking twice about it.

As sexy as it was to watch my girl square off with someone, this wasn't the time nor the place for it. That, and Vivian was about ten pounds wet, Jasmine would kill her.

"Look, Vivian. We need to talk and you really need to listen to the words I'm telling you."

She took a step closer running her hand down my chest. I grabbed her wrist harder than necessary before it went any further. She winced. Under normal circumstances I'd feel sorry for her, but she wasn't leaving me with much of a choice and it was the only thing holding her in place.

"Angel, I've missed you. You know we do much better at not talking than talking. How about we go to the back and I show you just how much I missed you."

## CHAPTER 24

Vivian looked like a cat in heat. The only thing stopping her from rubbing herself against me was my bruising hold on her. "Vivian I told you before and I'm going to tell you again: we're through. I was only interested in fucking you and I told you that." She went to speak up but I cut her off. "No. I'm not interested in sticking my dick in you either. I'm with Jasmine and I'm not going anywhere. I don't want anyone else."

*Jasmine*

I wasn't necessarily one of those girls who got jealous. I always believed jealousy had a lot to do with insecurities and I already had enough issues going on. I really didn't need to add anything extra to the mix.

So when I turned around to see Vivian stick her nasty claws into Angel, I naturally wanted to beat the shit out of her. But it had nothing to do with me being jealous. Nope. This was strictly because I was a territorial person. I had no problem with people looking, but I'd be damn if someone touched what was mine.

Vivian knew exactly who Angel was with. She clearly didn't understand the memo he handed out about it. I had no problem breaking each one of her grubby little fingers to help get that message clear. Maybe then she'd take the hint and keep her cunty ass away from him.

I sat back and watched Vivian practically rub herself against him. The more I stood back and watched the interaction, the angrier I became. I was already pissed with all the shit that had been going on. This girl was making things worse.

I closed my eyes, trying desperately to get my temper under control. This wasn't like me at all. I was usually the calm and laid back one. In a matter of seconds, I felt like I was ready to fly off the handles. I breathed deeply. I had to keep a rational head about all this.

Vivian, unfortunately, worked in this gym. Uncle Luke wouldn't take it well if I beat the shit out of her. I wouldn't be allowed back and I truly loved coming here. This place had become my safe haven. Coming here had been a better therapy than going to an actual therapist.

I heard a painful screech and my eyes snapped open. I saw Vivian smack Angel across the face, not once but twice. I watched as Angel went to grab her and she stumbled back swinging wildly and screaming; "Don't fucking touch me."

Any rational thoughts I was trying to hold on to went straight out the window. I hauled ass to where Angel and Vivian were. Words flew out of my mouth before I could actually think about what I was saying. "You stupid bitch. How about you keep your damn hands off my man already?"

I took a swing with every intention of pounding my fist into her face. That joy was quickly wiped away as I was swept off my feet. I looked down to see Angel's arm wrapped around my waist and he was pulling me back away from Vivian.

I growled, looking back at Vivian. All those tears she had been crying earlier when she was screaming at Angel were completely gone. The little twit had been faking the entire time and now she was wearing a triumphant smile. It annoyed me that she thought she won something.

## CHAPTER 24

I started struggling against Angel's hold. I wanted one tiny piece of her. It would be just enough to wipe that smile off her face.

Angel's hold tightened as he pulled my body flush against his. "Knock it off, Jas."

I stuck out my tongue at him. "Nobody likes you right now." The bastard chuckled as he continued to drag me away. "So you know, Angel. The second you let me go, I'm going to kill you, and then I'm going to come back out here and stomp Vivian's face in."

He grunted and I grunted back. I could speak caveman too. I turned my attention back to the cunt bucket who was still watching us with smug satisfaction. I had no way to physically wipe that look off her face. Since Angel insisted I be carted off like some misbehaved child. I did the next best thing I could think of, and it was something Kris and I liked to call old reliable.

I stuck both of my middle fingers up at her. I mouthed: "I will catch you, bitch." And then smiled. The fear that flashed in her eyes was enough to fill me with some type of satisfaction. Vivian knew she needed to fear me. Good. I watched her with my own smug smile now. She may have thought she won something today, but it didn't matter. She'd get what's coming to her in the end anyway.

*Marcus*

They never saw me. No one ever did. I was always overlooked, no one paid me any attention until it was too late.

## Into Pieces

That worked out fine for me. It allowed me to do what I wanted, when I wanted.

Vivian looked directly at me as soon as Angel swept Jasmine off into the locker rooms. She smiled nervously. She was starting to second-guess the plan. Somewhere along the way, she managed to pick up brain cells and questioned how any of this would get her Angel back. Luckily for me, she soon forgot about all those questions once I stuck my dick in her again. She was pathetically easy to manipulate; it almost annoyed me how I was able to bend her so quickly.

I nodded my head at her. Vivian knew what to do next. My plan was now in progress and Angel's dumb ass had fallen right into it. I knew I needed to leave to set the second part in motion, but I couldn't get my feet to move yet.

I had foolishly followed Jasmine here, wanting to end this cat-and-mouse game we were playing. I wanted desperately to claim her and rip her from Angel's hold. I looked between the girls' locker room and where Vivian stood. Why was it always him? He used and practically abused them and they all couldn't do without him. Why?

A bunch of girls left the locker room giggling. Their giggles stopped the second they looked at me. A couple gave me the once over, their eyes shone with avid interest. But there was one who shied away, my look making her nervous. I smirked. If I had the time, I'd make her my new favorite plaything. Lucky for her, I only had eyes for one.

My phone started ringing again. Tony had been calling me nonstop since Jasmine came back. Big brothers can be so annoying.

## CHAPTER 24

I picked up, hoping if I actually answered him one time, he'd stop bothering me. "Can I help you?"

"You really had to go and leave a note, Marcus? Why can't you leave her the hell alone already? She does not want you."

"You took the note?"

I yelled into the phone. A couple of people who had been wrapped up in the altercation between Vivian and Angel were now looking in my direction. I cursed. Shit. I didn't need to make a scene. It would place me here when I wasn't supposed to be.

I made a hastily exit, but I felt eyes burning a hole in my back. I didn't bother looking back. I couldn't. I was going to kill Tony if he ruined this for me.

INTO PIECES

# Chapter 25

*Jasmine*

We hit the locker rooms and there were a couple of females in there getting changed and grabbing their stuff. Angel politely asked the ladies to leave. They took one look at him and then me; they all had grins on their faces as they scurried out of the locker room. I even heard one mutter "Lucky bitch" as she passed by me. I rolled my eyes, if they only knew.

Angel released me. I turned around pushing him hard. He fell into the lockers behind him with a grunt.

"You should have let me hit her, Angel."

He grunted. "I've been on the receiving end of your fist, not once but twice. You'd have killed her. You out weigh her and even if you pulled your punch, you still would have knocked her out."

I rolled my eyes. "You had a *bendito* moment? You a sucka. Feeling sorry for her. Trust me, she'd have been aight."

"Jasmine."

"What? She smacked you twice. Twice, Angel! You should have let me bash her face in."

I was buzzing with energy, bouncing on my toes. I couldn't keep still. I felt like I hadn't spent half my morning pounding that punching bag into the ground. I desperately wanted to hit something, preferably someone by the name of Vivian. She was probably still standing outside thinking she won. I wanted to run out of here and hit her one time but I knew that wasn't the answer.

I turned, facing away from Angel. I closed my eyes, inhaling deeply. I was a rational human being; I had no real reason to put my hands on her. It wasn't like Angel wanted me to hurt her. He was being the gentleman that he was. He was trying to save her life. It was sweet of him, really it was. If I kept telling myself that, eventually I'd believe it and actually woosa a little bit.

Angel's deep chuckle interrupted my thoughts. My head snapped towards his direction. There was a crazy person living inside every female and men had a tendency to do little things that brought that crazy person out of even the most civilized female. For me? Laughing when you know I'm pissed off would do it.

"Something amuse you, Angel?"

"Na. You should calm down a little though, Love."

And that right there was the other thing that brought the crazy out. "Excuse me?"

### Angel

Oh shit! I realized as soon as the words slipped out of my mouth how badly I fucked up. You know that saying, the one about never telling an angry girl to calm down? Yeah, I was two seconds away from finding out why you should never tell a girl that.

## Chapter 25

Jasmine looked like she was a breath away from skinning me alive. I was man enough to admit, that while I wanted her wrapped around my cock, I was also a tad bit scared for my life.

"Oh no, Angel. Don't get quiet now. Speak up. What did you say to me?"

"I'm saying, don't you think you're making a big deal out of this?"

Her brown eyes narrowed into tiny silts as she turned fully to face me. Yep, I was about to die.

"I'm making a big deal out of all of this?" Her voice went up an octave as she approached me. "Not only did you get me in trouble with Uncle Luke. He was sweet enough to give me thirty suicides everyday for a week."

"Aw. Come on, Love." I reached out for her. She smacked my hand away and pushed me back into the lockers again.

"Nope. You don't get to touch me. That's what got me into trouble in the first place." I crossed my arms over my chest. I let my wolfish grin out as I watched Jasmine's eyes widen a little bit at the way my arms bulged in this position.

Jasmine enjoyed my body as much as I enjoyed hers. I loved that she couldn't hide from me physically. Her eyes were starting to give her away, every single time. She might have been pissed about the extra workout, but she damn sure enjoyed what led up to that particular consequence.

"You're going to deny you enjoyed yourself? You're a bad liar, Love."

Her eyes narrowed even further. "Don't be cute, Angel. You know I enjoyed it, but I'm not going to enjoy the suicides I have to do." She stepped closer to me. "And while we're on the subject of things I don't like, I damn sure don't like Vivian putting her hands on you. Or, being dragged away like a two-year-old throwing a tantrum." She looked at me for a second and grumbled. "Asshole."

I couldn't stop my smile from stretching across my lips. Jas honestly looked adorable angry. I would never tell her that to her face, though. I already made the mistake of telling her to calm down. I liked my balls right where they were, thank you. I didn't need to piss her off any further.

"Why do you keep smiling, Angel? In all honesty, it's pissing me off and makes me want to kill you."

I threw my head back and laughed. "Stop being an ass." Jasmine growled. She went to push me, but I caught her wrist spinning her into the lockers behind me. She winced as her back hit the hard metal.

"You okay?"

She nodded while she struggled against my hold. "I'm still going to kill you."

I pressed my body flush against hers and pinned her hands above her head. She let out a gasp. I waited, searching her brown eyes, making sure she was still with me. We may have come a long way, but we weren't past anything yet.

## Chapter 25

Jasmine licked her lips, making them wet, and I groaned, leaning my head against hers. I wasn't kidding when I said I was turned on. Jasmine had my dick trying to escape since we left the hotel room. This girl had me completely strung out on her, and it was intoxicating knowing she was right there with me.

"Angel," she panted.

I looked up into her eyes. "You good?"

She licked her lips again, and I wanted nothing more than to dive right in and kiss those lush lips of hers. But I held back. I needed to be sure we were on the same page.

"I'm good, Angel. Promise. Just let me touch you."

I chuckled. "You just threatened to kill me and you want me to let your hands go? I don't think so."

I gripped her wrists in one hand and trailed my other hand down to cup her cheek. "You truly are amazing, Jasmine. I don't think I've ever had someone defend me the way you were ready to defend me against Vivian." I leaned in, placing a small kiss underneath her ear and right by her erratic pulse. Jasmine's whole body trembled from the simple touch.

I hummed my appreciation. My girl craved the touch of her man. Her hunger for me only fueled my desire for her even more.

I pulled back, watching Jasmine's eyes turn a darker shade of brown and her breathing increase. I leaned in again, my lips precariously close to hers. Her breath hitched and I grinned. "I don't think you were really defending me. I think you wouldn't like any female putting their hands on me in general. Why is that, Jasmine?"

She didn't even hesitate. "I don't share what's mine."

"Good."

I bit down on her bottom lip and pulled it into my mouth, sucking on it gently. She groaned and her whole body relaxed into mine. The hands that held her wrist brought them down and placed them on my throbbing dick. The little minx that she was squeezed causing my own groan.

I pulled back again and saw her eyes were closed. She had a nice flush to her body. It was the same one she'd get when she was getting closer to an orgasm.

"Jasmine."

Her eyes flew open. "If I put my hands down your shorts, will I find you wet?" She bit her bottom lip and nodded. "Oh no. I want to hear you say it. Will I find you wet for me?"

"No. You'd find me soaked."

Just like that, Jasmine broke my control to shreds. I couldn't take it anymore. I picked her up by her waist and she instinctively knew to wrap those sexy-as-sin legs around my body. I pulled her hair, angling her face to mine, and devoured her lips. I was hungry for her, and judging by the way she was clawing at my shoulders, she wanted to feast on me as well.

I had both my hands under her shirt, making their way up to cup her breasts. We both moaned. In the back of my mind I

## Chapter 25

heard the door swing open, but I didn't want to stop. I had gone too long without tasting her.

"Angel Louis Torres. Did I not tell you to unhand the lady?"

We both groaned before we started laughing. I knew it was only a matter of time before Uncle Luke would come barging in. I was hoping I would have had time to get Jasmine off at least twice before that happened.

"And you, young lady, I guess you're up to fifty suicides for two weeks now. I'd give some to Angel but his ass isn't allowed back. I have half a mind to kick your ass but you're a grown man now not a child."

I slowly dropped Jasmine to her feet and cupped her face. "Sorry, Love."

She smiled that smile that light up her entire face and made me feel like the king of the world. "No worries, Angel. It was worth it."

I smiled back. "Always will be, Love."

"I said let's go." Uncle Luke came behind me, pulling me by the ear and dragging me out of the locker room. "You never learn, do you?"

I knew better than to grumble under my breath, and honestly, I was too happy to be upset. I didn't care that I was being dragged out of the girls' locker room like I had been in my teenage years. Like Jasmine said, it was worth it and with her, I knew deep down it always would be.

# Into Pieces

# Chapter 26

*Jasmine*

It had been a whirlwind summer. So much managed to happen in such a short time; it surprised me how quickly things could change. But I guess, given the events in my life, I should have been used to change happening within a blink of an eye. It seemed to be the way my life worked for the most part.

I leaned my head back against my brother's tombstone. I hadn't been here since that night I told Angel I was raped. Looking back on it now, I can say I was glad I told Angel here. I laughed. That didn't make me sound too crazy, right? What person would want to share their deepest secret in a place with a bunch of dead guys?

Hindsight. Hindsight was 20/20. And as creepy as it might come across, I was glad I told Angel everything here, with my brother close by. He was always there when I needed him when we were younger. It was only right that he was there in spirit when I told Angel what happened to me.

My hands dug into the dirt that sat on top of his grave. I missed him. This summer seemed to be the worst it had been since he first died. I could have used his wacky philosophy on life to help me weed through a lot of my battles. He had so much left to teach me, and he was taken away from me entirely too soon.

I had come here to apologize for living my life like a hermit these past few years. He wouldn't have wanted that for me. I also came to acknowledge and accept that his death wasn't my fault. Jay was my big brother and I knew it now; if he had to go back and do it all over again, he wouldn't change a thing.

I remember everything that happened that night. Marcus let me go and I ran straight to him. He was the only person I wanted to see and talk to. I knew he'd find a way to help me.

It was the first time I ever saw my brother angry. He punched a nice-sized hole through our living room wall. My brother never showed that type of aggression, ever.

*"Jasmine, I'm going to make this okay for you. I promise you. He will never touch you again. Just promise me you won't take a shower till I get back, okay?"*

*I didn't understand completely. I just nodded. "Where are you going, Jay?"*

*"Don't worry about that now, okay?" He ruffled my hair and grabbed his car keys heading for the door.*

*"Jay, wait!"*

*He turned and there was nothing but pain in his eyes. Tears sprang from my eyes as I realized exactly what he was going to do.*

*I launched myself at him, throwing my arms around him. I thought if I held on tightly, I'd be able to keep him here and he wouldn't leave me.*

*"Don't do this, Jay. I don't want you to go to jail. It's not worth it."*

## Chapter 26

*Jay pried my hands off of him and held my shoulders firmly. I put my head down, knowing no matter what I said, it wouldn't change his mind.*

*"Jasmine, look at me."*

*I slowly lifted my head to stare into brown eyes identical to mine. There was too much pain and remorse there. A complete contrast to his naturally light-hearted nature.*

*"I'm your big brother. I'd kill for you no questions asked."* *He laughed but it was void of any humor.* *"There's probably nothing I wouldn't do for you. It hurts me to know I couldn't protect you from this or from him. And I have to live with that for the rest of my life. But I will make this right for you."*

*Jay pulled me into a bear hug, and I squeezed back just as tightly. "Now, let me go do my big brother duties."*

I had watched him walk out that door with a promise to come back for me. He never made it back. I wished every day I had a few more moments with him. Just so I could tell him how much I loved him and needed him in my life.

I knew now that it wouldn't have made a difference if Jay stayed a few extra minutes or not. He still would have gone to Marcus' house and kicked his ass. And when Marcus came to, he still would have gotten in his car and gone looking for him. Maybe if Jay didn't blow past that stop sign, Marcus never would have had the opportunity to hit him dead on and Jay never would have lost control of his car and wrapped it around the pole.

The breeze blew around me. It was warm and oddly comforting. I closed my eyes, letting it blanket over my body. I didn't know what it was; maybe it was because I was sitting in a cemetery in the middle of the day, but the warm breeze felt like Jay's arms were being wrapped around me.

I inhaled deeply, soaking in the woodsy scent that surrounded me. A smile made its way across my lips. Maybe the stress of the summer had finally gotten to me and I snapped. I could swear my brother was here with me, right now. I felt his presence deep down in my soul. I was sure if I reached out a little, I'd be able to touch him.

A twig snapped in the distance and the breeze turned chilly. Whatever comfort I felt disappeared and dread quickly followed. I snapped my eyes open, scanning my surroundings.

And as I was quickly learning the ways in which my life worked, I was sure that seeing Tony standing in front me was a sign that something bad was about to happen or happened already. I stood up and crossed my arms over my chest, ready to face whatever it was that brought him all the way out here to my brother's grave.

### *Tony*

I came here to visit my mom's resting place and my feet led me to Jay's grave instead. I didn't expect to see Jasmine here, yet I wasn't all that surprised either. Jay had always been her hero, nothing happened in her life that she didn't run and tell him about. Given all the things that happened this summer, I was surprised the dirt that was above Jay's grave didn't have a permanent indention in it.

## Chapter 26

I saw her resting with her eyes closed and honestly had no intentions of bothering her. This was the first time in a long time she looked truly at peace. I didn't want to disturb that rare moment for her. It was the least I could do for her. But, like clockwork, Marcus was trying to screw that up too.

He was standing a few headstones away watching her and me. He was pissed. Probably pissed I ripped up that note before Jasmine got her hands on it. He was probably even more pissed that I was standing here this close to Jasmine.

Marcus took one step forward and a cold breeze rushed through the cemetery. Jasmine's eyes snapped open and landed right on me. I smirked. Her instincts were getting better. She slowly stood, eyeing me cautiously. "What are you doing here?"

I looked beyond her to where Marcus stood. His smile was anything but friendly, as he seemed to fall back and blend into the shadows. Jasmine turned around to follow my line of sight. I knew she wouldn't see him. He wasn't ready to show himself to her yet.

I couldn't suppress my annoyance with Marcus. No matter how much I yelled, talked and beat it into him, he couldn't let Jasmine go. There was no way to make him comprehended that she didn't want him.

My phone chimed, signaling an incoming text. I looked at the message and quickly shut my phone off. Marcus was relentless. He now thought I had feelings for Jasmine. He thought I was trying to push him out so I could take his place. I never noticed how bad Marcus' mind was until now. Did my father even know how damaged his son really was?

Jasmine turned back around to face me. She had this look of concern as she stepped closer to me, placing her hand on my arm. The slight touch was innocent and meant nothing to her but comfort, but my body reacted like it was an invitation for something else.

"You good, Tony?"

She looked at me with those beautiful brown eyes of hers, and I could see why she captured Angel's heart and was my brother's obsession. Jasmine was everything that was good and beautiful. Even as ruined as she thought she was, she still possessed an innocence about her that could draw even the worst of sinners in.

I captured a stray hair that escaped from her messy updo. It was soft in my hands, and I felt something inside me start to break. I would never have the love of a girl like Jasmine. My brother made sure to ruin that for me.

I tucked the strand behind her ear. "Yeah." I snapped my mouth shut and cleared my throat. Everything I was feeling was threatening to boil over. It was getting harder and harder to hold myself together.

I stepped away from Jasmine, forcing a smile. "I'm okay, Jas."

She smiled up at me, and there it was, that fucking look in her eyes. The one that showed you she trusted you. Even after everything that happened and continued to happen, Jasmine still believed I had her best interest in mind. I didn't though, I never really could. And just like that, I was breaking inside a little more.

## Chapter 26

"Jas, can I ask you a question?"

"Yeah, what's up?"

"Do you um–" I cleared my throat and shook my head. "Care to escort me to my barbecue?"

She laughed. "That's not what you wanted to ask me, Tony. What's up?"

I threw my arm around her shoulders and started walking with her towards the exit. "It's not important, not anymore anyway. Maybe in another life."

She looked up at me. But I shook my head, at her hoping she'd let it go. Jas shrugged. "Well, if you change your mind, you know I'm all ears. Now, let's go stuff my belly with some food."

We both laughed and the pain inside my chest manifested. I was winning the Asshole of the Year award with my performance. Marcus was going to destroy Jasmine if it was the last thing he ever did. The only thing I could do was sit back and let it happen.

INTO PIECES

# Chapter 27

*Jasmine*

Everyone I've ever known was sitting in Tony's backyard. I thought this barbecue was only going to be for a couple of us, not the entire neighborhood and then some. Tony never liked the big crowds. I mean, he went clubbing with my brother and Angel, but a party at his house? That never happened, and judging by the look on his face, he was starting to rethink the whole idea of inviting everyone he knew.

The gate swung open again and I tensed. Every single time someone came through that gate, my heart either stopped or sped up. I was anxiously waiting for Angel to show up. I was also nervous that Tony's pops would show up. That man still managed to creep me out and piss me off all in the same breath. Regardless, I really didn't want to have to deal with him today. I was in a semi-good place and I did not want anyone, especially not Mr. Marcelo, messing it up. I just wanted to have a good time, enjoy myself and step away from all the negativity.

I let out a loud burp that would put every male here to shame. Everyone stopped what they were doing to glance over at me. I smiled and patted my full belly. It had been a very long time since I had any barbecue food. The last barbecue I went to, I never even got a chance to touch the food thanks to Angel and that twat face Vivian. Today I made sure to make up for it.

As soon as Tony and I got here, I put him to work behind the grill while I helped set up. He promised me his famous ribs, and boy did he deliver. His ribs were always so juicy and the barbecue sauce was heaven in a bowl. He said it was his mom's secret recipe. All anyone was ever allowed to know was that it contained either beer or liquor in it. No one could replicate it. I didn't care as long as Tony kept making them with the barbecue sauce, I was a happy camper.

I stretched out on one of the lounge chairs we had put out. I smiled. I was happy and stuffed. I ate a lot and I wasn't even feeling the least bit guilty about it. Okay maybe a little bit, but that was only because Angel still wasn't here yet. He told me to save him a plate but I could only do so much against my appetite. Feeding my belly always came first.

I let out another loud burp. If I kept this up, I'd be able to make room for more food.

"Geez, Jas. You'd think you were a dude. Can you try to act like a lady?" Chase sat beside me in a huff.

Somebody was in a mood. "I am a lady. And ladies burp, loudly."

"Just take it down a notch, Jas." Chase started grumbling beside me.

I cracked a cheesy grin and patted him on his shoulder. "Aw, is somebody upset? Green is definitely not your color, Chase. It makes you grumpy."

"What are you talking about?"

"Oh, so you're playing the stupid card today too? Okay."

## Chapter 27

I sat back in my seat still grinning. My eyes followed Chase's line of sight. I already knew why he was in a mood, but it was still amusing to see it actually play out in front of me.

Kris had shown up looking hot per usual. Short shorts and a red halter top. She also showed up with a date. The hot Marine we met at the wedding, Damien. The man looked just as good in jeans and a fitted T-shirt as he did in his dress blues. His grey eyes still had a mischievous twinkle in them. When he caught me staring at him, he winked and I laughed in response.

Chase grumbled beside me. "You too?"

"What?"

"Nothing, Jasmine. Just forget it."

"Aw, someone's feelings are hurt." I patted him on his shoulder again and he turned to look at me. "I think it's time you suck it up, buttercup." Chase's eyes narrowed. "What? Oh you thought because I was rooting for you two that I'd be on your side?"

He rolled his eyes. "That would mean exactly that, Jas."

"And I would. But there's this one tiny little problem that keeps coming up. You don't want to be with her."

He went to speak but he shook his head instead. "Yeah, Kris told me what happened at the wedding. We both think you're being a dickhead." I sat back in my seat. "You boys keep playing these games and think a girl is going to sit around and wait for you." I shook my head. "That gets old pretty quickly,

Chase. Oh, and just so you know, I was the one who gave Kris Damien's number."

Chase abruptly stood up, knocking his chair over. "Are you fucking kidding me, Jas? After everything I've tried to do for you?"

I stood up calmly and faced him. I couldn't hide the smile on my face even if I wanted to. Chase may say he couldn't or wouldn't be with Kris, but his body and heart were saying something completely different.

"Look, Chase. I know you're feeling some type of way right now because Kris is here with someone else. But we both know it's selfish and stupid of you to expect her to wait for you to get your head out of your ass. Damien is hot and she deserves someone who isn't going to play the type of games you're playing with her."

"You guys okay here?"

I spun around quickly with a wide smile on my face. Angel smiled back opening his arms. I went willingly into them. He kissed the top of my head and we both let out a sigh of contentment.

Angel whispered. "I think we're honeymooning. I can't believe I missed you this much and I've only been away from you for a couple of hours."

I pulled back barely suppressing my laughter. "You think I'm gorgeous, you want to kiss me."

## Chapter 27

Angel threw his head back and laughed. "And no more *Miss Congeniality* for you."

"Best movie ever."

"Really? It's bad enough Kris is drooling over Damien. Now, I gotta deal with you two love birds?" Chase grumbled behind us.

I faked whispered to Angel. "Don't mind grumpy pants over there. He's jealous your sister moved on and doesn't want anything to do with him."

"I can still hear you, Jasmine. And I'm not jealous!"

I turned around and stuck my tongue out at him. "You're totally jealous and you have no one to blame but yourself."

Chase grunted and turned his back towards us.

"My point has been proven, thank you."

Angel pulled me to his side. "Do I need to separate you two?"

"He started it."

Angel laughed as Damien and Kris made their way over to us. I chuckled. The closer Kris got to us, the more agitated Chase became. Oh well, serves him right.

"What's up, Torres?" Damien gave Angel one of those manly handshakes that was a hug without them actually touching. When his eyes settled on me, he gave me his signature bad boy grin.

INTO PIECES

"Whatever you're thinking about, Damien, knock it off."

He laughed as he grabbed me right out of Angel's hold and off my feet. He squeezed me tightly against him.

Angel growled deep behind us. "I'd advise you to get your hands off my girl, Damien."

Damien and I both laughed as he set me back down. He pulled on one of the curls that escaped my bun. "You look good, Jasmine. Make sure I'm the first one you call when Angel fucks this up." He placed a quick kiss on my cheek that was entirely too close to my lips.

Angel's hand came down hard on Damien's shoulder. He growled his warning, "Knock it off already. She's mine. If you touch her again, I will hurt you, Damien."

Damien stepped back laughing with his hands held up high in mock surrender.

I crossed my arms over my chest. "You're horrible, Damien."

"It's what I do, sweetheart. I give guys too stubborn to realize what they have a nice little push in the right direction.

"Yeah, well, you need to cut the shit." Angel grumbled beside me. His hand came to rest possessively at my neck.

"That can't always work for you, Damien. Some guys, no matter the incentive, won't head in the right direction."

"Really, Jasmine?" Damien's lips spread into a wide smile. It really wasn't fair how good this man looked. "Who's hand is on your neck right now, while giving me his *'I will kill you'* look? And" He stepped further back, waving his hands across Tony's yard. "If you haven't noticed the other two love birds are no longer with us. My guess, he's groveling at Kris' feet right now."

I looked around and noticed there was no sign of them anywhere. My eyes met Tony's, and he pointed the spatula he was holding towards the front of his house. I looked back at Damien who had a very self-satisfied smile on his face. The smug bastard was too cocky for his own good. Rather than ever admit out loud that he was right, I completely ignored the fact that Kris and Chase were no longer here.

"You know, Damien. When you settle down, because we both know it's going to happen eventually, I want the privilege of meeting her. I want to be able to shake the hand of the female who brought your cocky ass down a few notches."

He scoffed and went to step closer, but Angel's deep growl stopped him in his tracks. "That's never going to happen, Jasmine. There's not a female out there who can handle me for more than a couple of nights."

Though I'm sure his statement was meant to come off as cocky, the look in his eyes gave him away. Hmm, so there was already someone out there giving Damien a run for his money. I guess that's a story for a whole other time.

INTO PIECES

# CHAPTER 28

*Kris*

Here we go again.

Chase walked closely beside me. His whole body was tense. I didn't want to go anywhere with him, but I couldn't necessarily kill him at Tony's barbecue. That was considered bad manners and everyone would have been a witness. It would have just gotten complicated.

Chase grabbed my arm, pulling me in the opposite direction I was walking in. I sucked in a sharp breath. Every single time he touched me, it was like sparking a match. My body went from cold to on fire in a matter of seconds. One stupid touch from him and I was putty in his hands.

I took a deep breath, trying desperately to steel myself against the unnerving emotions Chase enticed in me. I couldn't succumb to this with him anymore. It hurt too much.

Chase made a sound that was in between a groan and a grunt. I cracked a smile. It did good for my ego to know Chase wasn't as unaffected by me as he wanted to believe.

There was something here between us. Whether it was just physical remained to be seen. He enjoyed playing games that I no longer wanted to be a part of.

"Don't worry, Kris. I know what my touch does to you. I won't touch you for long. You were heading in the wrong direction."

"I didn't want to go with you in the first place."

"And yet, you're still here."

"That's only because I didn't want to kill you in front of Damien. It's too early in our relationship for him to see that side of me."

Chase growled beside me and then chuckled. "Kris, the last thing he wants with you is a relationship. He can't handle you anyway. You'd just be disappointed in the end."

I stopped short, wrenching my arm out of his hold. Chase turned around with a confused look on his face. "Why did you stop walking?"

"Seriously, Chase? What do you want?"

He went to speak, but he snapped his mouth shut instead. I rolled my eyes. He was unbelievable. "Whelp, this was fun. I'm leaving now."

I turned to walk away. There really was no need for me to be here, especially if Chase was going to continue with the same shit.

He reached out grabbing my wrist. "Kris, wait."

My body wanted to betray me and melt further into his hold. He made small circles against my pulse and it beat a little faster. Almost like it was jumping out to reach him.

"Beauty."

## Chapter 28

He groaned my name and I hated it. I hated that he said his pet name for me with such yearning and affection. I hated that, with a simple touch, my body came alive for him. I hated that he wasn't even that close to me but he still managed to surround me, engulf me with his scent and presence. And I hated myself the most. I couldn't stop wanting him.

"Chase," I whispered. It sounded more like a plea. A plea for something, I wasn't entirely sure I was ready to admit.

He stepped closer to me. His hand still held my wrist. His chest was pressed firmly against my back, and I shivered. I wanted to press myself into him, meld my body with his. But I couldn't. In my head I knew the games couldn't go on anymore. I was tired of them, even if my body was betraying my want right now. I knew this had to end.

"Chase," I said his name more firmly now. "What do you want from me?"

He bent down, his lips near my ear. "You, Kris. I've always wanted you." He placed a kiss on my exposed shoulder, and my knees buckled at the tenderness in his words and actions. *Don't break, Kris. Do not break.*

Chase abruptly stood up straight and let out a breath. And there he was, good ol' Chase in all his glory. It was always going to be the same shit with him.

"But–"

"But," I cut him off. I already knew what he was going to say. He said it all the time. "Let me guess. I can't be with you."

I turned around, pushing him hard. My frustrations with this situation, with him and myself were finally boiling over. "Enough with this shit already, Chase. Why the hell did you make me come all the way out here?"

"Because..." he stammered, and I pushed at him again.

"It's because you're a selfish prick."

"Beauty," he purred my pet name.

"Fuck you, Chase. You don't get to do this anymore."

Chase scrubbed a hand down his face. He let out a breath that sounded like he was frustrated. It made me angrier that he thought he had any right to be frustrated by any of this.

Either you want someone or you don't. You were either with someone or you weren't. Only kids played the games Chase continuously played. I was a fool for allowing it to go on for as long as I did. My heart was starting to hurt from all the back and forth. I couldn't take it anymore.

Chase reached out for me and I took a step back. His eyes flashed with hurt. I didn't care, mostly.

"I'm sorry, Kris. I know I can't be with you. But every single time I see you with someone else, I lose my shit."

I laughed. Something inside of me snapped. "I'm going to kill you, Chase."

I saw heat flash in his eyes, and he took another step forward. I stepped back. "Don't touch me, Chase. I promise you I will kill you."

## Chapter 28

Chase chuckled as he lunged for me. I didn't step back fast enough. Apparently my mind still didn't have any control over my body. I made a half-hearted attempt at pushing him away. He grabbed my arms, successfully pinning them behind me.

"Chase," I warned, or at least tried to. My voice came out entirely too husky for my liking. I hated that my body reacted to him this way. My nipples were sharp points brushing against the fabric of my shirt. I was wet, painfully wet. I was throbbing, desperate for Chase's hands to be anywhere than where they were now.

Chase leaned further into my body, doing a very successful job of completely surrounding me. He knew exactly what he did to me, and he was using it to his advantage.

"Beauty, Beauty, Beauty." Each time he said his pet name for me he swiveled his hip into my body, making me feel how hard he was. How hard I made him.

He leaned in, placing a kiss under my ear. It took all of my strength not to lean into him and seek more of his touch.

"You can't fight this attraction anymore than I can, Kris. You want me. That little hitch in your breath, the way your body is coiled so tightly, waiting for my touch."

He bit the bottom of my ear, and I had to bite my own lip painfully to keep from moaning out loud. I couldn't give into him anymore. This had to end.

"You want me, Kris. Why are you denying it now?"

## Into Pieces

"Chase, sweetheart." I was proud of myself. My voice came out steady. "Nobody likes you. In fact, I want nothing more than to wrap my hands around your neck and squeeze the life out of you."

Chase's deep rumble sent a new set of shivers throughout my body. "You're a horrible liar, Kris. You want to wrap your hands around something alright, and it sure as hell isn't my neck."

"Chase, I swear. Just let me go." I started struggling against his hold. This was ridiculous. Why couldn't he leave me alone already?

He switched his hold on my arms to a one-handed hold. The other hand came up to grab my chin. He forced me to look up at him. "That seems to be the problem, Beauty. I don't know how to let you go."

His lips came crashing down on mine with enough force to knock the wind out me. I didn't care. I didn't want to breathe if it meant Chase would keep kissing me like this.

He let go of my arms and fisted my hair in his hands. He angled my mouth in a way that suited him best. He was devouring me, consuming all of me. I held on for dear life.

This is what I wanted. It was what my body craved from him. Chase and his hunger finally unleashed on me. I kissed him back just as viciously. I wanted to consume as much of him as possible. This way, when I walked away, I'd have something to hold on to.

## CHAPTER 28

We both pulled away at the same time, breathing heavy. Chase was the first to speak. "Kristal," he said my full name on a groan.

I knew what was coming, and if he was having problems stating the facts yet again, I'd have no problem lending him a helping hand. It's not like I hadn't heard it a million times before.

"I'll save you the speech, Chase. I know what it is and what this won't ever be."

I turned around quickly and walked away from him. I wanted to stay and wrap myself around him. I wanted that kiss to be the start of what could be, but I knew Chase a little too well. He didn't want this. Well, his body did, he just couldn't let go of whatever was holding him back. I knew I couldn't take the back and forth with him anymore. It was a waste of time and it was starting to take its toll on me emotionally.

I didn't bother going back to the barbecue. I didn't want to bring my joyous mood around other people. I decided to head home and have a night with my two favorite boys: Ben and Jerry. Those two never let me down. Tonight's poison would be Cheesecake Brownie, the perfect flavor to drown my sorrows in.

I made it two blocks when I realized a car was crawling up the street behind me. I initially shrugged it off, thinking the person was just looking for an address. I quickly darted across the street, going down a one-way block just in case. I picked up my speed trying to get off this block in case the car was following me and double backed.

INTO PIECES

I was practically running now. I made it to the next block a little winded and relieved the car wasn't there. I set my regular pace and started laughing to myself. Why the hell was I so freaked out? People drove that slowly all the time when they were either lost or trying to find an address. I shook my head. That incident with Chase must have really thrown me off.

I turned the corner and came face to face with the car that I was trying to escape from. Dread crept up my back when I saw who was lounging on the hood of it. Marcus.

He sat there with his arms crossed and a smile on his face. This guy always creeped me out now, more so then ever. This was wrong. Why was he here? Why was he following me?

I took a step back and Marcus shifted. It was subtle. If I wasn't looking at him I would have missed it.

"Don't run, Kris. It will just piss me off more. I have a timetable to follow and you killed most of that time talking to Chase."

I took another step back. I had to give myself a head start if he was serious about running after me. "What are you talking about?'

His eyes narrowed. "Didn't I tell you not to run?" He let out a breath and stood straight. He unfolded his arms and I realized he had a gun in his hand.

"This is what's going to happen, Kris. You're going to get in this car with me."

"And if I don't?"

## Chapter 28

There was no way I was getting in a car with him. There was something off about Marcus. His eyes weren't all that focused. I knew I shouldn't piss him off, but something in my gut told me if I got in that car with him my chances of coming out were slim to none.

"Well, it's simple, Kris. You don't have to get in. In fact, I really don't need you; you were just an incentive. I'll still find away to hurt your dipshit brother and Jasmine."

His smile was anything but friendly and his cold eyes zeroed in on me. There was something in his stare that told me he was serious. I was confused as to why he was here and why he would go after my brother or even Jasmine. But if I could do anything to help distract him from going after them, I would.

I put my hands up and walked slowly over to him. Maybe once we got to wherever we were going and he didn't have his hands on that gun I'd be able to escape or something.

"Okay. We do it your way, Marcus. I'll go with you."

He reached out grabbing hold of my arm. I held back my wince. His hands were cold and his grip was bruising. I sent a silent prayer to whoever was listening that Angel, Jas and myself got out of this in one piece.

Marcus led me to the backseats and opened the door. He leaned in, whispering in my ear. "You always were a stupid bitch. I think I'll have some fun with you first."

Fear hit me first and then my world went pitch black.

INTO PIECES

# Chapter 29

*Chase*

I stood there a little dumbfounded that Kris actually walked away from me without so much as a backwards glance. I stood there like an idiot staring after her until I could no longer see her. Every fiber in my body demanded I go after her, but I couldn't get my feet to move. When she finally disappeared from my sight I turned and headed back towards the barbecue.

I should have gone after her. I shouldn't have let her leave like that, and if I was being honest with myself, it hurt like hell watching her walk away.

I mean, Kris was right with what she said: we couldn't be together, not right now at least. As long as this pending job loomed over my head, I wasn't about to start something with her, especially since I'd be gone more than I'd be home. That wasn't a relationship.

I was annoyed with myself now. I shouldn't have brought her out here. I should have just left her alone to be with Damien.

As soon as the thought crossed my mind, I growled deep in my chest. That primitive part that resides in all men knew Kris belonged to me and demanded I go after her and claim her. The logical part that dominated knew that could never happen.

## Into Pieces

I opened the gate to Tony's backyard. I was surprised to see that the amount of people had dwindled a little bit. I guess with Jas hogging all the food, there wasn't much left for everyone else to hang around for.

Speaking of Jasmine, I heard her girlish laughter followed by Angel's deep rumble. My eyes followed the sound, and I saw the two of them huddle together in a corner completely oblivious to the world around them.

A small smile tugged at my lips. Those two looked extremely happy. I'd say the happiest they'd been in a very long time. Angel had this look in his eyes; it was there every time he looked at her when he thought she wasn't paying attention. He looked in awe of her, like he couldn't believe she was his.

I envied what they had. If I continued to take on these jobs, I'd never be able to have what those two had, especially not with Kris. If I kept hanging out with those two love birds, I'd start admitting out loud that I wanted what they had. Even with all the bad shit they continued to face, I'd take even a fraction of it if it meant I had the one I wanted by my side.

Jasmine laughed again and a pang of guilt hit me hard. I'd been so caught up with Kris and this job, I completely forgot to follow up with the lead I thought I had on the break in at her house. The lead would probably pan out to nothing, but it never hurt to check. When it came to Jas, even Kris, I'd rather be safe than sorry.

I pulled out my phone, looking for the contact I needed to hit up. Damien came and stood by me. I didn't bother

## Chapter 29

suppressing my snarl. The asshole had gotten to touch what should have been mine.

Damien laughed beside me. "Going by your reaction and the fact that Kris isn't with you, I'm guessing you didn't grovel properly and she kicked your sorry ass to the curb."

"If I ignore you, will you go away?" I snapped.

"Nope. I'm going to stand here till you tell me how you managed to let a girl like Kris slip through your fingers. I mean, shit. I thought Jas was something special when I met her, and don't get me wrong, she is. But Kris? That girl is all passion. The amount of fire–"

I rounded on him, grabbing a fist full of his shirt. "Don't you dare talk about Kris. You don't know anything about her."

The bastard that he was cracked a wide smile. "And something tells me neither do you, Chase."

"Fuck you," I snarled at him.

The mood I was in, I wanted to bash this shithead's face in. He had no right to talk about Kris like he knew what type of woman she was. Just because he went out with her this one time did not mean he had any knowledge or claim to her.

I let out an annoyed breath. Clearly I had no claim on her either. I had no right getting in Damien's face about Kris. If this was who she wanted to be with right now, I had no choice but to grin it and bear it.

I let go of his shirt and started to walk away when Damien grabbed my shoulder, stopping me in place. I turned around to face him. "What do you want, Damien?'

"Oh, you think you're going to get off that easy? I'm an annoying little shit and a prideful man."

"What are you talking about?'

"You and Kris, you idiot."

I looked at him completely baffled. Here I was thinking he wanted to be with Kris, but he was trying to have a conversation about her and me. Who was this guy and why the hell was he so invested in our lives?

"I'm going to ask this again. What do you want from me? Are you looking for my blessing to go out with Kris or something? 'Cuz' that shit's not gonna happen. Kris can do much better."

"And I'm sure she's done a lot worse."

I took a step toward him and he smiled holding his hands up. "Easy, killa, your emotions are showing. I can't seem to understand why you're reacting like this, but you refuse to be with her."

"That's really none of your business."

Damien shrugged. "You're right, it's not. But I'm a sucka for a pretty girl who's hung up on a schmuck who fronts like he doesn't want her. Kris told me what your baggage is. She didn't go into the gritty details, but I'm going to give you my two

## Chapter 29

cents anyway. Have you even bothered to ask Kris if she's willing to stand by you while you're off playing superhero?'

I went to speak but I shook my head.

"Yeah, I didn't think so. Let me let you in on a little secret, being a Marine and all. At the end of the day, if she wants to be with you, she's going to move heaven and high water to make it happen. The distance isn't going to matter as long as you come home to her."

Damien had not only taken on a serious tone but his facial expression lost that hint of amusement. This was probably the first time since I met him that he didn't have a smile on his face. "Who's the lucky girl that made you have all the answers?'

He clapped me on the shoulder. "No lucky girl. Just one big mistake, one that I can see you're about to make. How about you let Kris decide how she wants to live her life." With that he walked off to grab a beer and whatever food was left.

I let what Damien said sink in. I never really discussed our options with Kris. I mean, sure, it'd be difficult to maintain any type of relationship taking on these jobs. But it was something that Kris and I could have figured out a way to work through. I also had to wonder why I never thought about it before. No, I knew why. I didn't want to tie her down so early in life that she'd end up resenting me later for it.

This was frustrating. First things first, Kris and I had to have a conversation, an actual conversation. One that was void of either one of us touching the other and probably in a public setting. Any time we got too close to each other, we became animals only focused on the basic need to claim one another.

I pulled out my phone again. I dialed Kris' number, not expecting an answer. We needed to talk and soon. Her phone went straight to voicemail, and I left a message begging her to call me back.

Feeling somewhat better about my situation with Kris, I could finally focus on Jas' situation. I went to dial my contact when Officer Santos and his partner Officer Hayden showed up. I knew Tony had friends on the force, but I didn't think he knew these two like that.

I approached them, forgetting about my phone call when I realized why they could be there. "Santos, Hayden, it's good to see you guys again. I take it you have some news about the break in?"

Officer Santos looked back at Hayden and then back at me. "Um, that's not why we're here, Chase." His eyes scanned the backyard and landed on Angel.

"Why are you here then, Santos?"

He cleared his throat. "We're here to arrest Angel."

# Chapter 30

### *Jasmine*

A hush had fallen over the backyard. There weren't that many people left at Tony's barbecue. Whoever did stay behind was avidly watching Chase and Damien's heated debate.

Angel wanted to intervene but, I held him hostage and kept him seated. There wasn't anything he could do, and honestly, there wasn't really much to be worried about. Boys were going to be boys, and I was pretty sure that whatever they were discussing had everything to do with Kris. My money was on Chase thinking he still had some type of claim on her and didn't appreciate Damien getting anywhere near her.

Boys and their pissing contests––always trying to see who was better for a girl without ever actually asking the girl what she wanted.

I knew Kris wanted Chase, but he chose to be an idiot. I learned quickly this summer the importance of seizing the opportunities you wanted. You never knew how quickly they would be gone.

Chase chose to drag his feet no matter how direct Kris was about what she wanted from him. Now, it was his loss, and Kris needed to enjoy the rest of the summer with someone as delicious as Damien.

"You sure I shouldn't go over there?" Angel asked.

"I'm positive. They'll work it out themselves non-violently. No worries."

I hoped. I prayed Chase didn't do anything stupid. He was usually the most level-headed of the bunch. It took a lot to get him to a level that required him to act violently. But I've been around Damien enough now to know he knew exactly what buttons to push to get a rise out of anyone.

I took another look back and saw Chase finally letting go of Damien's shirt. I let out a relieved breath. That meant no fighting, which worked great for me. All I wanted to do was stay wrapped up in the little bubble Angel and I managed to lock ourselves in.

I was trying my hardest to ignore the rest of the world. Angel and I rarely ever got these moments that weren't filled with bad news dwelling in the background. I was learning slowly that when things were going good between us, I was going to sit back and enjoy it. I'd worry about the bad stuff when it came. And it was sure to come, no sense in spoiling a perfectly good moment on things that hadn't happened yet.

Angel surprised me with a quick kiss on the lips. I smiled, pressing my fingertips against my own lips. I still wasn't use to how his lips felt against my skin. The spark that it ignited every single time he touched me always left me feeling light-headed.

"What was that for?' I asked breathlessly.

He reached for my forehead, massaging a crease. "You always get this crease––well, I like to call it your hulk vein––in your forehead when you start stressing about things. I've never

## Chapter 30

noticed it before, not until recent events. Given some of the circumstances, it's actually cute."

I pulled away. Angel's hands on me did deliciously disastrous things to any self-control I thought I had. "You watch me entirely too close for my liking, mister."

Angel chuckled. He grabbed my legs, pulling me off my chair and onto his lap.

"Angel," I warned.

He rubbed his nose against mine before taking my bottom lip in between his and biting down gently. My breath hitched ever so lightly but Angel still heard it. He growled low in his chest. My body started to hum in anticipation.

"I think you do like it when I watch you closely, Love." His deep rumble sent a nice rush of liquid to my core. "You see, it lets me know exactly what it is you like and exactly when to give it to you."

He pulled me even closer to him. Our breaths mingled with each other. "I bet if there was no one here, you'd let me make you cum, wouldn't you, Love?"

I bit down on my own lip, not wanting to voice what it was he did to me. Angel laughed, reading me entirely too well. "You're not supposed to be hiding from me remember, Jas? You're wet for me, aren't you? It's okay to be honest."

Angel's hands moved from my ass to rest in my lap. I was torn between scooting further away from his touch because we weren't alone and rubbing myself against his hands that rested precariously close to the ache that was slowly building inside of me.

I still had my teeth digging into my lip to stop me from making any type of noise that would alert the party goers to what was going on here.

Angel brought one of his hands up and gently pulled my lip from between my teeth. "You're going to destroy your lip like that."

He rubbed his thumb across my lip. I was feeling anxious and a little hot. I let my tongue take a tentative swipe at Angel's thumb. I watched as his eyes darkened and his nostrils flared. "Love," he groaned low, "I have a million and one things I'd much rather have you do with these lips." He traced my lips once more with his thumb. "And," he pressed his thumb into my mouth, "that tongue of yours." He leaned in closer, taking my hand and placing it on his hard erection. "I'm already hard. You see what you do to me."

Feeling incredibly sexy and wild, I gave Angel's hard on a little squeeze as I sucked his thumb further into my mouth. I watched as his eyes turned mossy green and were set ablaze by my actions. I didn't bother hiding my smile. I enjoyed having this affect on him. It turned me on knowing I was the one making him lose his battle with his rock solid self-control.

Angel slowly pulled his thumb out of my mouth on a pained groan. He brought his lips down to my ear and whispered. "You think you're slick? The only thing that's stopping me from ripping your shorts off and sliding my dick inside you is the fact that I don't want anyone to see how you look when you cum. That is only for me."

## Chapter 30

He pressed a kiss on my neck and I shivered, inching closer to him. Angel chuckled into my neck as he smacked me on my ass. "Behave before you get us both in trouble."

His laugh abruptly stopped as he lifted his head out of my neck. His whole posture went rigid as well. I tried to pull back so I could turn and figure out what caused his swift switch in mood, but he held me firmly against him.

"What's wrong, Angel?"

Like clockwork, bad news never stayed away for long. This was just a reminder as to why I needed to focus on the good when it came, even when it wasn't often.

I was trying not to panic. I was thinking worst-case scenario when I noticed it got really quiet. Then I remembered Chase and Damien were in a heated discussion before I shut the rest of the world out and focused on Angel.

I groaned dropping my head on Angel's shoulder. "Did Chase actually hit Damien?"

If anyone got Chase to act violently, it would be Kris and a really annoying Damien.

Angel sat back, forcing me to raise my head and look at him. "What? Why would?" He laughed. "I kind of almost wish this was about those two fighting. It would be nice if things weren't about us for once." He nodded in the direction behind me. "The cops that were at your house are here."

"What? Why?"

## INTO PIECES

I quickly detangled myself from Angel and stood facing Officer Santos. I wasn't too sure who the other officer was, as I only remembered Santos. He was the one who asked me all those obscene questions at my house.

I took a step forward and then stopped. I didn't want to deal with this crap anymore. I was tired of all of this, honestly. I know I said I was going to fight back, but couldn't I at least get a little break before I had to?

I looked to the heavens, praying for something––strength, guidance, anything at this point. I didn't want to walk up to them and have them tell me they had no answers for me. On the other hand, I was more nervous to find out if they did have answers for me. I wasn't sure if I could deal with another blow.

A warm hand engulfed mine, giving it a tight squeeze. I turned to face him. His eyes had softened back to their original green, but they shone brightly with love. He leaned in, placing a gentle kiss on my forehead.

"Whatever this is, Love, I got you. We face it head on and together."

I placed my hand on his chest, mentally absorbing some of his strength. He was right. I was going to put my big girl pants on and face whatever this was with Angel by my side.

I let out a breath. "Okay, then. Let's go see what Officer Santos could possibly want now."

We walked over to the officers and Chase. When Chase heard our approach, he turned to face us. He looked angry and worried. Oh no. Immediately panic seized me. I tried to

## Chapter 30

breathe through it. I had no facts yet. There was no reason to get ahead of myself.

"What's wrong, Chase? What happened? What did they find?"

Officer Santos spoke up as he unhooked a pair of handcuffs from his belt. I looked back at Chase confused. What the hell was going on?

Chase shook his head. "They're not here for you, Jas."

Officer Santos spoke up. "We're here to arrest you, Angel."

INTO PIECES

# Chapter 31

*Jasmine*

"I'm sorry, what?"

There was a loud ringing in my ears, and no matter how many times I shook my head, I couldn't get it to stop. I was sure I'd heard Officer Santos wrong. Why the hell would they need to arrest Angel? He didn't do anything.

Angel remained as still a statue beside me. I couldn't figure out if he was worried or not. Then it dawned on me: Angel was late to the barbecue. He said he had to take care of something before he came here. I felt my face pale as I realized what it could have been.

I rounded on Angel before Officer Santos could get close to him. "Did you find out who did it? Who broke into my house?" I whispered. I didn't want to incriminate myself or Angel if this honestly wasn't anything more than a misunderstanding.

Angel grabbed my face and pulled me towards him giving me a deep and desperate kiss. I felt my knees weaken as he poured everything he had into this kiss. He pulled back entirely too quickly and it left me yearning for more.

"I didn't find the person who broke into your home, Jas. I'm not sure what this is about. But, going by the look on Chase's face, this is something serious."

"Angel Luis Torres you are under arrest for the assault against Vivian Sepia. You have the right to remain silent."

I blocked out the rest of Officer Santos' voice as I watched him handcuff Angel like he was some criminal. I held on to one word and one word only. Assault? He didn't even touch Vivian. That little altercation at the gym was nothing. She hit him. All he did was grab her arms to protect himself. This was bullshit.

The other officer whispered something to Chase before she grabbed Angel's other arm. He looked at me one last time before they pulled him away and out of the backyard.

The walls around me were threatening to crash and crumble. This was honestly too much to deal with. All I wanted to do was curl into a ball and cry. Why did these things keep happening to us?

I stared at the gate Angel was hauled off out of. He looked as defeated as I felt. If it wasn't one thing, it was something else.

I took a long deep breath. *Get it together, Jasmine. Angel needs you.* I let everything Officer Santos said sink in. Angel was arrested for assault, one that never happened. He was innocent and we had to clear up this misunderstanding.

I looked back at Chase as he stood there and watched. I grabbed him and pushed him towards the gate. Chase had connections and so did Tony. Shit, Tony's asshole of a father was a lawyer. I'm sure he would have no problem helping us out. It was the least he could do.

## Chapter 31

"Chase, go. You have to help him. Get Tony to help too. Angel didn't touch her. He's innocent, trust me. Though I can't promise you my hands won't be around her neck once I catch her.

Chase grabbed my arms, stopping me from pushing him further out the door. "Jasmine, wait. You need to stay put. No going after anyone or doing anything. I know Angel would never do something like this. It's just that Vivian is in pretty bad shape. Like, in the hospital bad. Angel being a combat veteran, suffering from PTSD and that altercation at the gym the other day, this doesn't look good."

I crossed my arms over my chest. "You're telling me you believe her over Angel?"

He held up his hands. "Easy. I'm not saying that. I'm telling you this is going to get worse before it gets better."

I rolled my eyes. That seemed to be the resounding theme of my life. "He didn't do anything, Chase. She's lying."

"I believe you, Jas. Look, I'm going to go down to the precinct and see what I can find out. Hopefully, I can pull some weight and get Angel home to you tonight. But I can't make any promises. I need you to stay here. You good to stay by yourself?"

I looked at Chase like he was stupid. I wasn't aware I needed a babysitter. "I can take care of myself. Just focus on figuring this crap out with Angel. I want him home."

Tony walked by us and stood next to Chase. He still had this worried look on his face, but it seemed to have intensified once the cops showed up. I guess if both he and Chase were this worried about the situation, it had to be serious.

"Hey, Tony. You think if Angel needs it, your pops would represent him?"

I didn't think Angel would need it. But right now, it was Vivian's word against his. I hated that I had to ask Tony's father for help. I wanted to demand that he do it. I felt like his father owed me something that he could never truly give me back.

Tony reached out, giving my shoulder a reassuring squeeze. "I will make sure he does, if Angel wants it. Don't stress. Everything's going to be okay, promise."

I didn't believe him. Tony didn't bother to look me in the eye when he said it. Which meant he didn't believe it either. But I wasn't going to worry. Not yet. I knew Angel didn't touch Vivian. This would go away. The truth would come out.

"You ready to go, Chase?" Tony asked.

"Not really. I'm not comfortable leaving Jas by herself. Given all the shit that's been going on. I think someone should keep her company."

"I can stay with her."

I groaned at Damien's voice. I thought I saw him leave with the rest of Tony's guests.

"Hello! Need I remind everyone that I am an adult with the capacity to take care of myself?"

## Chapter 31

Chase cracked a smile. "Maybe we should just take her with us?"

"Holy shit. Just go already. The more time you sit here discussing my babysitting situation, the more time you waste getting Angel back home and the charges cleared. Now go."

Both Chase and Tony smiled before giving me a hug. "Yes ma'am. This new bossy side of you can be charming, sometimes." Chase chuckled.

He turned to Damien. "She manages to get into any trouble, Angel's going to kill you and then me." He turned back to me before leaving. "Behave, and I will call you with any information I have, okay?"

I watched as Chase and Tony walked out of the gate. The second they left, my nerves came back. I had this feeling something bad was about to happen.

I laughed to myself. If Angel and I survived this summer intact, there was nothing we couldn't survive together.

I turned around, needing something to do, to focus on. I couldn't have all this nervous energy bottled up. I'd drive myself crazy. I turned, slamming right into Damien's chest. He didn't even budge when I collided into him. I completely forgot he was here. It was ridiculously quiet after Tony and Chase left. I thought I was alone.

I looked up at him and he had this serious look on his face. It was at odds with the mischief look he always had. "What?"

He reached out and touched the crease in the middle of my forehead. "You know you have this—"

"Yes, I know. My hulk vein." I used air quotes around the words hulk vein. I never noticed it until Angel pointed it out today.

I side-stepped him and started cleaning up what I could of Tony's yard. I grabbed all the empty plates and soda cans off the table and threw them in the garbage. Again the backyard got eerily quiet. I turned around and Damien was right behind me, practically on top of me.

"How the hell do you move like that?"

He shrugged. "I figure you'd be used to it by now. Angel moves like that." He cracked a smile like he was in on a secret only he knew. "Well, actually, I think you're probably so in tuned with him you'd be able hear him shift slightly from all the way across the room." He laughed. "How do you deal with it when Chase moves like that?"

"What are you talking about?"

"Oh come on, I'm almost positive Chase can move just as quietly as I can. What's his deal anyway? He's not a Marine. I can sniff out my own kind."

I shrugged. I really didn't know. Come to think of it, I didn't think anyone of us knew what exactly Chase did. I was just grateful, especially in times like this that he had the connections he had. I'd have to ask him the next time I talked to him. My curiosity was peaked. I wonder if Kris knew what he did.

# Chapter 31

"I don't know what he does. Did you really want to know? Or were you just trying to make conversation?"

"I wouldn't have asked if I didn't want to know, Jasmine."

I rolled my eyes. This was going to be a painfully long day. I had to wonder what was going to drive me crazy first. The insistent waiting for information or dealing with Damien and his charming personality. Who knows, if Damien played his cards right, I might end up killing him and landing myself in the cell next to Angel's.

I continued to clean up the rest of the backyard. I needed to grab some Tupperware and more garbage bags. I also had to clean the grill. I looked at it and decided that was the last thing I was going to touch.

I looked over at Damien who stood silently with his arms crossed. He watched me zip around the backyard but did not once offer to help or continue with the conversation. "Hey, Damien. How about you quit staring and help me clean up?"

Damien scoffed. "You seem to be doing fine all on your own, Jas. Besides, I'm too pretty to clean."

I stopped what I was doing and looked at him. He had a serious look on his face. Like I offended him for even asking the question. I threw my head back and laughed. Laughed a full belly laugh complete with an un-ladylike snort.

Of all the people they could possibly stick me with. Damien was a fool, but he was a fool who would no doubt keep my mind from worrying about the situation going on. Thanks to Damien, that laugh eased some of the tension I was feeling.

Into Pieces

Everything was going to work itself out. There was no other option. Angel was innocent. Chase and Tony were going to help prove that quicker, and Angel would come home to me.

Damien chuckled as he walked up to me. He threw his arm over my shoulder. "You feel better, Jas?"

"Yeah, I do. Thank you. Now, seriously, help me clean up."

Damien groaned, and I laughed as I sent him into the house for the things I needed.

# Chapter 32

*Angel*

I went from worried to pissed to annoyed and right back to worried. I decided to settle on being pissed. I gave the arresting officer my statement not once, not twice but three times. Then I had to give my statement to another police officer and then another one.

They all shoved photos of Vivian's banged up body in my face like it was supposed to mean something. All it did was piss me off more. Any man who put their hands on a female should be beat repeatedly with a two by four.

I felt bad that someone did that to Vivian; no one should have to go through that. But I wasn't the person who did it to her, and I was pissed I was even being brought in here based on some hearsay because we had an altercation at the gym.

Honestly, this was bullshit. Half the people in this precinct knew me and knew I wouldn't do anything like this. But everyone was following procedure and blah, blah, blah. I didn't even get to see Chase or Tony. They asked if I wanted to call someone, like my parents. I declined. They were out of town, and I didn't want to bother them with this nonsense. It would be cleared up soon; there was no reason to make any phone calls.

So, I sat with stale coffee and crappy donuts, waiting patiently to be released. The door to the interrogation room they left me in opened and Chase and Tony finally strolled in.

## INTO PIECES

"Please tell me you two are here to spring me out."

They both looked at each other before Chase spoke up. "It's going to be awhile before we can get you in front of a judge. You know why you're in here, right?"

"Yeah, some prick beat the shit out of Vivian. They think that prick was me because some idiot saw me get into a small altercation with her."

"No, bro. Vivian said you were the one who beat her to a pulp. We were just at the hospital to see if she woke up yet so we could question her. But the docs aren't letting anyone in until she's stable."

"So what are you two doing here? One of you need to go back and wait. This is bullshit that she's saying it's me. I didn't fucking touch her." I snapped.

I scrubbed a hand down my face. I was tired and frustrated. I couldn't fathom why Vivian would say that it was me when it wasn't.

Every single day I regretted sleeping with her. Today more than ever I wish I never touched her. It would have saved me this massive shit storm I found myself in.

I let out a breath. "What's our next move?"

"You're next move is to sit here and be patient."

"Like I really have a choice, Chase?"

"Take the attitude down a notch; we're trying to help you out here. I always told you your dick would get you into

## CHAPTER 32

trouble. I just thought it would have been when we were younger. Not now."

"Save the I-told-you-so for when I get out of this mess. What do you think, Tony? Think it's time I call your pops in as my lawyer? You think he'll represent me if Vivian insists on framing me?"

Tony was staring off into space. I wasn't sure he even heard what I said. I called his name twice before he responded.

"Huh?"

Chase turned to face Tony. "What's with you? You've been a space cadet since we left your house. I need you to get your head in the game here."

Tony's phone chirped and the sound made his face scrunch up. It looked like he was in pain. I was concerned for him. I couldn't take any more bad news. "Seriously, Tony. You okay?"

He nodded. "Yeah, yeah, I'm good. Just this whole thing." He tapped his skull. "It's mind blowing that we're here for something like this." He shook his head. "It doesn't sit right with me, you know? I mean, I know you didn't do it; I'm not saying that, I just…"

He blew out a breath. This situation was hitting him hard. I saw the photos of Vivian's face, I could only imagine how worse for wear she looked in person. Tony was a big guy, but he was a softy when it came to the opposite sex. It probably destroyed him to see Vivian like that.

"Don't worry, Angel. My father won't have any problems representing you if this gets any worse."

I nodded my head. "I appreciate that."

His phone chimed again and he swore under his breath. Something was wrong with him. Now, that I watched him more closely. Something outside of my case and him seeing Vivian was weighing down on him. He was fidgeting, which was something he never did, and he had sweat trickling down the side of his face.

Now, granted, it was hot outside but the AC was blasting in here. There was no reason he should have still been sweating like that. This wasn't how Tony acted, no matter what was going on. He was as level-headed as Chase when shit hit the fan. Something was off. My gut was starting to scream it out to me. I just couldn't put my finger on it yet. His phone chimed yet again and he pinched the bridge of his nose.

"Is that some girl you're trying to avoid? If you didn't sleep with her, I'd advise you not to. You don't want to end up in my predicament."

Chase laughed. "Ah, I see we're feeling better about the situation if you have time to make jokes."

"I gotta make jokes. Going a little stir crazy just sitting here."

Tony's phone beeped again and he excused himself. I nodded in his direction. "What's up with him?"

## Chapter 32

"Damned if I know. He's been twitchy since we left his house. I'm guessing his ass probably got some crazy chick on the side and he's not trying to end up like you."

"Fuck you." I laughed. "You're not allowed to make jokes yet. Something's up with him, though. I can feel it."

"Yeah, but I can't afford to look into it right now. I can only deal with one crisis at a time."

Chase sat down in the chair opposite to me. "Look, I'm working through a few favors right now. I'm trying to see if I can at least get you out on bail tonight. Don't worry about the cost, I got it. If Tony's pops is willing to represent you, then we let him worry about all that stuff when the time comes. Right now, I just want to get you home to Jasmine before she comes down here and beats me."

Just hearing her name set my blood on fire. I missed her. I hated that I was putting her through this. I hated that my decisions made a mess of everything. I wanted to go home and spend the night holding her in my arms. I wanted to put this behind us already.

"How is she?"

Chase shrugged. "Last I checked in with Damien, she was doing fine. You know I'm not much of a fan of him for obvious reason, but he sure knows how to come through when you need him. He said he's doing a great job at distracting her."

I heard myself growling. I knew Damien from our time served together overseas and when we were stationed stateside. The man fucked anything that had legs. I knew what his particular brand of distraction was.

Chase chuckled. "I'm sure he knows you would kill him. He's not distracting her like that. When I called, I couldn't tell who was driving whom crazier. They seem to be bickering like brother and sister. I think he's got a soft spot for her."

"Better not be too soft a spot. I'd have to kill him." I blew out a breath. "Speaking of siblings, anyone heard from Kris yet?"

I didn't hear her mouth running around outside. Which was good since I knew she'd be driving everyone in here crazy. I was worried, though, since she wasn't here, she might be out looking for Vivian. That wouldn't be good either.

"You know your sister isn't talking to me. I'll call Jas and ask her if she's heard from her. In the meantime, let me see who I can strong arm into getting you home. I was going to send Tony back to the hospital to wait for Vivian to wake up. But he was a wreck when we both went to see her. I'll see if I can get them to send someone else and hopefully she wakes up and IDs someone else as her assailant."

Chase stood up clapping me on my shoulder. "Hang in there, bro." He walked towards the door and opened it. I called his name before he could leave. I had one question for him that needed an answer.

He turned around to face me. "What's up?"

## Chapter 32

"I've been brought into this precinct enough times with Jay and you and Tony to know when someone's the top dog around here. What the hell is it that you do?"

Chase laughed. "Sit tight, buttercup. I might tell you one day if you're lucky."

He closed the door and I shook my head. I couldn't believe he still wouldn't tell me what it was he did. If he got me out of this, I'd think he was on the government's payroll. It was the only explanation for his connections.

INTO PIECES

# Chapter 33

*Tony*

I went through the billion text messages from Marcus. He kept texting to see how far things were going in the investigation against Angel. I knew my brother was fucked up, but this whole situation took the cake. I was baffled he was able to get Vivian to go along with his plans. She had to know doing this to Angel wasn't going to get him back.

I sat down in an empty chair in the far corner of the building. I needed some time alone to process all this shit that was happening. I wanted to close my eyes and rest but I couldn't. I couldn't get the image of Vivian's bashed up face out of my head.

Every time I closed my eyes, every single time my phone beeped, I saw Vivian laid up in that hospital bed hooked up to a bunch of wires and machines. The bruises on her face and around her neck made me sick. I couldn't stay in that room. I couldn't see her like that. I didn't know her personally, but no girl deserved what she went through.

How many other people were going to get hurt at the hands of Marcus? How many more incidents would I need to cover up for him? I felt like this was never going to end.

Something inside me was breaking. I was sick to my stomach by all of this and Angel saw it. He knew something was up with me. I saw it in his eyes, the way he watched me. He was waiting for me to have a breakdown. I was starting to suck at hiding what Marcus did to people. I couldn't hold the bad in anymore. It was starting to seep out of my pores.

My phone rang and I jumped, startled by the sound. I didn't even bother to check the Caller ID. I knew who it was, and I must have been a glutton for punishment because I actually answered it.

"What do you want, now?"

"If you would actually text me back, I wouldn't have to call you."

"What do you want, Marcus?" I snapped, my impatience with him growing.

"Is he locked up? Rotting in a cell for the assault on that poor defenseless girl?" Marcus chuckled to himself. "You know, I almost feel a little bad for Vivian. The dumb ass that she is really believes this is going to bring Angel to her."

"You know you beat her to an inch of her life, Marcus?"

I was still blown away by the violence Marcus could inflict on anyone. I knew he raped girls, I saw them all after it happened. They all ran to me. They all thought I could protect them. But I couldn't, I never did. He always got to them first. But Marcus never beat them this way. I couldn't understand how doing any of this would bring him Jasmine.

"Yeah, well, I had to make it believable, big bro. Angel is a Marine after all and suffering from PTSD. He wouldn't just smack her up, now would he? He would lose control. Vivian's face was an outlet for his sufferings."

## CHAPTER 33

I hung up, tempted to throw my phone. The only thing stopping me was the too many questioning eyes I'd have on me.

I really couldn't take this with him anymore. I hated my father for not giving a shit about what his son did. I called him the second I left that hospital room. I tried desperately to get my father to do something, anything. He wouldn't though. He was even annoyed I was calling him with this bullshit.

I heard some female in the background and knew my father wouldn't help. Before I hung up, my father told me, "Find out how much this is going to cost me and I'll cut the check." I was disgusted that he thought money would fix anything this time.

My phone rang again. And again I picked it up. "What?"

"You're a little touchy today. What's the matter? Are you annoyed that I ruined all of your chances with Jasmine? I told you she belongs to me, Tony. No one will be able to touch her again."

I stood up. "What did you just say?"

"Oh, you heard me. You know, I have to say, she looks really good cleaning up the mess you left in the backyard. I knew she'd make an excellent housewife. I can't wait to break her in again."

"Marcus," I warned, "don't you dare go near her."

"She's at our house, Tony. You really make things too easy sometimes."

I heard the click and then radio silence. "Son of a bitch." I yelled, hurling the phone across the room. I watched it smash into a million little pieces. I cursed again. There went another phone and my only way to contact Jasmine. I hauled ass back to the interrogation room, praying Chase was still there. I had to reach out to Jasmine. I had to warn her this time.

This was too much. I could no longer sit back and watch Marcus destroy her again.

### *Jasmine*

I rolled my eyes as my phone rang for the millionth time today. It was Chase calling again. If he wasn't calling me, he was texting his new BFF Damien. It wasn't like he was calling to give me a play-by-play on Angel. Nope, he was calling to check in on me every few minutes. Dude worried more than a mother hen.

I picked up my phone on the third ring. I didn't bother to keep the annoyance out of my tone.

"What can you possibly want from my life now? I told you don't call me unless you're telling me you're bringing Angel home."

"Well, hello to you too, brat. I wasn't calling to check in, this time. I was calling to ask if you heard from Kris."

"Oh shit! I completely forgot to call her."

"Well, aren't you the best friend of the year."

## Chapter 33

"Bite me, Chase. If you didn't have your head so far up your ass, Kris wouldn't be ignoring you and you would have heard from her by now."

Chase laughed over the phone. "Geez, Jas. I don't miss your sass at all. Just make sure you get in touch with her. Don't need her finding out from someone else about Angel. You know how she gets."

We both laughed. "Yeah, I'll call her now and let her know. Hey, how's he doing?"

"Bored and missing you, of course. Let me go I have people I need to bully."

We hung up and I cracked a smile. It was nice to hear Angel missed me. Chase could have been lying about his predicament but I was going to choose to believe he was doing as well as could be expected. He'd be home soon and all this would be cleared up.

I looked through my contacts for Kris' number. I was going to send her a text but I figured this was something that needed to be discussed over the phone. She was going to hit the roof when she found out why Angel was locked up. She was definitely going to be pissed she pulled her punch when she hit her at the last barbecue.

The phone rang a few times but she didn't pick up. I hung up and dialed the number again. As the phone rang I heard the ring tone Kris had for me somewhere in the background. That's odd. I cleaned this whole backyard and didn't come across any lost phones.

The ringing stopped and her voicemail picked up again. I left a message this time. "Hey, Kris. You know I don't like it when you ignore me. Pick up already, you little gremlin. I'll just keep calling."

I heard the gate swing open and I hung up. I turned around. "Hey, Damien, you didn't find a--oh shit."

My heart slammed to a standstill and my lungs forgot to work. "No." That smile and those cold dead eyes were staring back at me. I was stuck, frozen in place by my fear. I couldn't get my body to run, scream, do anything. I was reliving the nightmare. He wasn't supposed to be here. Tony promised he was gone.

"Hello, Jasmine. I see you're happy to see me."

"Oh, God. You're really here."

Marcus chuckled. "Yes, Jasmine. I've missed you too."

# CHAPTER 34

***Tony***

I walked by the interrogation room but Chase wasn't in there anymore. I was torn between going in and waiting out here for Chase to come back. I needed to reach out to Jasmine, but my phone was sitting at the end of the hall in tiny little pieces. I couldn't go in there yet. Angel would know for sure something was wrong. And his freakishly spot-on instincts would assume something was wrong with Jas.

I didn't want to set him or anyone else off. I wanted to diffuse this situation on my own. It would give my brother the time he needed to let this obsession go. He was my blood. There had to be some good left in him.

Hayden, one of the police officers who arrested Angel, walked by. I grabbed her before she walked off into the Captain's office. "Hey, can I ask you something?"

"Well, that depends on what it is?"

She smiled brightly at me. On more than one occasion she'd not so subtly asked me out for drinks. I had turned her down time and time again. I couldn't afford to hit it off with someone and bring her around my family. Everyone knew who my father was; no one knew who my brother was and the problems he caused.

Hayden was sweet outside of the uniform and pretty inside and out. She was exactly the type Marcus went after.

It sucked; we might have been great together. But I'd never get the chance to know as long as Marcus was running loose.

"Have you seen Chase?"

Her smile dimmed a little. "One day when you ask to speak to me, it's going to be because you're taking me up on my request for some drinks. Chase said he'd be back in about ten minutes––that was ten minutes ago––something about having to talk to someone. I don't know; he just told me to tell you if I saw you to wait."

I smiled at her and let her go into the Captain's office and waited. That was all I could do right now. It wasn't like Angel had Jasmine's number memorized anyway.

\*\*

**Marcus**

Oh, my sweet, sweet Jasmine. This was the face that haunted my dreams. I was finally here with her. There was finally nothing and no one keeping us apart. Angel was out of the picture. My brother wasn't here; he was busy keeping Angel contained. That idiot Chase was running around trying to push whatever weight he had into freeing Angel.

That wasn't going to happen. If I was lucky, Vivian would die and they'd leave Angel to rot in a cell. Then I'd have all the time in the world to enjoy Jasmine.

She looked just as sweet as she did the day at the gym. She was paralyzed with joy at seeing me stand before her. She kept

## Chapter 34

muttering, "It's you. You're here." Yes, my sweet girl, I was here. I came back for her just like I told her I would. Now there would be no more games. It was time for Jasmine to come home.

I took a step towards her. I was anxious to close the distance between us. I was dying to touch her. Four years and I felt like I forgot how soft her skin was.

Jasmine took a step back. "Don't come near me, Marcus. You're not supposed to be here." She trembled over her words. Her excitement was overwhelming her. "Your father, made me sign a contract. You're not supposed to be here."

"Shh. It's okay. I couldn't stay away from you, Jasmine. You belong to me. Now come here and greet your man properly."

### *Jasmine*

There were a lot of things that I was scared of, clowns and bugs in particular. But there was nothing that terrified me more than the man who was standing in front of me. I was prepared to deal with everything getting thrown my way, everything, except seeing Marcus again.

Any progress I made, everything I worked hard to overcome was completely shot to shit as Marcus stood in front of me. He reduced me back to that scared little girl I was the night he raped me.

"Jasmine."

## Into Pieces

He called my name and it made my skin crawl. I started scratching at my arm. I felt dirty and suffocated by his smell, his presence. I wanted to shower again. I needed to wipe the filth he left on me. Why was he here?

I hated the way he said my name. He said it with possession, like he owned me. He kept taking steps forward and I kept backing up. I didn't want to give him a chance to get close to me. I didn't want him to touch me anymore.

I backed up right into the table and I jumped. *Get it together, Jasmine. Do not show fear. He likes fear.* I heard a noise in the house and a glimmer of hope sprung through me. I wasn't alone. Not this time. Damien was in the house. He'd see that someone was out here with me and come to investigate. This was the first time I thanked Chase for not wanting to leave me alone.

I thought about Tony again. I looked down at my phone, expecting to see a missed call from him, but there was none. Did he even know Marcus was home?

I looked back at Marcus as he took another step forward. "How long have you been home? Tony's not here. Your father isn't either."

He laughed like one would laugh at a child who asked a ridiculous question. "Oh, my sweet Jasmine. I've always been here. I stayed close, always keeping an eye on you. I know what lies Tony told you. He did that for me. He understands that we belong together and was doing anything he could to help me achieve that."

## CHAPTER 34

A wave of sickness hit me. I was nauseous and I felt faint. The loud drumming was back in my ears. Tony knew. Tony always knew Marcus was here.

I had this shooting pain in my chest. I rubbed at trying desperately to make it ease. This was what betrayal felt like. My heart hurt, threatened to break out of my chest. I trusted him with everything. Every word Tony ever uttered had been a lie. He looked me right in my eyes and lied. I never saw the truth. I really didn't know how to trust the right people.

I heard Marcus move and my gaze snapped to his. He had taken a few more steps closer to me. Now there wasn't much distance between us. I was starting to panic even more. There was no controlling the hysteria I was feeling.

"Stay––stay back, Marcus. I mean it."

My voice came out weak and unsteady. I hated that I was reduced to this, but I didn't know where the strength I thought I had disappeared to. And where the hell was Damien? Why hadn't he come out here yet?

I shot my gaze to the house and back to Marcus hoping he wouldn't take that as an invitation to move closer. Why the hell couldn't I get my feet to work? My gaze shot back to the house, praying I'd find some sign of Damien.

Marcus laughed as he made a lunge for me. I slid across the table quickly, avoiding him. "I told you, don't come near me," I screamed, sounding hysterical.

"Why do you keep looking towards the house, Jasmine? Hoping someone will come out and save you?"

INTO PIECES

I turned back to face him and watched as he pulled out a gun with a silencer attached to it. I felt the blood drain from my face. My heart beat a million miles an hour, and the pain in my chest intensified. I was completely defenseless against Marcus.

I stood up a little straighter, trying to get my breathing under control. I couldn't go out like this. Not this time. I was older and stronger now. *Just breathe, Jasmine. Keep breathing. Calm down and stay level. You're in control here.*

I took a look at the facts. Marcus wasn't here to kill me. He didn't want me dead, at least not yet. He was here because he had some sick twisted obsession with me. The gun was just to scare me. He would have hurt me already if that was his goal.

I crossed my arms over my chest and gave my best bored expression. "Is the gun supposed to scare me, Marcus?"

He laughed. "Ah, and there's that defiance I missed. No, Jasmine. This gun isn't to scare you. It's to keep you in line. And since you keep looking back at the house, I will tell you a little secret. Your friend isn't coming to the rescue. He's currently bleeding out on the kitchen floor. So, this is what's going to happen, Jasmine." His voice took on a menacing tone. "I'm all for the cat-and-mouse game. You know how much I love a good chase, but not today. I've already wasted enough time."

He leveled the gun at my face. "You're going to come with me right now and if you don't?" He pulled a phone out of his pocket and tossed it in my direction. I fumbled to catch it. When the picture on the screen righted itself I felt the contents of my stomach threaten to come up.

## Chapter 34

Kris was bound and gagged and bleeding down her face. "Where is she?"

"She'll be dead along with your friend in the kitchen if you don't come with me, Jasmine. I only want you. I've always only wanted you. People like that idiot in the kitchen and this bitch and her brother were always in the way. Come with me now and they might have a chance to survive."

This was what I didn't want. I didn't want more people hurt because of me. I knew Marcus wasn't bluffing either. He went out of his way to slam his car into Jay's. He'd do the same or worse to the people I loved if I didn't go with him. I wasn't sacrificing anyone else because of Marcus. If it meant keeping Kris and Damien alive then that meant I was walking out of here with Marcus. I couldn't let him hurt the people I cared about anymore.

"You win. I'll go with you. But we need to call an ambulance for Damien. I'm coming with you so no one gets hurt."

He smiled. "Oh, Jasmine. I knew you'd see it my way. Throw both phones on the table." He took a step towards the table and grabbed the phones. The gun was held steady in his grasp. I had taken some self-defense classes. I knew I stood a chance at removing the gun from his hands. I just didn't know how good of a chance I had of not getting shot in the process.

"I can see the fire in your eyes has only gotten brighter. Extinguishing it this time around is going to be twice as fun."

He motioned with the gun. "Walk and don't think about running or screaming. I may not want to kill you yet, but that won't stop me from putting a bullet in you. And while you're suffering from the wound, I will kill Kris in front of you."

I walked at a painfully slow rate, praying someone, anyone, would come barging in and end this.

"You know, Jasmine. I don't think I can resist touching you much longer."

"What?" I tried to turn around but pain laced through my head. The world spun and everything went black.

# Chapter 35

*Chase*

I made my way back to the interrogation room pissed off. I couldn't get Angel out, not without me taking that damn job. I was torn. I knew Angel was innocent and he shouldn't have to spend a night in lock up. But honestly, I didn't want to have to take this job in exchange for his freedom.

I scrubbed a hand down my face. I hated being in this position. I'd just have to discuss it with Angel and see how he wanted to handle this.

I got to the room and saw Tony pacing outside of it. He looked nervous like something happened. My first thought was that shit just hit the fan and Vivian went from critical to life support. I had a feeling this day was going to get better and better.

I stepped into Tony's line of sight. He abruptly stopped and his face hardened. "Where they hell have you been? Hayden said you'd be back in ten minutes and that was…" he looked at the clock on the wall "…twenty-five minutes ago."

"Whoa, what the hell happened?"

"When was the last time you spoke to Jasmine?"

INTO PIECES

"About twenty-five minutes ago when I told her to call Kris. What's wrong with you? You've been acting crazy since we left your house. What's up?"

He put his head in his hands a second and was breathing heavy. He looked back up at me and his eyes were watery. What the hell was going on? Tony started patting his chest with his hands. "It hurts, man. You guys...it hurts too much now. I can't keep it in."

Now I was worried. Never have I ever seen Tony crack like this. Aside from Jay and Angel, Tony was the strongest guy I knew. He dealt with a lot. I never knew is whole family dynamic, but I knew his father was an asshole who use to ride him hard. Never in all my years have I seen Tony break like this.

I reached out to offer comfort to a situation I didn't understand. I still had no idea what was going on. I just knew I couldn't be the only one level here. There was too much going on. I needed Tony as level as I was. "Hey, man. I don't know what's going on but I'm sure it's nothing you can't handle."

Tony let out a breath. "I fucked up, Chase. I hurt so much. We gotta go inside. Too much time has passed already, and honestly, I'm not sure what to do."

He opened the door to the integration room and I stared dumbly at his back. It was in this moment I missed Jay. He would have known how to handle both situations. I was flying blind here. I had no idea how to deal with Angel and whatever the hell was going on with Tony. Jay had that knack about him. He knew how to read everyone and how to handle whatever it was someone was going through.

## Chapter 35

I looked to the heavens. I didn't really believe in much, but I hoped Jay was watching over us and that he'd find a way to help me help both of my friends.

I walked in and Tony was standing in the corner with his hands in his pockets. He looked ill. I looked at Angel and he shrugged. I stood at the wall opposite Tony but close to Angel. I crossed my arms over my chest. Well, here we go.

"Okay, Tony. We're all ears. What's up?"

He took a steadying breath. "I've been lying to you guys this whole time in order to protect my brother. Actually, the lying has been going on since as long as I've known about my brother. I mean, you have to understand, you know how my father is. It's very difficult for me to go against him and what he's taught me."

Angel and I exchanged very confused glances at each other before we looked back and Tony. He was sweating profusely now. He was nervous. Whatever he had to tell us was a big fucking deal. "Look, Tony. Whatever it is, start from the beginning. Or give us the short version. You're kind of talking in circles here. We don't know what you're talking about."

He visibly gulped. "I know why you're in here, Angel."

"Yeah, I think we've all been caught up to speed on that one, Tony." Angel quipped. I guess his humor on the situation was wearing thin.

"Yeah, but I know the real reason. You're being set up, the fall guy. I also know who broke into Jasmine's house and trashed it. I even know who sent that package to her in the beginning of the summer."

I saw Angel stiffen. What the hell was this? Tony walked towards the table and leaned on the chair opposite Angel.

"I know everything, Angel. Everything that's happening has to do with Jasmine."

Angel moved subtly. His breathing completely changed too. Oh shit. I was getting nervous. Whatever Tony had to tell us, I hoped there were enough cops in this precinct to help keep Angel from killing Tony.

"Somebody isn't too pleased with you being with her, Angel. That's why her house was trashed. It was in retaliation for being with you. You're in here so you can be out of the way." He took another breath. "This is also the same guy who raped Jasmine and had a hand in killing Jay."

The room went really quiet except for the vents pumping air into the room. If there was anyone listening on the other side of the glass, Tony just kissed his law enforcement career goodbye. He covered up evidence to what was apparently a murder and rape.

I watched Tony struggle to tell us this. When he first started, I felt a little remorse for him. But now? I felt nothing for him. Why did he wait all this time to tell us what happened? Was he only telling us now because of Angel's predicament?

## Chapter 35

I looked at Tony. I knew him my whole life and yet, standing in front of me was stranger. I didn't know who he was. How could he ever cover up Jay's death like that?

"Look, Tony."

He put his hand up, cutting off what I was about to say. "I'm not done, Chase." Oh, great, there was more bad news. "The person who raped Jasmine is my brother, Marcus. And I think he took her."

I moved, thinking I'd stop Angel from bashing Tony's head in. If he touched him, I knew no amount of favors would get him out of here tonight. But Angel never moved from his seat.

If a stranger was looking at him, that stranger would mistake Angel for being calm and rational. But I saw his eyes. They were locked on Tony and they promised him death.

I also saw the hurt in his eyes too. He was feeling the betrayal as much as I was. Tony was family. Shit, they all were. Tony, Angel and Jay were the closest things to brothers I had. A very specific type of rage began to bloom inside of me as Tony told us he helped cover up Jay's death. I didn't realize I lost two brothers that day Jay was killed.

Angel spoke. "This is what's going to happen, Tony." The calm in his voice sent a chill down my spine. Even Tony felt what Angel was saying underneath his words. This wouldn't end well for him. Tony stood up taller and began to sweat even more.

"You're going to find out exactly where he took her. Then you and Chase are going to bring her home. I would go myself but, thanks to you and that scumbag, I am currently shackled in here."

"Tony, I fucking promise you. I swear it on everything. He hurts her again; you better pray they keep me locked up in here forever. Because I will hunt you down and make you understand exactly what it is Jasmine went through."

"Angel, I'm--"

"You're what? Sorry? I can't even look at you right now. I don't even want to speak to you. My concern is Jasmine. I want her home and safe. Find her, now."

Tony shuffled out of the room with his head down. As soon as the door closed, Angel's head fell into his hands. I walked over to him, giving his shoulder a reassuring squeeze.

He looked at me and the worry was written all over his face. I knew what he felt because it vibrated through me. He felt helpless yet again to save Jasmine because he was sitting here.

"Chase, I hate to ask you."

"No, don't even sweat it. Jas is family, man. I'll bring her home. She's not going to hurt again like before. I promise you. I'm also going to get you out of here tonight. So when she comes home, she'll come home to you."

Angel nodded his head, and I gave his shoulder one last tight squeeze before I headed out of the room. I pulled out my phone and looked for the contact I needed. I guess I was taking

## CHAPTER 35

the job. Angel needed to be out helping to find Jasmine. It would kill him if he couldn't at least be there for her.

The phone rang only once and the person on the other end didn't bother to speak. He already knew why I was calling. "I want him out. The sooner the better and I will take the job, but I'm going on the assignment the first week of September. I want to be home as long as possible."

My contact laughed before he answered. "That's not a problem on either count. Just be aware I can't release him right this second but he'll be home tonight."

I saw Tony sulking. It took everything in me not to punch him in the face. I needed to stay calm. Jasmine needed someone who was level-headed and not going to let his emotions get the better of him.

I had taken numerous jobs where I didn't get along with those in charge but I still handled the job. This would be no different. This was about getting Jasmine home safely. If that meant working with this piece of shit, then so be it.

I walked over to Tony. "Let's go. We're wasting time. I want Jasmine out of Marcus' hands, like, yesterday."

## Chapter 36

*Jasmine*

*Get up, Jasy. You have to wake up. Come on, Jasy. Wake up and get out. If you can't, then you gotta fight back. Do not give up, Jasy. Just get up, please.*

"Jay."

I woke up with a start and a pounding headache. I snapped my eyes shut. The room was spinning. I grabbed my head, trying to make it stop. I had the weirdest dream. I thought Jay was here with me telling me to get up. I peeked one eye open, testing to see if the light would increase the pounding in my head. When it didn't, I opened up both eyes and took a look at my surroundings.

I was in Uncle Luke's gym. I cracked a smile. This was a poor choosing on Marcus' part. Well, poor choosing for him, beneficial for me. I felt completely at home and totally in control here. Whatever fear I had before he knocked me over the head started to disappear. I was walking out of here today, alive, and so were my friends.

A heard something stir beside me. I turned, not able to hide my gasp. Kris' entire face was swollen. Her hands were tied behind her back and she was gagged. She looked like she was struggling to open her eyes and sit up.

## Chapter 36

I reached out for her, but she flinched. "Hey, Kris. It's me. It's Jasmine. I'm going to get you out of here." She relaxed a little and the eye that wasn't swollen shut opened. I removed her gag and she smiled at me.

"I am so happy to see you, Jasmine. He didn't hurt you, did he?"

I chuckled. Kris looked like she went through the ringer with Mike Tyson and she was worried about me. I took in her bruises and noticed she wasn't wearing the halter top from earlier. I got this pit in my stomach. I couldn't live with myself if Marcus hurt her the way he hurt me.

I grabbed the shirt she wore. "Kris?" I questioned. I couldn't physically voice what I wanted to know. I was scared to hear her response.

Kris shook her head. "He didn't have time. I attacked him when he brought you in. Me looking like a truck hit me is the result of it. I thought he was going to do it when he pinned me down and ripped my shirt, but you must have stirred or something. Whatever you did, he completely stopped and walked away from me."

I let out a sigh of relief. I already felt like shit. I got Damien shot and Kris caught up in this mess. I'd never be able to make it up to her if he violated her like that.

"Jas, I don't mean to cut this reunion short, but we should get out of here while we still can."

"Yeah, you're right. Can you walk?"

"I think so."

"Okay, let me untie you and we can get out of here."

I heard a gun cock and I turned around to see Marcus stroll in. He was just as bruised up as Kris was. His right eye was starting to swell, and he had a nasty cut on the side of his face. I nodded my head in approval. Kris got him good.

"I wouldn't set her free if I were you, Jasmine. The bitch has already pissed me off; I don't need much of a reason to kill her now."

I stood up in front of Kris. No one else was dying, not if I could help it. "You said if I came with you, you'd let her go. Did you even call an ambulance for Damien?"

"I left a note for my brother to find. Stop worrying about everyone else, Jasmine. I came back for you, damn it."

His hand was shaking and he no longer had that cold calculated look in his eyes. He looked nervous and not all that stable. This wasn't the same man who raped me when I was younger. Where was the guy who made me fearful of my own shadow?

"Marcus."

I was proud I said his name without wanting to puke. I had to keep my head about me in all of this. One wrong move and either Kris was going to get shot or we both were. My goal was to get us both out of this alive and in one piece.

I walked towards him and he started lowering the gun. A smile spread across his face and it caused me to falter in my

## Chapter 36

footing. His smile made me nervous. This whole situation made me nervous. I heard my heart thunder in my ears. *Steady, Jasmine.*

I got close enough to touch him, but I left some space between us. I wasn't sure if I would be able to control my features if he reached out and grabbed me.

"I knew it, Jasmine. I knew you'd come back to me. I told Tony, you know. I told him you were meant to love me and you would love me. I'd do anything for you. You know that, right? I didn't mean to kill Jay, but he was in the way. He didn't want us together, Jasmine."

The mention of my brother's name took me back to that night I was raped. *Breathe, Jasmine. You must stay focused.* Marcus went to reach for me and I instinctively took a step back.

The features of his face contorted in pure anger. He brought the gun up to swing, but I was able to dodge the hit. I went to counter the dodge with my own hit, but Marcus swung low and punched me in the stomach. He knocked the wind out of me, and I hit the ground cradling my stomach.

"You stupid, bitch."

He kicked me in the same spot that he had punched me in, and I saw stars. I cried out in pain. Holy shit. That hurt. Marcus bent down and grabbed my face. "You really haven't learned, have you? I told you I've been watching you for months. I know how you move."

He pushed me on my back and straddled my waist. I couldn't hold off the panic. I was choked by my fear. This was going to happen again. I started thrashing against him. Trying to my hardest to get him off me. But he forcefully pinned me down.

"That's right, Jasmine. Keep fighting me. Keep that fear in your eyes. You know how much I love it."

I felt him get harder on top of me. The tears started trickling down my eyes. I was right back to that night four years ago, helpless, alone and afraid. And again I could do nothing but sit back and take it.

"Hey, asshole. How about you pick on some who's gonna fight you back."

I turned and watched Kris awkwardly stand up. I had loosened the rope enough that her hands were now free and balled into tight fists.

"Kris, don't." I tried to warn her off. She looked like she didn't have much strength to fight him off this time.

"Shut up."

Marcus backhanded me hard enough that my head slammed into the mat. I started seeing little black spots and the pounding returned. A wave of nausea overtook me, but I breathed deeply through my mouth trying to fight it off.

Marcus rubbed himself against me once before he got off of me. He put the gun in his waistband. He slowly made his

## Chapter 36

way to Kris as I struggled to stand up without the floor coming up to meet me.

"Hmm, if I didn't know any better, I'd think you have a thing for me, Kris. What happened? Chase can't give the brand of sex you crave? You like being held down, don't you? You like being forced to cum by a strong male?"

Kris laughed at him. "You're nothing but a weak pathetic little bitch who probably sucked his mom's tit for too long. You're a loser, Marcus. I don't want you, and Jasmine sure as shit doesn't want you."

I watched as Marcus closed in on Kris. He reached out fast and wrapped his hands around her throat. "I bet you liked to be choked while you're being fucked. How about I just choke you now?"

"Hey, Marcus!" I screamed. He turned around to face me but his hand was still firmly wrapped around Kris' neck. Her eyes were rolling to the back of her head as she made half-hearted attempts to punch and kick at him. I had to think fast.

"I have a proposition for you."

He smirked. "I'm intrigued. Go on."

"A one-on-one match. You beat me, you leave Kris alone and I will willingly go with you and be yours. I win, you crawl back into that hole you came out of and leave me and everyone I love alone."

He threw Kris up against the wall. I watched her body slide down and slump over. I watched closely, desperately, looking for any sign of life. "She's fine, Jasmine. You always care about everyone but me."

"Shut up. Are we doing this or not?"

He took his shirt off and discarded it on the floor. I redid my ponytail, making sure no extra hair slipped out. I couldn't afford any distractions.

We walked towards each other, both circling one another. "This is like our first time, Jasmine. Do you remember? You fought me then too. Just like you want to do now. You succumbed to me though, just like you're going to do now."

"I don't think so, Marcus."

I swung hard and fast. He dodged my attempts easily and landed a blow to my ribs. I sucked in a sharp breath. This was going to be harder than I thought.

We circled each other again. I faked a right jab, and he dodged it like I wanted him to. I spun around, shooting my leg out and catching him in his side. I heard his breath seize.

I cracked a smile. He was able to predict my swings but not my kicks. I swung twice, and he went exactly where I wanted him to go to set up for a kick to the same side. Marcus stumbled back, grabbing his side. My goal was to get him on his back and kick him till he was unconscious.

## Chapter 36

He looked up at me then, smiling. "You've gotten stronger, Jasmine. I'm pleasantly impressed, but let me show you how much stronger I still am."

He swung first and I dodged it, but he moved with me and charged his whole body into mine, knocking me off my feet. I hit the mat hard with a *whoosh* as the air left my lungs. Marcus sat straight up, and swung catching me in my face. I was sure the hit was meant for my already throbbing skull but I was able to move my face upward, catching the blow on my cheek.

The pain was enough to make me black out but I kept my eyes open, sucking in as much oxygen as I could. Marcus jumped off of me and placed his shoe on my chest, pressing down hard. It was difficult to breath.

"I told you, Jasmine. You belong to me. I will kill everyone before I let anyone else have you. Looks like I win and you lose."

He took his foot off my chest and I gasped for air. "I guess it's time to say goodbye to your friend."

I summoned whatever strength I could possibly find and swung my leg out, kicking him behind his knee hard. He went down and the gun fell out of his hands. I struggled to get up. But I couldn't move fast enough.

Both Marcus and I lay there on the gym floor for a second trying to catch our breath. I saw him start to stir and I knew I had to get up. I struggled to my feet and quickly walked past him.

Marcus grabbed my foot, bringing me down to the mat again. I kicked back with my other leg and he let go. He rolled over towards the gun and grabbed it. Not bothering to struggle with standing up, I crawled over to Kris and pushed her body as far behind mine as I could go. If he wanted to kill another person I loved, he was going to have to go through me this time.

Marcus stood up spitting blood. He wiped his nose as it gushed blood. That cold dead stare was back. He raised the gun and pointed it in my direction. "Move, Jasmine now."

I stood slowly, making sure Kris' body stayed behind mine. "No. You're done taking from me, Marcus."

He laughed. "Is someone always more important than me? I love you! You're supposed to love me, Jasmine. You have to, you're the only one that could."

He wiped his nose again and paced back and forth in short bursts. "This wasn't supposed to happen this way. You picked me. You belong to me."

He stopped pacing and turned to face me. "If I can't have you, Jasmine..."

I saw the resolve in his eyes. With Marcus, I should have known, this was only going to end one way.

An eerie calm settled over me. So this was the way it was going to be, huh? For the first time in my life, I wasn't scared of the outcome. Marcus was done taking people from me. I stared into his cold eyes and felt a certain type of

## Chapter 36

determination. He wouldn't win. He never really could, not anymore.

A smile spread across my face. "Oh, Marcus. I never belonged to you. And I never will."

I closed my eyes waiting for what I knew was coming. *See you soon, Jay.*

I heard the gun go off and everything became still.

INTO PIECES

# CHAPTER 37

*Chase*

My gun went off and I stood still, in shock by the scene before me. If I had gotten here a second too late, a bullet would be sitting in Jas' chest instead of Marcus' back.

"Chase?"

Jasmine's voice broke me out of my trance. "Yeah, Jasmine?" My voice came out raw and full of emotion.

"Am I dead?"

I laughed at Jas' silly question. The absurdity behind it made this situation unbelievable. "No, Jas. You're very much alive."

"I am?"

"Yes, brat."

I stepped further into the gym and Jasmine ran towards me. She jumped into my arms, and we both held on to each other tightly. She started crying, and I held on even tighter. "It's okay, Jas. You're finally okay."

We both let go at the same time. "If I ever in my life have to save you again, please don't be standing in front of a guy with a gun. I can't take the heart attack you almost gave me."

"I couldn't let him hurt Kris."

My phone chimed and I grabbed it to see who it was. I smiled. "Go outside, Jas. There's an officer and an ambulance, okay."

She nodded and walked away, but she came running back and slammed herself into me. "Thank you for showing up on time, Chase."

I pulled her off of me and kissed her forehead. "Any time."

She ran outside and I turned to face Kris. I walked over to her. I checked Marcus' pulse first to confirm what I had hoped was a kill shot. Marcus was finally put down. Just wished it had happened sooner.

I took in Kris' injuries and wanted to kill Marcus all over again. "Beauty, what am I going to do with you?" I softly scooped her up in my arms and she turned her body towards mine. Even in her unconsciousness she knew I was there for her.

I placed a kiss on her forehead, feeling relief that not only was Jas alive but Kris was as well. It was going to suck to leave her.

### *Angel*

An officer had filled me in on all that Chase had done to get me out. He also filled me in on what was happening with Jasmine. Right now we were breaking all traffic laws to get to Uncle Luke's gym. I prayed she was okay. I couldn't take it if her or my sis were seriously hurt. I'd kill Tony and end up right back behind a cell.

## Chapter 37

As soon as the officer pulled up to the curb, I was out of the car and barreling through the cops and firefighters and EMTs. I was desperate to see Jasmine. I needed to be sure she was okay.

Officer Santos saw me and called me over. Jasmine was wrapped in a blanket sitting in one of the ambulances. The second she saw me, she threw the blanket off and ran full force towards me.

I met her halfway. Our bodies collided and I swear I thought I was going to cry. Jasmine was safe and alive and in my arms and whole. I've never been more relieved in my life to have someone in my arms. I heard her muffled sobs, and I couldn't hold back my own tears.

I've fought overseas in a war that killed many of my brothers. Yet, I'd never been more scared in my life than when I was sitting in the precinct knowing some crazy person had her and all I could do was wait.

We finally untangled ourselves and Jasmine quickly wiped away her tears. "I thought I wasn't going to see you again."

Her statement echoed the very real fear I had. I couldn't help it. I grabbed her face and pulled her lips to mine. I needed to make sure she was real and alive and in front of me. I drank her in, devouring her taste. She pulled away first, gasping for air.

"What's wrong? Did I hurt you?"

She smiled. "No, my ribs hurt. Still can't breathe properly."

I scooped her up in my arms and lead her back to the ambulance. "She's saying her ribs hurt did you check her out yet?"

"Yes, he did, Angel. They need to take me to the hospital to get a full check."

"Then let's go. What are we waiting for?"

"I was waiting for you to show up. I didn't want to leave without you."

I kissed her forehead as the two EMTs hooked Jas up to a couple of machines.

"Just so you know, Jas, I'm going to be annoying these next few weeks. Like up-your-ass annoying."

She groaned. It started off as an annoying groan then it sounded like she was in pain. "What happened?" I wanted to touch her, but I was fearful that I would hurt her more.

"Let's get her to the hospital and checked out okay?" the EMT suggested.

"Yeah, let's go." I grabbed her hand and squeezed, letting her know I wasn't leaving her side. Not now, not ever.

# Chapter 38

*Angel*

The charges were finally dropped. I was no longer being charged for assault. Vivian sang like a canary once she heard about Marcus. She told the cops his whole master plan to basically take me down and get me out of the way so he could get to Jasmine.

The plan would have worked too, seeing as my DNA ended up under Vivian's nails thanks to the little outburst at the gym. I had not only been IDed by Vivian, but there were a bunch of witnesses who saw our little altercations and had reason to believe I would want to hurt her. Being that I was a combat veteran, they were really playing up the PTSD card.

Chase had to use whatever connections he had to get me out on bail before seeing a judge so I could get to Jasmine. And thanks to this sick bastard and Tony covering for him, Chase had to take a high-profile job he didn't want to take. Chase just got home; he wasn't ready to leave, but now he had no choice in the matter. I hated that he got dragged into this situation. But I was grateful he was willing to do whatever he could to help; he really was my brother.

I was still having a hard time believing Tony could lie to us like that the entire time. I trusted him, and I trusted him to look after Jasmine, and he betrayed us. You think you know somebody and then one day they do or say something, and it's like you're looking at a stranger.

## Into Pieces

We've been friends since we were in diapers. Blood couldn't make us any closer. Tony mourned with us when we buried Jay. It hurt my heart knowing Tony covered up his death and made it look like an accident all to protect Marcus. A fucking scumbag who didn't deserve the air he breathed.

My hands flexed into tight fists. I was getting pissed all over again. If I didn't get my temper under control, I knew I'd end up back on the train and heading straight to Tony's house to do what I couldn't do at the precinct. Tony magically disappeared after he helped Chase pinpoint where Jasmine and my sister were. He knew I was coming for him and the coward that he was hid.

I let out a breath. I had to remind myself it was over. Marcus had finally been put down. Not by my hands, unfortunately, but either way he was no longer a problem for anyone. I found out he not only raped Jasmine but he raped my ex Janet too. There was a long list of girls he hurt, but it was finally over and he couldn't hurt anyone anymore.

I heard Jasmine laugh and I turned in the direction she was in. Her, my sister and Damien were off walking the boardwalk at Coney Island. Kris was currently trying to stuff a shitload of cotton candy into his mouth. I laughed. Kris was finally back to her old self. She still had a few bruises and she had to wrap her wrist every once in a while, but she was healing and she was okay.

Damien was touch and go there for while. Marcus missed his heart by an inch. He had to go through two surgeries, and then we sat and waited for him to wake up. Jasmine wouldn't leave his side. She blamed herself for getting Damien shot.

## CHAPTER 38

When he finally woke up to Jasmine asleep in the chair at his beside he smiled and looked at me.

We didn't speak, but I knew what he was telling me: I was a lucky bastard for snatching a girl like Jasmine up. He was right, I knew I was and I planned to never let her go.

Her laughter rang out through the crowded boardwalk. She was having a good time. I was glad I was able to give this to her. It was such a small piece of happiness compared to everything that happened. She needed this; we both did. It was about time we had some drama-free, uninterrupted happy time.

I was watching her as she watched the fireworks light across the sky. Coney Island was notorious for their firework display in the summer time. All the bright lights shone across Jasmine's beautiful face, transforming it to an array of bright brilliant colors. I was in a trance watching her. I counted my blessings everyday that I realized early on that I needed her in my life. She truly was my greatest strength and my greatest weakness. Jas had become an extension of me.

She must have sensed me watching her; she turned around with a goofy grin spread across her face. My heart sped up and my lungs seemed to constrict, fighting for air. Would she ever stop taking my breath away? She walked over to me, and my arms opened for her on their own accord waiting to accept her. The second she came into my arms, her body immediately melted against mine. We both let out a sigh of contentment.

This was supposed to be a simple embrace, innocent, but every time Jasmine was near me she had complete control over my body. She had the ability to set it on fire, filling me with a need to always touch and taste her. I tugged at her hair, tilting her head up towards mine. She instinctively sought out my lips with hers. I couldn't hold back my groan of appreciation. Jasmine's taste was my own personal addiction, intoxicating. The more I experienced it, the more I craved, the more I knew I'd always want and need it.

I pulled back to cup her face. Her big brown eyes were filled with so much hope. We survived the summer of our demons. They came out in full force, and they seemed to have gotten along well with each other. We no longer were pushing and running away from each other. This summer proved we were stronger as a unit and we were ready to face whatever the world had for us. We'd get through anything.

She pulled me back down for a quick kiss and bit my lip.

I chuckled. "You know what biting is going to start, Love."

"Yeah, well, I'd rather you thinking about that than what's going on in your head."

"How do you know what I'm thinking about?"

"It's your eyes. You're not here with me. Your eyes are a million miles away. Come on let's go for a walk."

*Jasmine*

I intertwined my hand in his and pulled him to walk along the boardwalk. Angel was worried. He was worried this ease wasn't going to last. We faced a lot in such a short time. I worried too. Our demons had come out to play this summer.

## CHAPTER 38

But they didn't drive us apart like I thought they would. No, they actually pushed us together. I was glad I was still standing here with him by my side. I loved Angel, and there wasn't anyone else I wanted to go through all of this with.

He tugged at my hand abruptly, stopping me from walking any further. "You yell at me for being in my head and look at you."

"I did not yell, you big baby."

He laughed. "You totally reprimanded me." He pulled me close to him, wrapping his arms around my waist. "Where's your head at?"

I went to answer but he shook his head. He gave me that devious smile of his, the one that always put my mind at ease. "Actually, never mind. I want you to do something for me." I raised my eyebrow at him and he chuckled. "You're a dirty bird. It's nothing bad. Scouts honor."

"Your ass was never a scout," I grumbled.

He laughed, smacking my ass. "Just shh. I want you to listen to something." He tilted his head a little bit and had this twinkle in his eyes. "Can you hear it?"

I mimicked his movements, trying to hear what he heard. All I heard was the sound of the water hitting the shore and the rides running at Coney Island along with the chatter and laughter of those enjoying themselves here. "Um, I think you've been out in the sun too long, Angel. I don't hear anything."

## Into Pieces

"That's because you're not listening. Close your eyes."

I closed my eyes, still struggling to hear what he was hearing. But I couldn't make anything out. Maybe his mind finally went. This had been a very long summer, after all.

"Angel I don't hear––"I was cut off by a sweet simple kiss that had my knees going weak and goose bumps spreading across my flesh.

"I think we're spending too much time thinking, Jasmine. It's summertime. It's supposed to be our carefree time. It's time we just enjoy things. I think we deserve it. Don't open your eyes yet."

He spun me around and began to dance. I started laughing as I peeked up at him. "You know, you went from someone who had no type of rhythm to dancing all the time. Even when there's no music playing."

He chuckled as he spun me again. "The music's there, Love. You're still thinking too much. It's okay to let go." His face grew serious as he cupped mine with his hands. "We've both gone through a lot in such a short time. That would have broken anyone, and we managed to survive it. It's time to let go and be silly and enjoy life for what it is. What was it your brother used to say?"

Angel smirked and I responded with a smile of my own as I stated my brother's famous words verbatim: "Life is and will always be meant to be lived. Taste it, savor it, consume it and let it consume you. Get lost in it. Life is intoxicating if it's lived right. You should never be afraid of life. You should never hold anything back. There's entirely too much to explore and

## Chapter 38

experience and taste and touch, and we're never given enough time to do it all."

This time I was filled with the same joy that Jay always had when he was alive. He may have lived a short life, but it was a fulfilled one. Marcus may have had a hand in taking him away from me, but I finally believed Jay would do it all over again just to protect me. Jay lived with no regrets, and I didn't want to have any either.

I smiled up at Angel, the man I planned on experiencing all of what life had to offer with. The good, the bad and all the in between, I wanted it with him. Whatever life had in store for us, we'd face it together and survive it. We were warriors and that was what warriors did.

INTO PIECES

# Chapter 39

***Chase***

My bags were packed. I was used to goodbyes in my line of work I never stayed in one place long enough to have any ties. But this was home, and it always hurt a little more each time I had to leave.

This time killed me especially, since I had no choice but to take this job. Thanks to Tony and his brother, I had to pull in some favors. I couldn't keep Angel locked up while Jasmine was out there with Marcus. I couldn't see Angel helpless like that when I had the power to do something about it.

Honestly, I didn't regret helping them. I'd do it again in a heartbeat, but now I'd lose time I'd never get back. Don't get me wrong, the job had its perks. I got to see the world. I loved the fact that I was the youngest and still the best at what I did. But I was losing my desire to travel abroad and tackle new tasks. I wanted to give it up or at the very least take a sabbatical. I had other interests now that were occupying all of my attention, but it was too late to do anything about it.

My door swung open and Tony stepped in. Well, speak of the devil. He looked worn out. It was nice to see he was just as affected by what transpired as everyone else was.

"Can we talk, Chase?"

I dropped my bags and crossed my arms over my chest. I had to rein in my temper. This bastard had a lot of nerve. We had nothing left to discuss. He put not only Jas in harm's way but Kris too.

I didn't know who he was anymore. I couldn't understand how this kid I grew up with who never raised his voice to a female could ever allow Marcus near any girl. How did Tony allow all this shit to go on as long as it did?

From the information I was given, Jasmine wasn't the only girl Marcus raped and Tony covered up for. How did he ever think this was okay?

"You need to leave, Tony. You know you're no longer welcome in this house."

"I know. I just came to say I'm sorry."

"I'm not the one you owe an apology to."

He made a move to sit at the table. "Did you not hear what I said? You're not staying."

He let out a breath. "Look, man, we use to be boys. I just need to apologize. I tried to apologize to Angel and Jasmine, but they won't hear me."

I started laughing. He couldn't be serious. He played a major role in the torment that Jasmine went through, and he expected people to welcome him with open arms?

"Tony, you can't be this fucking dumb. Apologizing is going to do what for Jasmine? It doesn't erase what she went through. Shit, if you wanted to do something for her, you should have put that damn dog down a long ass time."

## Chapter 39

"That's so easy for everyone to suggest, Chase. He's family."

My temper got the better of me, and I marched right up to Tony and got in his face. "No, Tony. He wasn't family. We were your family. Jay opened up his home to you when you couldn't deal with your father. His mom fucking fed you and clothed you. Are you fucking kidding me right now? Jay was family and you sat there with the rest of us as we mourned him. Was that fake? Did you even give a shit?"

Tony backed up and scrubbed a hand across his face. "You know I care, Chase. You guys were the closest thing to family I had. Jay's death hurt me just like it hurt everyone else."

"Yes, Jay's death destroyed you so much you falsified that police report. Jay didn't blow past that stop sign or whatever the hell you put down. Marcus hit him dead on because he knew Jay was going to bring him down and your father wouldn't have been able to dig him out of that hole."

Tony looked at me with surprise. "Yeah, asshole. I had to do some digging, but I know. I know the whole truth behind that fake accident. Nice cover up, I must say."

I took a step back and crossed my arms over my chest. The need to hit Tony was starting to override my rational side. I was livid and hurt that we ever let Tony into our tight circle.

"How were you ever capable of looking Jasmine in the eye? You must not sleep at night. And if you actually do, you're more like your father and Marcus then you care to admit and I truly never knew who you really were. Marcus should have been put down a long time ago, Tony. Jasmine and all those other girls never would have experienced what they did."

"It's not as easy as it seems. Look, I came here to apologize, Chase. You know, you use to be the reasonable one."

"Trust me, I am being reasonable allowing you to even be here right now. Understand something: I would have laid down my life for you. Any trust, any love, anything I had for you is gone. You fucked up the second you allowed Marcus to come anywhere near those girls. I really hope you can live with yourself after all this shit is said and done. But don't you dare fucking come back around. You come anywhere near those girls, especially Kristal, I will break your neck. Now, get the fuck out my house, we're done."

I turned around; I couldn't stand the sight of him any longer. I wanted nothing more than to beat the life out of him. How the fuck could he have covered up Jay's death like that? How could someone do that to Jasmine, to her mother?

It hurt to know that Tony had allowed this to go on for so long. Almost every single girl Angel had been with Marcus went and raped.

I really didn't want to leave. The threat was gone I knew that, but it still felt wrong leaving Kris alone.

I heard the door swing open again. Unbelievable. What could this dense bastard want now? I swung around. "Did you––oh, um, Kris." My words were cut short at the sight of her standing in my doorway.

## Chapter 39

The air instantly shifted around us as it always did. My clothes felt too tight and too constricted for my body. I yearned to reach out and touch her one last time, but I remained where I was. There was a reason I didn't want to see her before I had to leave. Not only did she tell me to stay away while she healed. But I knew, looking at her now, I wouldn't have been able to leave her alone. Not without fully knowing how she tasted.

Seeing her unconscious in that gym and then lying in that hospital bed made me hurt in ways I never thought were possible. The caveman inside of me demanded I take her just to make sure she was really here and then be the one to nurse her back to her vibrant self. But she told me she didn't want to see me, and I tucked tail and left.

Now she was standing in my doorway in shorts and a big ass T-shirt that swallowed her. It did nothing to hide the body underneath, however. Her hair was down and in disarray around her face. She looked messy, and I had never seen her look more beautiful.

I would miss her smile, her spark, and that fire. I'd miss every nuisance that made Kris who she was. I wasn't even gone yet and I missed her already.

Our timing truly sucked. I'd never get the opportunity to know her intimately and privately. And the way our last conversation went, I'd never know the privilege of being her man.

"What are you doing here, Kris?"

She slammed the door and stomped straight towards me. There was that legendary Torres temper; it shone in her hazel eyes. She was pissed. Probably because I was running out of here without so much as a backwards glance.

Kris pushed me, but it wasn't enough to make me budge. I saw it in her eyes. She was ready to lay into me, and I couldn't do much but stand here and take it.

"You really thought you were going to leave without even saying goodbye? Goodbye to me? I don't mean anything to you now?"

"Kris," my voice was pleading. I didn't seek her out because I couldn't say goodbye to her. I didn't want to go through what we were about to go through right now.

"Please, Kris. It's easier this way."

She pushed again. "Easier for who, you? You've never run from anything. Now, that seems to be all you do." She pushed harder. "After everything that just happened, you really weren't going to say goodbye?" She kept pushing. Her hands became fists as she pounded into my chest. "I can't believe you're leaving me again."

"Last time we talked, that's what you wanted."

Her punches came down harder. "Don't be a dickhead. Not right now. You know that's not what I meant." She let out a huff. "Everything we've just been a part of, you didn't think I deserved a goodbye?"

Her hazel eyes became misty as her hands fisted my shirt. "You tell me all the time some jobs you take can be dangerous.

## CHAPTER 39

I didn't get to say goodbye to Jay. I can't believe you would do the same to me. What if you never come back, Chase?"

And the resolve I was trying so hard to hold on to began to slip as I snatched her up and placed her on the counter. "This is why I didn't come and say goodbye to you, Kris."

On a groan, I covered her lips with my own. Her body relaxed against mine, and I was lost to her. All summer long I held back because the timing wasn't right. I was learning that, with our lives, we'd never get our chance.

Her lips were so soft and so enticing. I needed to stop this before it got out of hand. I tried to pull back, but Kris held on and pulled me closer to her. She wanted it just as much as I did, and I always held back from her. I should have never waited. But now wasn't the time for would have's and could have's. I had to leave.

Kris' hands slid down my chest, and I caught her before I really couldn't stop myself. I pulled away. "Tsk, tsk, Beauty. You know better than to touch before I give you permission to."

She pouted her bottom lip out, and it made me want to suck it in between my own lips. Or rub my dick against it. Yep, it was definitely time to go. I tried to disengage myself from her hold, but she wrapped her legs around me and pulled me back towards her.

"You're really going leave it like this, Chase?"

"I have to."

"Why? All we ever did was wait. Wait because either I wasn't right or you weren't right. You just came back and now you have to leave again. And you're not going to some bullshit desk job. This could be something that can be dangerous. You're really okay with leaving just as we are?

She shook her head. "I really thought this summer would have taught you time was something we didn't get back. All that shit that went down between my brother and Jas and you haven't taken anything away from it?"

Kris pushed at me and jumped off the counter. She walked past me, and I reached out grabbing her wrist to keep her from going further.

"You know I want you, Kris. That has never been an issue. But I really can't do this. It wouldn't be fair to me or you."

If Tony had handled Marcus a lot sooner, I would have been able to turn this job down with no consequences. But thanks to him and his backwards loyalty, I had no choice but to walk out of this kitchen and away from Kris for who knows how long.

I wanted her to wait for me. But I wasn't that much of a prick to do that to her. She had a life to live, and sadly, it wasn't going to be with me in it.

I moved my hands to cup her face, looking into those beautiful hazel eyes of hers. I leaned in, intent on placing a kiss on her forehead, but the little minx moved getting high on her toes and smashed her lips against mine.

## Chapter 39

Her wandering hands were a lot faster this time and found exactly what they were looking for. I was already half hard when Kris walked in, now with her hands stroking me and her lips on mine, the blood left my brain and headed south. I groaned into her mouth. I truly was a fool to give this up without even getting a small taste.

She bit my bottom lip before she broke the kiss. "One night, Chase. I'm not asking for forever. I just want one night with you before you leave."

She chuckled more to herself than out loud. "Look at you, got me practically begging to have my way with you."

I let myself laugh at the absurdity of it all. "Come on, Beauty. I will walk you home."

I was at the door when I realized she didn't follow me. I turned around and sucked in a sharp breath. Kris had chucked her oversized shirt and shorts and was standing in my kitchen in a red lacy bra and sheer boy shorts.

My knees buckled as I gasped for air. "What, what." My voice came out in a groan. I cleared my throat and shook my head, trying to clear it.

"What are you doing, Kris?"

She shrugged nonchalantly as she twirled a piece of her hair between her fingers. "You may enjoy walking around with a hard on, Chase. But I like to satisfy my needs when they arise."

"You wouldn't."

Kris smiled. "You can go. I'll let myself out when I'm done."

She turned around, and I don't remember how I moved as fast as I did. But as soon as I was close enough, I grabbed her and spun her around. She smirked, and I hauled her little ass up against my body and backed her up against the nearest wall.

Kris wrapped her legs around me as she breathlessly said my name.

"You wanted me, Kris. You're finally going to have me. I'll be damned if any pleasure you receive tonight is coming from anything but my hands, my mouth and my dick. And you're not allowed to cum until I say so, agreed?"

She didn't respond right away and I smacked her ass. Kris let out a gasp as her eyes narrowed into tiny slits. I couldn't hold back my chuckle. This was going to be a fun night.

"I asked you a question, Beauty."

Her hands, which were wrapped around my shoulders, curled into the hairs at the back of my neck and she pulled. I winced at the sharp pain and my dick twitched.

"This isn't going to go your way, Chase."

I smiled as I leaned in and bit her bottom lip. I pulled back far enough to look into her eyes. "I don't have anywhere to be for at least eight hours. At least half of that time, I'm going to be buried deep inside of you."

## Chapter 39

Her breath hitched and I smiled. "Understand something, Beauty. I'm about to ruin you for anyone who comes after me. Anyone else will pale in comparison. I'm a selfish asshole because I am perfectly okay with that. I can let you have your way for at least ten minutes and then the rest?" I winked at her. "The rest of the time, I'm going to show you exactly how many ways I can get you to cum for me."

**The End**

# Sneak Peek at Chase and Kris' Story:

"Come on, Jasmine. Can you hurry up already?" She came barging out of the bathroom looking pale as a ghost. "Dude, you okay?"

"No, you impatient little gremlin. I keep throwing up the contents of my stomach even though there's nothing in it. You believe I just finished brushing my teeth and my stomach decided it was time to hack up some more."

Jasmine slowly walked over to the couch to sit down. She looked like she had the flu. but in all my life I've never seen Jas sick. "You want to postpone this?"

"Yeah, and your brother would have a fit. Something tells me he's been planning this since before we left. The sneaky bastard that he is."

I laughed; Jas was definitely in a mood. "Are you PMSing?"

She mumbled under her breath, "If only it were that."

If only it were that? Huh? Then it hit me. Oh shit. "Hey, Jas, are you–"

Before I could finish my question there was a knock at the door. Jasmine jumped up and headed to the bathroom. "If that's your impatient brother, tell him I'm getting dressed and I won't be late, promise."

I couldn't fight my grin. I grabbed Jasmine before she could escape and pulled her into a hug. She stood there a second before hugging me back. "Don't say anything yet okay?" She whispered.

"Don't worry, I won't. But I'm super stoked. I hope it's a girl."

She laughed and ran into the bathroom. I walked towards the door, genuinely happy for Jasmine and my brother. Angel did good and they deserved all the happiness in the world, especially after their rough start.

This day couldn't get any better. There was another knock and I chuckled. If this was my brother, he was getting extremely impatient in his old age. "Hold your horses, I'm coming."

I swung the door open and time came to a standstill. It had been a long time since I saw him, but the second I did, my body remembered in detail the devastating things he can do with his hands and his mouth. My nipples hardened and heat pooled between my legs.

I would never ever admit this out loud, but I missed him. Seeing him now brought that emotion barreling through the wall I had built up around my heart. I wanted nothing more than to throw my arms around him and kiss him senseless. But that wasn't going to happen. He chose to walk from us, from me. There really wasn't much left for us. Once my body and heart got on board with that plan, everything would be fine.

"Angel told me I'd find you here, Kris." The deep rumble of his voice sent a shiver through me. This was going to be a long week if his voice alone could send my body spiraling.

Chase saw the shift in my body and his eyes darkened. "I've missed you too, Beauty."

He grabbed my face in his hands and pulled my lips towards his. Yep. This week really was going to suck.

Into Pieces

CPSIA information can be obtained
at www.ICGtesting.com
Printed in the USA
LVHW05s0001050718
582631LV00002B/290/P

"Angel told me I'd find you here, Kris." The deep rumble of his voice sent a shiver through me. This was going to be a long week if his voice alone could send my body spiraling.

Chase saw the shift in my body and his eyes darkened. "I've missed you too, Beauty."

He grabbed my face in his hands and pulled my lips towards his. Yep. This week really was going to suck.

INTO PIECES